# Toward That
# Which
# Is *Beautiful*

## A Novel

## MARIAN O'SHEA WERNICKE

She Writes Press

Published 2020
Printed in the United States of America
Print ISBN: 978-1-63152-759-3
E-ISBN: 978-1-63152-760-9
Library of Congress Control Number: 2020906873

For information, address:
She Writes Press
1569 Solano Ave #546
Berkeley, CA 94707

Interior design by Tabitha Lahr

She Writes Press is a division of SparkPoint Studio, LLC.

For Michael
Love always

# $\mathcal{D}$ios

*Siento a Dios que camina*
*tan en mí, con la tarde y con el mar.*
*Con él nos vamos juntos. Anochece.*
*Con él anochecemos. Orfandad.*

I feel God who walks
so much in me, with the evening and the sea.
We go away together. Night falls.
We go into the night together, Orphanhood.

—César Vallejo

***Achirana:*** a canal bringing fresh water from the highlands to the desert area around Ica in Peru. According to an ancient Inca legend, the Inca ruler Pachacutec became enamored of a beautiful young girl from the region of Ica. The maiden spurned his advances, but the ruler was so smitten he told her to ask any favor of him. She asked him to build a canal that would bring water to the parched lands around Ica. The word *achirana* means "that which flows cleanly toward that which is beautiful."

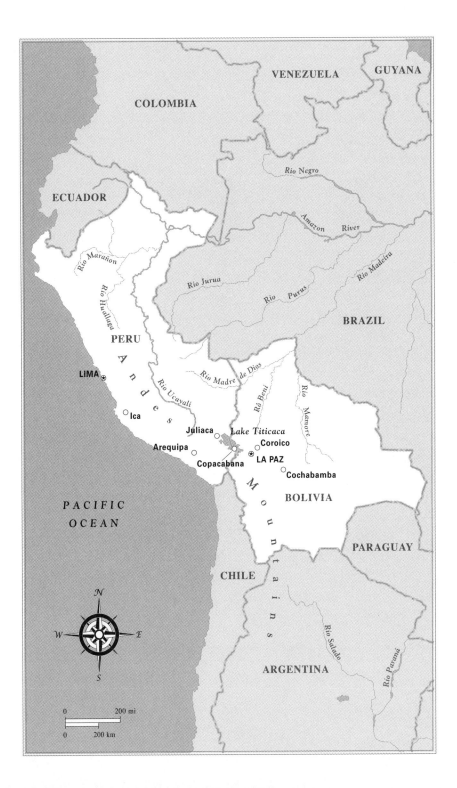

# $\mathscr{C}$hapter One

## Thursday, June 25, 1964

$\rightsquigarrow$

$\mathscr{A}$t noon on a brilliant June day in the highlands of Peru, called the Altiplano, Sister Mary Katherine slips out the back door of the convent of Santa Catalina. She crosses the courtyard, gliding past fat little Tito playing in the shade of the eucalyptus tree near the convent wall. He looks up expectantly, but for once the tall nun does not return his grin. His mother Marta, the convent cook, comes to the door to check on her son, and, as she wipes her hands on her faded blue apron, watches in silence as Sister Mary Katherine pulls the large wooden gate open and disappears.

Sharp angles of sunlight fall on her black veil and white habit. She walks swiftly, inhaling the olive oil and garlic smells of noonday meals in the village, her footsteps echoing in the hushed streets. Not even a dog barks. She crosses the dirt road heading north of the parish, past the infirmary, shuttered now for the siesta, and enters the main street of Juliaca. The market stalls are still open, but only a handful of women and children squat in the shade, half-heartedly guarding their baskets of potatoes, onions, carrots, and mushrooms, their dogs huddling together for warmth in the early winter sun. A young girl in a green poncho greets her shyly, *"Buenas tardes, madrecita."*

Soon Kate—for she has never stopped being Kate beneath the long white habit and black veil of the Dominicans—reaches the edge of town, where one rusting taxi is parked in the shade of the train station, the driver lounging in the shadows. She thinks briefly of buying a train ticket, but, smothering a laugh dangerously close to a sob, realizes that she has no money—and even worse, that she has no destination. You have to buy a ticket to somewhere, after all. All she knows is that she is running away.

The nun walks at a steady pace down the dusty road winding through sparse fields. By late afternoon she realizes she is headed toward Lake Titicaca. Solitude hangs over the land like mist.

Kate has heard the Aymaras' stories of the great hungry god of the lake. Once she and the other sisters went out on a Sunday afternoon in a balsa boat with a local guide. Raul was paddling gently around when the sky darkened and the wind picked up. In a determined voice, he announced that they were heading back to shore. Kate remembers how she protested, but that Magdalena, their Peruvian novice, shook her head and put her finger to her mouth.

"Don't insist," she whispered in English. "Raul says that storms are very bad here on the lake. If we capsize no one will come to rescue us, for the native Andean prople believe that the god of the lake gets hungry—and we'd be his lunch!" Her eyes laughed. She was from Lima, and the ways of the highland people were as foreign to her as they were to the American nuns she had joined. But her face stayed serious as she nodded to Raul in assent. Despite the other sisters' grumbling, Raul's back remained straight beneath the wool of his poncho, and his slender hands gripped the oars firmly as he brought them safely to shore.

By now Kate's feet hurt. Her sensible black oxfords were fine for everyday work in the parish, but they aren't right for hiking; she wonders what she'll do if she gets a blister. She finds a dry spot in the reeds encircling the lake and sits down to take off her shoes. She is thirsty and hungry, too. By now they would have missed her at the convent.

She gazes at the sun's slanting red rays, glinting on the lake. Sister Josepha will be at Vespers now, trying to chant the psalms by herself. Kate murmurs the opening verse:

> The morn had spread her crimson rays,
> When rang the skies with shouts of praise,
> Earth joined the joyful hymn to swell,
> That brought despair to vanquished hell.

Despair. What's happening to her? She lies back among the reeds—so tired, tired of fighting herself, of trying to live the life she had vowed, of trying not to love. Trying not to love.

Lying on her back, she sees a condor circling the lake in a wide leisurely arc. His white throat gleams in the dusk. *He is a good omen,* Kate thinks as she closes her eyes. *He will watch over me.*

# Chapter Two

*K*ate wakes, feeling the damp ground beneath her. Now it is night. How long has she slept? Her face and hands are freezing, and her feet in the cotton stockings are numb. She pulls on her shoes. She has to get up, to move. This is crazy, she knows, this panicked flight. Suddenly she thinks of Jane Eyre fleeing from Rochester. She finds the road again.

In the black sky, the stars shine icily remote and unfamiliar. She meant to study these constellations of the Southern Hemisphere ever since she came to South America, finding it so strange at night not to see the Big Dipper and Orion in their familiar spots. Tonight there is no wind, and above the distant peaks of the Andes, the moon is rising. She holds up her watch—eight thirty. It will get much colder, she knows, a twinge of panic tightening in her throat. Somewhere along this road is an old colonial Spanish house that the local manager of the train station refurbished. But the family moved out last year, and Kate doesn't know if anyone lives there now.

Finally, off to the right, she sees a light flickering through some scrubby bushes. She follows the wooden fence up to the gate and reaches through to unlatch the iron bar within. She pauses for a moment, waiting for a dog's bark, then makes her way quietly up the flagstone path that leads to a wide veranda. As she knocks on the door she thinks she can hear music. The door opens and the outline of a man is framed in lamplight.

"Bloody hell!"

Kate, surprised to hear a British accent, sticks out her hand.

"Sister Mary Katherine, from the Dominican Sisters at Santa Catalina," she says in what she hopes is a firm voice.

The man steps aside to let her in; now she can see his dark hair, graying along the temples, the angular face. His eyes are shadowed in the dim hall. As Kate shakes his hand, his wool sweater scratches her arm.

"Come in, come in. I'm sorry this place is such a mess." Confused, he looks around the room. Her glance follows his. On a table with two kerosene lamps burning are several notebooks piled neatly next to a typewriter. A fire flickers in the great stone fireplace across the room. Now the music is clearer—Mozart, Kate realizes as she notices the short-wave radio on a table in the corner. It is the familiar music that does her in, hearing it in this desolate foreign night. Her voice trembles.

"I'm sorry, it's just that I'm so tired and cold. I fell asleep on the ground. My habit is damp . . ." She tries to keep her voice steady.

Her host, looking closely at her, seems to relax at the sight of her tears. "Okay, mysterious sister of the night, come in. I'm going to get you warm clothes. While you change, I'll reheat some lovely soup that I have left from my supper. A hot toddy might be in order, too."

The man leads her down the hall to a back bedroom, unused it seems, except for an open suitcase that lies, neatly packed, on a love seat. When he leaves the room, she walks over to the peeling gilt mirror above the dresser. It is a Peruvian mirror in the colonial style, made of mahogany, and framed by tiny irregular pieces of mirror inlaid in the dark wood. The pieces glitter in the lamplight and reflect her image in a thousand broken fragments. She stares, her face pale beneath the black veil, and the white scapular that hangs straight from her shoulders to the hem of her long skirt is smeared with dirt.

"These should do all right." His voice is brisk, and he does not meet her eyes as he thrusts a pair of soft, faded flannel pajamas, a red checked bathrobe, and a pair of cotton socks into her arms. "Freshen up now. There's a sink and a toilet in the courtyard off this room. I'll have something hot ready in a moment."

Kate walks back to the mirror. She unpins the black veil from the white cap covering her hair, folds it neatly in a square, and places it on a chair. Then she pulls off the tight cap and runs her fingers through short, curly brown hair. She takes off the wimple covering her neck, the scapular, and finally her skirt and blouse. The image staring back at her is almost boyish, a tall slim body in a white cotton T-shirt.

She grabs the towel he has left and pushes open the door to the courtyard. The thin crystalline air stings her as she hurries through her wash at the sink. She returns gratefully to the bedroom, which, although chilly, is well lit and comforting with its maple single bed, so much like her old bed at home in St. Louis. Tucking her hair behind her ears, she cinches the bathrobe tightly around her waist and pads back to the living room in the Englishman's warm socks.

He is stooped over the stove, stirring the soup. "I forgot to introduce myself," he says, not looking at her. "I'm Peter Grinnell, on loan from Cambridge University to study Andean history and culture. Actually, I'm leaving tomorrow. I'm off for a month or two of vacation in Surrey. Summer's quite green and pleasant there."

She is grateful for the easy way he chatters on. Somehow he's sensed her deep embarrassment at appearing before him without her habit and veil.

He hands her a glass of amber liquid. "It's whiskey and

honey. There should be lemon too, but try finding lemons any-where up here."

Kate thinks of her father. A hot toddy was always his favorite cure for a cold or the flu, or even for the desolation of a windy February night. "Thanks. May I help?"

Unsure of protocol, Kate sits clutching her glass of whis-key. After a sip, she feels the warmth invade her empty stomach.

Peter serves the soup carefully and sits down across from her. He pushes his chair back from the table and lights a ciga-rette. "You don't mind?"

"Of course not."" Kate knows she is devouring the soup greedily, but doesn't care. There are biscuits, too, hard but filling.

"Well, Sister Mary Katherine, you frightened me a bit when I saw you all white and ghostly in the moonlight. I thought you were a spirit. The Aymara talk about the mountain gods who sometimes appear in the form of animals, birds, often the condor, but also as people—even as foreigners."

Kate remembers the condor she'd seen over Lake Titicaca. She grins at him, relaxing for the first time that day. Fortunately, this cool, middle-aged Englishman doesn't seem shocked by an American nun sitting by his fire in his pajamas, enjoying his whiskey and soup.

He squints through the cigarette smoke, and asks abruptly, "How old are you?"

"Twenty-five."

"Ah, a little young for the solitary life of the Altiplano, I suppose."

Solitary? Since she'd left St. Louis she hadn't been alone for a minute, and yet she realizes with a jolt that there is a deep core of loneliness inside. She answers slowly. "Well, I suppose I am still pretty green. I came to Peru from our Motherhouse in St. Louis a year ago. Then a month in Lima, followed by five months in Cochabamba at the Maryknoll Language Institute. I've been here in Juliaca since January."

"Did you study Aymara in Coch?"

"Very little—most of the course was Spanish. I had about three weeks of Aymara."

Peter gets up abruptly and paces across the room. "I must say, you Americans can be damned naive at times. Green, happy, middle-class innocents flocking in droves to do good—not understanding the people or the culture, putting up buildings, bringing in U.S. dollars and medicine." He glances over to see if she is offended. "What do you do up here anyway? You're a nurse, I suppose?"

"No, but I wish I had studied nursing." Kate shoves her empty bowl away and takes another drink of whiskey. "At least then I could be sure I was really doing something useful. Of course, Sister Jeanne Marie—she's our nurse—says that by the time she sees the patients it's usually too late to do much—T.B., cholera, dysentery." Kate knows she is rattling on but is unable to stop. *Is it the whiskey?* she wonders. "Anyway, my job is teaching the children to read in Spanish, and I give catechism classes to the women and teenagers, with an interpreter who translates my halting Spanish into Aymara. God knows what message comes out!" She falters, "Actually, I don't know what I'm doing."

She looks up to find his eyes on her; they are green, she sees, fringed by thick dark lashes, like a girl's. "What made you want to be a nun in the first place?"

Kate stares into the fire for a few moments. "I felt called somehow."

He laughs at this. "Okay. Second question: What are you doing wandering around the Altiplano alone at night?"

She looks up, catching his ironic stare. She looks away. *Because I'm burning up with love*, she wants to say. She thinks of St. Augustine's Confessions: "Burning, burning, so I came to Carthage." Would he recognize the quote? In the firelight she sees a face—Father Tom's as he had appeared that morning in his gold and white vestments at Mass. His dark, unruly hair slicked back, his eyes closed as he raised the Host at the consecration. His hands had gripped the Host as if willing God's presence into the damp old church. And she, a nun, drowning with love and desire for him.

Peter waits. The music rises and falls, a stream rushing out to the sea.

"I had to get away. I was suffocating."

"Do the other nuns know where you are?"

"No." She doesn't even know where she is.

Kate watches him as he gets up and walks over to a table beside the front door. He picks up his keys. "I'll take you back now, if you like."

She begins to shiver. The warmth of the fire cannot reach the cold within. He walks over and stands in front of her. "Sister Katherine—whatever your name is—they'll be worried about you."

She rises to face him. She forces herself to speak calmly; he must not think she is crazy. "Peter, I'd be so grateful if I could stay here tonight."

"Look, I have to leave in the morning. I'm going in to Arequipa to stock up on some film, get my mail, and see a few friends. Then on Saturday I go to Lima for the flight to London."

"Do you think I could catch a ride with you to Arequipa?" Kate strives for a light tone—as if she were a college girl going away for the weekend.

Peter gazes into the fire, avoiding her eyes. "You really ought to go back to Santa Catalina, you know. They'll be worried about you."

"No, I can't." She tries to keep the edge out of her voice. "I just need to get away so I can think. I'll let them know some- how that I'm all right. Please, Peter, you've been so kind." She stops, afraid to say more.

He comes toward her. "All right. I'll probably be arrested for abducting a nun. We'll leave here in the morning at six thirty sharp, when the fog's burned off. I want to make Arequipa by nightfall." He reaches out as if to touch her hair, then drops his hand. "Good night, Sister," he says with just a touch of mockery.

After the warmth of the fire, the guest room is freezing. Kate flings the bathrobe on the foot of the bed and slips between the sheets. She pulls the rough woolen blankets around her. They smell musty; Peter mustn't have much company. In the dark, she starts to tremble. What is she doing? She has taken the coward's way out, she knows. Running away from Santa Catalina isn't helping her think straight. She is only worrying a lot of good people who have other, more important things to do than chase after a twenty-five-year-old nun who should know how to handle falling in love. *Falling. Yes, fallen.*

# *C*hapter Three

*In* the strange bed, Kate is restless, turning from side to side, smoothing the pillow. She was so excited about coming to Peru just one year ago. She did well during the five months in language school in Cochabamba, earning the praise of her teachers as well as of the other students who were struggling. Now, after only six months in the Altiplano, she is out of her depth.

She remembers her first glimpse of Tom. It was in December, just six months ago, after she'd traveled all night on the bus from language school in Cochabamba to La Paz. At the train station, she was to meet the team of priests and nuns she would be working with in Juliaca. Cold and tired, she'd felt relieved to see the tall form of a Dominican nun waiting for her in the crowd. When Sister Josepha embraced her, Kate breathed in the clean, unmistakable scent of Palmolive soap. Then she noticed two men standing by, waiting to be introduced.

Sister Josepha led her over to the priests. "This is our pastor, Sister, Father Jack Higgins." Kate felt her hand crushed between the rough hands of a tall, gray-haired man in a black windbreaker. Beneath it she saw a gray sweater, but no evidence of a Roman collar. He motioned to the man beside him, and

Kate looked up into blue eyes that reminded her of a winter sky in Missouri.

"Tom Lynch," he said, and she recognized the tones of the west of Ireland, the lilt of her grandfather.

"Sister Mary Katherine O'Neill," she found herself saying in her most prim nun voice.

"Well, Sister Mary Katherine O'Neill, let's get the hell out of here. It's freezing, and we haven't had breakfast." Grabbing her suitcase, he strode ahead as Sister Josepha and Father Jack walked beside her through the crowded bus station. She'd had the faint impression that Tom Lynch was making fun of her, but soon forgot about him in her struggle to breathe. Her heart racing, she had to stop several times to catch her breath.

"It's the altitude, my girl. You're at 12,000 feet now," boomed Father Jack. "You'll soon get used to it. Why, look at Josepha here. She's a pro by now."

Sister Josepha smiled slightly and took Kate's arm. "Don't worry, Sister. We all felt that way at first." The nun led her to the street where Father Tom was already in the jeep, waiting.

He drove fast through the winding, narrow streets of La Paz, barely missing several *campesinos* heading for market with baskets of potatoes and beans. They pulled up in front of a two-story brick bungalow on a shady street that angled sharply up a steep hill.

"Now don't get used to all this luxury," warned Father Jack. "Juliaca is nothing like this. We're having breakfast with the St. Louis priests and nuns at the convent of Cristo Rey; then we'll drive on to Juliaca later today."

Tom had already hopped out and was at the front door, greeting the two nuns who stood there and slapping the backs of a couple of priests in the entrance. He looked more like a politician than a priest.

During breakfast the whole group wanted to hear the latest gossip from Cochabamba and the language school. Kate told them about her teachers, especially the ruthless nineteen-year-old Mirta who had made her life miserable for the two weeks she had taught Kate Spanish. Then over bacon and eggs and strong coffee, the men and women traded stories of their own struggles to learn the language. Many had studied Aymara and Quechua as well as Spanish. Kate was stunned by the easy camaraderie among them; some called each other by first names, unlike the stiff "Yes, Sister," "No, Father," repeated endlessly at home.

Kate found herself glancing too often down the table to where Tom Lynch was engrossed in a quiet conversation with a white-haired priest for much of the meal. Once she heard the younger priest raise his voice and pound his fist on the table.

"Well, the gobshites that did this will pay. Kennedy was a great man, and you Americans will see to your shame what follows."

The group quieted suddenly at the mention of the luminous young president, the first Catholic to hold the office, gunned down in Dallas in November. Father Jack said they were waiting anxiously for copies of *TIME* and *Newsweek* to arrive with the news they had only gotten in bits and pieces over the shortwave radio from Maryknoll in New York. Though Bolivian papers were full of the news, Father Jack complained about the confused accounts he read. "Or maybe it's just my Spanish that's confused," he said with a sigh.

Kate hadn't believed the news of the president's death at first when the young Chilean teacher who was her favorite had told her gently that morning at language school. How could he be dead, their young president, who had stood hatless among the sober old men on the morning of his inauguration? She'd seen all those pictures in *LIFE* Magazine, Kennedy scooping up his daughter, playing on the beach with his son, grinning down at his dark-haired wife. To her he seemed everything a man should be. Secretly Kate had felt a fierce tribal pride that he was Irish

Catholic. And now he was gone. Today was the first chance she'd had to talk about the assassination with Americans. They felt shame and confusion, as did Kate. What was happening to their country?

The meal broke up quietly, and soon Sister Josepha was loading the jeep with supplies for the infirmary in Juliaca as well as groceries for their house.

They left the city slowly, winding up the bowl-like city streets in a cloud of mist for half an hour. Kate felt nauseated, light-headed.

Father Jack turned around, his arm draped over the seat. "You know, Sister, it's summer here now, so that means the rainy season."

Kate pulled her black wool cloak tightly around her and reached into her bag for gloves. The damp cold was penetrating, and she was glad for the hearty breakfast that still warmed her.

"Just think of the Altiplano like Scotland, and you'll always be dressed right," said Tom, not taking his eyes from the treacherous road. "Summer is never summer here."

"I've been spoiled by Cochabamba," said Kate. "The weather was perfect there—cool nights and warm hot days." Kate thought wistfully of the garden in back of the Maryknoll house where she had studied each afternoon, a glass of iced tea at her side.

"Ha—that's our strategy, young Sister," laughed Father Jack. "We soften you up for the kill in Coch and then we let you see Juliaca."

Sister Josepha took out her breviary; Father Jack was snoozing in the front seat. It had begun to rain, and Kate found herself watching Tom's long white hands on the steering wheel and the way the black hair on them curled. Occasionally he would glance at her in the rear view mirror, but he looked away when their eyes met.

She stared out through the rain. The flat treeless pampas were deserted. They passed a little boy, about seven or eight, herding his scraggly bunch of sheep with a stick. Kate wondered how far he had to go. After a while the sun came out and white clouds appeared and disappeared in roadside lakes made by the rain. Blue and white and gray, an alien landscape flashed by with nothing familiar. Nothing seemed real except the snow-capped mountains in the ever receding distance. Then, at last, she fell asleep.

Kate awoke with a jolt to hear Father Jack exclaim, "What the fuck?" He leaped out of the jeep. A taxi, actually an ancient American Ford, was on its side in the ditch. The five or six passengers stood around the driver who sat on the ground holding his head in his hands. As she climbed out of the jeep, Kate saw the stream of red oozing from a gash over his eye.

Walking to the edge of the road, Kate heard a faint sound below. Down a steep incline, she saw six dead sheep scattered like stuffed toys on the brown field. A small boy—could it be the one she had glimpsed earlier?—stood nearby, weeping helplessly. Kate came over to him as the priests went to see if the taxi driver was hurt. The child wiped his runny nose on the back of his hand and gazed dully up at her. A blue stocking cap was pulled down over his head; the sharp lines in his face made him look like an old man. Around his mouth was a patch of rough white skin. His aqua sweater, with its carefully mended patches at the elbows, was too small. Gray pants, baggy and torn, fell down over his rubber sandals. He had a dirty white cloth wound around his shoulder and chest. Kate guessed it held his lunch. When he began to wail, Sister Josepha came over to where Kate stood watching helplessly.

"*Nene, que pasó?*" The older nun knelt in the dust next to the boy, her face close to his. He began talking rapidly in Aymara. Kate caught only some of his words, but gradually it became clear that the taxi had hit his flock of sheep as it was rounding the curve in the road. Now his father would beat him, for he had lost the sheep he was guarding. Kate saw a man in the distance approaching from the fields, dressed in black with a felt hat pulled down over his face. As he neared, the child ran to him and threw himself at his feet.

The father bent over and brushed the boy's head with a swift gesture and then gently disentangled himself from the boy's grasp. He looked at the carnage impassively, then slowly walked up the hill to the taxi and the two priests. A long conversation took place, with the taxi driver gesturing wildly and motioning toward the child. Kate couldn't tell what was happening, but finally she saw Father Jack take out a notebook and write down something as the two Bolivians looked on. Everyone shook hands then, but the eyes of the farmer looked murderous to Kate. By now the boy had gathered together the few remaining sheep; he followed his father down the steep bank toward the faraway hills.

Back on the road, the two priests discussed the incident for a long time. Kate could think only of the child's despair. In her poor Spanish and non-existent Aymara, she hadn't been able to comfort him. By noon they came to the border crossing at Desaguadero. Stiff and cold, Kate was relieved to climb out of the jeep. She stretched and looked around for a bathroom. Suddenly Father Tom appeared next to her. He motioned for her to follow him into the office of the guard.

"Have your passport ready to be stamped," he said over his shoulder. "You need the *salida* from Bolivia, and then you'll get the *entrada* into Peru."

She handed the priest her passport. He opened it idly and read aloud: "Born May 1st, 1938. 5'6", 118 pounds. Hair, light brown, eyes, blue." He grinned and handed it back. "I wonder if they'll be checking your hair color now, Sister Mary Katherine."

Why did he always say her name like that, drawing it out sarcastically? It was irritating. She shot him a look that was meant to be defiant, but it was wasted, for he had already walked over to the guard's desk to begin negotiations for stamping.

Kate was beginning to realize that nothing official in this country would be easy. It seemed that the man in charge of stamping had gone to lunch. He would most certainly be back in two hours, but the visitors, the guard emphasized, were more than welcome to wait in the office chairs or take lunch at a nearby café.

As Kate followed the Irish priest out of the office, she tried not to hear the good-natured curses that flew between Father Jack and Tom. She hoped no one passing by understood English. Then the two priests decided to get beers at the only bar in town. "Sisters, care to join us?" asked Father Jack.

"Oh, no thanks, Father," said Sister Josepha. "Sister and I will look around town and get a little snack."

Kate supposed this tour would take no more than five minutes. Gazing at the shabby gray buildings, she stepped carefully around the muddy puddles in the dirt road, holding her habit above her ankles.

They found a cramped cafe with a few tables huddled in one corner. The meal for the day was rice and beans with a small piece of dried codfish plopped in the middle. The nuns ordered *una gaseosa*, soda, to drink, knowing it would be safer than tap water. Kate was relieved to see the owner of the cafe, who apparently doubled as the waiter, bring two bottles of Coca-Cola to their table. Her stomach felt rocky. "I'm not feeling so well," she said.

"It's *soroche*, altitude sickness," Sister Josepha said. "It can really be very bad. Mother Mary Margaret had to have oxygen when she visited us here last year."

"But I've noticed that neither you nor the priests seem to be bothered by the altitude. How long will it take me to get used to it, do you think?" Kate hated to think of herself as weak and sickly. It had scared her that every few feet they walked she had to stop and catch her breath as if she'd just run a race.

"Oh, but we've been here for years. Give yourself time. Your body will accustom itself to the rarefied air, little by little.

Jeanne Marie says that the people who live here have more blood than we do. Their lungs have expanded, too."

Sister Josepha poured her Coke into one of the two smudged glasses the owner brought on a tray. Kate decided she'd drink hers right from the bottle.

Sister went on, "The funny thing is that when the people from the Altiplano go down to the coast, they get sick. Their bodies can't take the thick, humid air." She looked closely at Kate, her light blue eyes narrowing beneath almost invisible blond eyebrows. "You're in a different world here, Sister."

Around two-thirty the customs official strolled toward his office, picking his teeth meticulously as he unlocked the door. Peering over his wire spectacles, he read slowly, mouthing each word silently. Finally with a flourish, he stamped their documents. Soon the group crossed the bridge into Peru, where another wait was in store as their passports were carefully inspected and stamped again. "Damn it to hell," Father Jack muttered as he climbed in the driver's seat. "We have at least another four hours to Puno. I don't think we'll make Juliaca by dark, do you Tom?"

"It depends on what's ahead. The rain seems to have cleared." Suddenly Tom turned around and looked at Kate. "Would you by any chance know how to drive a jeep?"

Before she could answer Sister Josepha intervened. "Oh Father, you know she just got here. We can hardly expect her to drive these strange roads."

But Kate was determined to prove herself to the Irishman. "Of course, I can drive. My brother taught me years ago in our old Chevy Nova. One of the first things I did when I got to Lima last June was to get a driver's license. It took at least five trips downtown and a whole month before I could take the test. I'll be happy to drive."

"Good. You can drive when Jack gets tired. We have a long way to go."

In the dim light of the back seat, Kate examined Tom's profile, his high forehead and thin curved nose. She watched as he settled into his seat, hunkering down in his wool jacket. He turned around to look at her.

"It's grand to meet a nun who has a brother. Now maybe you won't be so shocked by the male crudeness around here." When Tom laughed, Sister Josepha hit him smartly on the back with her breviary. He pulled his collar up and yawned, "I'm going to sleep now. The beer has caught up with this one, I fear."

Kate closed her eyes, too, only to wake in darkness to the screech of a train. "We're here," Sister Josepha whispered. Kate looked out the window. She could see the outlines of a few buildings. The town was dark except for the lights of the train station at the end of the street.

Father Jack turned into a driveway on the side of a squat solid church and drove past several buildings, dark and silent. What time was it? Kate wondered. Lights burned in one long low building at the edge of the compound.

"The sisters are still awake," Sister Josepha said. "They shouldn't have waited up. They'll be dead tomorrow morning." But she sounded happy nonetheless, and before the jeep stopped, the front door swung open and Kate saw two nuns silhouetted in the light. Soon everyone was milling around, unloading supplies and chattering. The smaller of the two nuns introduced herself as Sister Jeanne Marie. Kate had a blurred impression of brown eyes and a soft rounded body.

"We're so glad you're here, Sister. It's lonely up here and we've been needing some young blood. We've been counting the days until you finished language school." She grabbed Kate's arm and gestured toward the white-veiled novice who was carrying groceries into the house. "And you'll be good company for our latest addition, I hope. Sister Magdalena doesn't quite know what to make of life up here."

Kate was puzzled by this, but in the confusion of unloading the jeep there was no time to ask questions. She turned to thank the two priests for bringing her to the mission, but all she saw were the jeep's red tail lights receding in the distance.

Now in this stranger's house, Kate tries to remember if even then she noticed that her world seemed flatter and less luminous after Tom Lynch left them that night. She does remember being surprised by the warmth and good taste of the convent.

The house she entered that first night in Juliaca was one she never would have expected to find in the Altiplano. In the States, it would be regarded as a modest brick bungalow, one in which a blue-collar family might be comfortable. But in this country, where the people they passed lived in mud-and-grass huts, it was a palace. She thought with confusion of her vow of poverty. To the people of the Altiplano, the foreign nuns and priests must seem rich, privileged like the landlords they worked for.

The small front parlor was austere enough, a few stiff wooden chairs and a large crucifix on one wall. But then beyond the translucent glass door, where few were admitted, Kate entered a rectangular room lined with bookshelves on one side and dark red plaid curtains on the other. At the far end of the room was a fireplace, with an old sofa and two easy chairs arranged around it; Kate saw a basket of red knitting on one of the chairs. The wide planks of the wooden floor gleamed.

"What a lovely room," Kate said uncertainly.

"Yes, we've tried to make it comfortable," said Sister Josepha, looking around proudly as if she were an industrious housewife. "But you can see everything else tomorrow. You'll have your first day off to get used to the altitude. Then we'll put you to work. Oh, the bell will ring at five thirty. Lauds and meditation are at six in the church. Sister Magdalena will show you to your room." She looks carefully at Kate. "Will you be all right? You look a little pale."

"I'm so tired, but thanks, Sister. Thanks for bringing me here."

Sister Magdalena looked shyly at Kate and picked up her suitcase. Kate followed the novice down a hall past several closed doors on either side. She pushed open the door to Kate's room, smiled up at her, and whispered, "*Bienvenida a Perú, Hermanita Catalina. Nos vemos mañana.*" She closed the door of Kate's room quietly.

Glad to be alone at last, Kate sat on the thin mattress. Her room was spare, just a bed, a small nightstand, and a desk with an iron reading lamp. On the desk, someone had put a few dried branches of eucalyptus in a clay ceramic vase. She walked over to the desk and inspected the vase. She saw that it was a woman's body, squat and powerful with full breasts and a swollen belly. The two handles on either side were arms. What an odd decoration for a nun's room. She wondered who had put it there.

During the night she awakened and sat up several times, gasping for air, her heart hammering beneath her ribs. When she lay back, she could feel blood surging through her veins. Her dreams that night were of riding, riding along a twisting road, where the mountains slipped in and out of high clouds so that she could not tell where she was going.

After breakfast the next morning, Sister Josepha clinked her spoon against her glass. "*Benedicamos Domino*," she said, indicating the end of the Grand Silence of the night before.

"*Deo Gratias*," the three intoned, and everyone looked at Kate.

"Did you sleep all right? I listened at your door a couple of times, but I didn't hear anything," said Sister Jeanne Marie. She looked fresh and efficient in spite of the interrupted night.

"Not really," Kate said. "I felt like I was drowning several times."

Jeanne Marie stood up to clear her place. "That's the altitude. I've got pills if you need them. Marta can make you a cup of *mate de coca* after a while, too. That's the remedy the people here swear by."

"*Mate de coca?*" Kate had been told how the people of the highlands chewed coca leaves to deaden the hunger and cold of their days. Their teeth were often stained and dark from the leaves. Did the nuns use it, too?

Jeanne laughed at the expression on Kate's face. "Don't worry. It's pretty harmless when taken in tea. I don't think you'll get addicted."

Kate noticed that Sister Josepha had a hint of a frown playing around her blond eyebrows. The older nun spoke softly. "Try to get through the day without medicine. Just don't exert yourself too much. I thought you might like to go with Marta to market this morning. I think I hear her in the kitchen."

When Sister Josepha pulled back the plaid curtains, Kate saw that one wall of the living room and dining room was a series of French doors opening to a patio. Although there was no grass in the courtyard, neat gravel paths had been raked and bordered with clumps of pansies, splashes of purple and yellow in the dusty courtyard. A single eucalyptus tree shaded a corner where two wooden chairs faced each other.

"Wow! How did you get these flowers to bloom?" asked Kate. "I read that the soil was so poor up here."

Sister Josepha smiled. "You know, I'm just a farm girl from Cottleville. Every time I go back to the States, I look for seeds of plants that I think can make it here."

"It's that Madre Josepha has the touch, as the people here say," Sister Magdalena said, stirring her coffee briskly. In the morning light she looked more sturdy and confident then she had the night before.

With a crash the swinging door to the kitchen bounced open and a small dark shape hurtled into the room. "*Buenos días, madrecitas.*"

Kate saw a dark, fat little boy of about three dressed in a

Mickey Mouse T-shirt and homemade pants. His bare chubby feet were covered with dust. He ducked behind each of the nuns, plucking their veils with a sly grin as he passed. When he stopped at Kate's chair, she found herself staring into dark-rimmed pools of light. His straight black hair fell over his forehead, and Kate longed to slide it back to feel its silkiness.

"This is Tito, the son of Marta and Alejandro. They make everything function around here—so we put up with this little urchin." Sister Josepha's gruffness was undercut by the way she held the child close to her body.

Sister Magdalena abruptly pushed her chair and began gathering dishes with a loud clatter. Her lips were tight as she went into the kitchen.

Watching Magdalena's retreat, Jeanne Marie whispered: "She thinks we spoil the child dreadfully. I'm afraid she doesn't approve of the way Tito's allowed to run wild around here."

The door opened again and a young woman of about eighteen with straight black hair pulled into a pony tail stuck her head in. "*Buenos días, madres.*" Kate noticed the sibilant quality of the young woman's speech, so different from the liquid music of Magdalena's coastal Spanish. This teenager must be Marta, Tito's mother and the convent cook.

While gathering up books and papers for the school day ahead, Sister Josepha called to Marta in the kitchen, "Come in and meet our newest Sister, Madre Catalina. She'll go with you to market today."

"*Mucho gusto, madrecita.*" Marta smiled, her broken teeth the only flaw in her young face. "*La madre es muy jovencita, no?*" She looked slyly at Sister Jeanne and winked. Kate sensed that Marta and Tito were an integral part of the household, and she'd have to adjust to the already existing alliances. Kate had never lived in a house with servants before. Having someone cooking for her and cleaning up after her made her self-conscious.

She thought of her mother, with three kids and a part-time job. Wouldn't she have loved a Marta? Kate remembered that her mother had finally hired a slight white-haired lady named Miss Elsie to iron and babysit once a week while she escaped to go shopping and visit her mother.

Well, she'd learn a lot of Spanish and maybe some Aymara while living in the house all day with Marta and the child. But was this living the vow of poverty?

After helping Marta with the dishes, Kate set out with her and Tito on the daily shopping trip. "Do you go to the market every day?" she'd asked the young woman in Spanish, struggling to remember her Spanish verb tenses.

"Oh *sí, madre*. I must go each day to find what is fresh. Then I will decide what to put in the soup."

They walked down the shady side street that the parish church faced, and soon came to the main street of the town. It was already bustling with business, for the morning began early in the mountains. As they walked the four blocks to the market, Kate stayed behind the mother and child, listening to Tito prattle in both Aymara and Spanish.

The market was a series of stalls where vendors spread out their wares and sat all day trying to sell hard potatoes no bigger than plums, beans, nuts, and sometimes fruit and onions. In one section dangled chickens and rabbits, plucked and shining. Kate wondered why they attracted no flies—perhaps because the cold dry air was inhospitable. She also saw a few barrels of fish, which Marta explained had been brought by truck from Puno very early that morning. In Kate's honor, she explained, she wanted to buy a nice *trucha*, but fish could only be bought on important feast days because Sister Josepha held the purse strings tightly. Marta gave a short wicked laugh as she said this, which made Kate wonder what she thought of the Americans she worked for. She watched Marta make her way haughtily through the crowd, ignoring the many calls from vendors wanting her to look at their wares. Kate guessed that Marta's position as convent cook gave her a status in the town that she relished.

After Marta selected the few things she needed for their meal, she guided Kate to a more chaotic section of the square. Aymara men and women squatted helter-skelter, their goods spread out on bright red and blue cloths on the ground. Here one could find *curas*, Marta explained, herbs, and potions for every need. In one area, Kate saw tiny curled-up dried creatures.

"What are those?" she said, gesturing. Marta explained they were llama fetuses, meant to be placed in the foundation of a new house or in a newly sown field.

"They make sure the house will bear fruit," she said, and lifted one up for Kate to inspect. Kate was transfixed by the tiny figure of the unborn llama nestled in Marta's rough palm. Suddenly her stomach heaved, and for one awful moment she felt she might vomit right there in the crowd. But the moment of nausea passed, and she hurried to catch up with Marta, determined to see everything.

There were ponchos for sale, made of llama wool and the softer, rarer wool of the alpaca. Kate examined the beads, fingering the amulets and clay figures. She remembered the vase in her room and wondered if Marta had placed it there for her.

After lunch Kate went with Sister Josepha to the school, to meet the *directora* and the other teachers. Sister Josepha told her about Father Jack's struggle with the government three years before to build a public school on the parish property with teachers paid by the government. The religion classes were taught by the nuns. "We won that battle," Sister said, striding briskly across the courtyard, her veil sailing out behind her, "but now the problem is getting the children to come. Their parents need them in the fields, and the little girls have to stay home to tend the babies while their mothers help herd sheep or work the fields. Babies . . . too many!"

Kate wondered at that. Was Sister implying they should use birth control?

"The teachers are always complaining that they have to re-teach everything every two weeks because half the class is usually missing. But Señora Montoya, who grew up in Puno, runs a tight ship and the school has grown over the past three years."

Sister Josepha hurried across the sunny gravel courtyard as the bell rang for afternoon classes. Kate struggled to keep up with her, her heart hammering fiercely from the effort. She knew Josepha had to be in her sixties; how was she able to move so fast?

"Señora Montoya is from Puno?" Kate asked, puzzled.

"Yes, she's a graduate of the University of Cuzco. Father Jack stole her from a Maryknoll school in Lima to start his school up here. She knows and understands the culture of the Aymara so well, she is priceless here."

They entered a one-story concrete building with a long hall. Kate heard the mingled sounds of songs and chants coming from several classrooms. A small woman in a gray suit walked quickly toward them.

Sister Josepha bowed slightly to the woman. "Señora Montoya, this is our new sister, Madre Catalina. She'll begin teaching the religion classes tomorrow. And Sister, this is our very capable director, Señora Luz Montoya."

Kate found herself looking down at the woman's smooth oval face; Señora Montoya stood stiffly erect before giving Kate a slight bow. "*Bienvenida*, Madre Catalina. We have been waiting for you with much anticipation. Would you like to see the school?"

Kate walked beside her down the hall, trying to adjust her stride to the tiny quick steps of Señora Montoya.

"Please feel free to wander around and sit in on the classes. You will find an interpreter in each room who can speak both Spanish and Aymara, so just talk to them if you have any questions." Señora Montoya bowed slightly again and walked into her office, motioning to Sister Josepha to follow her.

Kate wandered down the hall and saw that the school

was really only four large classrooms and a cafeteria with long tables. At one end of the cafeteria, several women scoured pots and pans while talking and laughing. They quieted when they spotted Kate at the door.

"*Buenas tardes, madrecita,*" the women called out with smiles. Realizing that they probably spoke only Aymara, Kate simply bowed and smiled. This was going to be so frustrating, she thought. She should have studied Aymara for months instead of a few weeks. Even her Spanish wasn't very good.

When Kate entered one of the classrooms, the children—rows of them in white coats—stood up and shouted greetings to her in unison. She looked into a sea of dark eyes. These were the youngest children; fifty or so were crammed at tables that reached to the back wall. They had pencils and notebooks in front of them, but no books that Kate could see. At the front of the room was a blackboard, and a map of South America was tacked to the wall. High over the teacher's desk hung a crucifix, and just below it a picture of a suave, gray-haired white man in a dark suit—President Belaunde, Kate realized. Tomorrow she would be expected to teach this class, as well as classes in the three other rooms. Though an interpreter would be at her side, how would she know what the kids were really thinking and understanding? Her head began to ache.

Later, crossing the courtyard, she ran into Father Jack and a stocky young man dressed in khaki trousers and a blue work shirt. "Ah, it's the newest addition," Father Jack said with a grin. "And how did you survive the first night in Juliaca?"

Kate smiled in what she hoped was a sporting way, saying that she had at least survived. She held out her hand to the young man. "You must be Alejandro. I spent the morning with Marta and your son, Tito."

Alejandro smiled widely, showing fine white teeth that contrasted sharply with his dark face. His eyes crinkled in the same way as his son's, and his hand was rough in hers.

"*Mucho gusto, madrecita. Bienvenida a mi pueblo.*" His voice was low and his Spanish very careful. Father Jack had explained yesterday in the jeep that Alejandro was a local boy who, six years earlier, had gone off to school in Arequipa at the suggestion of the priests. They had recognized his intelligence and hoped he would become a leader in the community. He was now an essential part of the parish team, able to teach the ways of his people to the American missionaries and, in turn, skilled at explaining the priests' teachings to the *campesinos.*

Kate wondered how he felt as he slipped continually from one world to another. As he walked away, Kate watched him snap his fingers at some boys who were chasing each other around the courtyard. Then he said something to them in Aymara, and they fell in behind him, matching his stride like soldiers.

Kate looked at the crinkled face of Father Jack, noticing the creases around his eyes and mouth for the first time. "I think I feel a little overwhelmed right now," she confessed.

"Of course, you do," he replied with New England briskness. "Give yourself time. With a name like O'Neill I know you're a fighter. Have you seen the clinic yet?" Without waiting for her answer he walked quickly toward a low building beyond the priests' house on the far side of the compound. As they passed the rectory Kate looked for Father Tom Lynch. But there was no jeep, and she felt oddly disappointed.

Entering the building from the bright midday sun, Kate was momentarily blinded. Then she noticed several women sitting on folding chairs around the room. They all had babies tucked into the shawls slung around their backs. Through an open door she glimpsed Jeanne Marie, her sleeves pinned up and a white apron stretched across her plump body. Bending over a baby, she listened intently to her stethoscope. The baby's mother, with her sunken, toothless mouth, looked more like the child's grandmother. When Jeanne noticed Kate and the pastor, she sighed as she straightened up.

"This one is hungry," she said quietly, motioning toward the baby. "See how distended the belly is? And the arms and legs are pitiful." She spoke rapidly in Spanish to a young woman who then spoke softly in Aymara to the impassive mother. The woman nodded and began wrapping the infant in a long white rag. Jeanne brought out two boxes of dried milk and explained carefully to the mother how she was to prepare it each day. She looked directly into the woman's face, but the woman kept her eyes lowered, nodding her head as if she understood. She then wrapped the baby tightly in her shawl and shuffled off, clutching the boxes in her hand.

"She's nursing the baby, but thinks she may be pregnant again. Her milk is drying up, she says. The baby cries all the time, and her husband is not patient."

Jeanne looked at Father Jack. He was moving restlessly around the room, picking up things and then putting them down.

"She'll probably be pregnant again in another month," Jeanne added.

The pastor avoided her pointed look. "Well, I'm off," he said. "I'm on my own for the next two weeks as Tom has gone out to the *campo*. He'll make the rounds of baptisms, weddings, Masses, and probably some funerals. He left this morning at dawn."

Kate felt a small drop in her heart, as if someone had deflated a balloon. She tried to convince herself it was the altitude.

# $\mathcal{C}$ hapter Four

$\mathcal{A}$fter their first meeting on the trip from La Paz to Juliaca, Kate hadn't seen Father Tom for most of December except on the days when he celebrated early Mass in the freezing church. She'd spent those first weeks trying to learn how to teach the children of the Altiplano, frustrated by being removed from them by not one but two languages.

So it was a considerable relief from teaching when Sister Jeanne Marie asked her to go along on a sick call a week after she arrived. Alejandro picked them up in the jeep, and they sped across the plains under billowing clouds, the sunlight sharp and unrelenting in their eyes. The mountains gleamed purple in the distance, receding endlessly from them, luring them on. Kate shut her eyes; later she opened them on golden fields with llama and alpaca grazing in the stubble. Dust swirled around them. From nowhere a cluster of huts appeared and a dog came running out to greet them, barking furiously. Kate stayed outside with the children while Jeanne Marie went into the dark hut with Alejandro to see the sick old man, Hernán. Kate could hear him coughing, and when the two emerged from the hut, Jeanne Marie's white apron was spotted with blood.

"Tuberculosis," she said. "There isn't much I can do except make him comfortable."

As they drove off, Kate looked back. The family stood still in the dying day, silhouetted against red clouds. All around them stretched vast plains. She watched until their figures merged with the plains and disappeared.

That night after supper, Kate and Jeanne Marie had talked about their day while they cleaned up the kitchen. Jeanne complained wearily, "I get so tired sometimes of rushing off to see someone when it's too late." She was bent over the sink with her sleeves rolled back, scrubbing the iron frying pan with desperate vigor. "Three years ago there was an outbreak of diphtheria. Whole families were wiped out. I had plenty of vaccine in the clinic, but we couldn't persuade the people to get the shots." Polishing the faucets, she continued. "Many people in the sierra prefer to go to their own *curanderos*."

"Yes, but at least what you're doing is concrete, real. I'm not sure that my classes are doing anything. Heck, half the time I'm not sure that Elva is really translating what I say. She goes on and on, and I just have to hope that she's not making up her own catechism lesson." Kate leaned against the counter, admiring the thoroughness of her companion as she scrubbed the sink with soap.

"Listen," Jeanne Marie insisted, "you teachers are teaching them to read. If the Aymara people become literate, they can solve their own problems."

"Tell me about the coca leaves, Jeanne. Today I watched a group of men in the market. They sat in a circle and passed around what looked like a lime, squeezing the juice over the leaves."

Jeanne laughed. "Well, what you saw is the equivalent of the men back home who go down to the corner tavern for a couple of beers after a hard day in the factory. Or at least that's what men did in Newark where I grew up."

Kate had known that Jeanne was from somewhere in the East, and now she could place the accent, her clipped speech. "Okay, but why the lime juice?"

"They wad the coca leaves up in a ball after they've sprinkled them with the juice, and then they chew it. Slowly the drug gets released from the leaves and suppresses hunger." She sighed as she took off her apron.

Once a month the whole team met in the priests' house to discuss their work and evaluate what they were doing. Kate found herself looking forward to her first meeting, getting a glimpse into the priests' house. She'd wondered at her excitement on the day of the meeting. It had been the week before Christmas, a clear day that ended in numbing cold. She and the other nuns arrived at the rectory at five o'clock as the mountain dusk fell quickly. Señora Montoya and Alejandro were waiting on the porch and greeted them as they came up the steps.

Before they could ring the bell, the door was flung open and Tom Lynch stood there, tall and welcoming in the doorway. As Kate passed close to him she saw that he had on a soft blue shirt. She was perplexed by the rush of warmth she felt as he helped her off with her cloak. He seemed surprised to see her, almost as if he had forgotten she existed. "Well, I haven't seen much of you except at early Mass. How have you been?"

"Okay, I guess. I know I fall into bed exhausted every night. They told me you've been out in the *campo*."

"Yeah, I love to be out there in the mountains. I get restless if I'm cooped up around here too long." He looked at the drink in his hand and ushered her into the living room. "I'm forgetting my duties as host," he said. "What will everyone have? There's coffee or hot tea, beer, whiskey, Scotch. You can see Father Jack and I are way ahead of you."

Kate glanced at a table covered with bottles of liquor. *All the comforts of home*, she thought. Alejandro accepted a beer, and Señora Montoya and the nuns all settled for hot tea. She would have liked a glass of wine but felt self-conscious about being the only woman to have a drink. Father Jack was smoking a pipe, and its fragrance made Kate think sharply of home and her father sitting in his red chair in front of the fireplace. She took the chair furthest from the center of things. She was new; she should try to keep quiet today.

Father Jack opened the meeting with some statistics on the numbers of people coming to the clinic and the school. He then called for reports from each team member and finally sat back with a grunt. "Well, the big news we have this month is that the government is starting a new program of redistribution of the land. Tom has been trying to find out how this will affect our people here. As you know, many of them work on the lands of Alfredo Muñoz Pacheco. Few families here own more than an acre of land for themselves. Tom, will you fill us in on the situation?"

Kate watched the face of the Irishman as he spoke for a long time about the government's new plan. Growing vehement as he spoke, he argued, "What we have done here is build a parish on the model of those in the States. I don't think that's what's needed here. We need to go out in the *campo* and talk to the men, get them in groups to listen to their problems, see what they think they need the government to do." His eyes were blazing, and his hands trembled a little as he brought his drink to his mouth.

Father Jack sighed and shifted in his chair. "Tom, we know what you think. You've told us a million times. Remember that our goal here is to work ourselves out of a job. In a few years we hope to turn the parish here over to the people."

Sister Josepha nodded. Kate noticed how flushed the older nun's cheeks had become, but when she spoke her voice was steady, controlled. "Father Tom, we're not all called to promote a revolution. The sisters and I just go on day by day, healing the sick, teaching, visiting—something like Jesus did, I suspect."

Frowning, the Irish priest's tone was icy. "Just remember that I come from a country where my people were denied ownership of land for centuries. We're not here to make everyone comfortable and at peace with the status quo. We have to provoke and unsettle and bother the hell out of the powers that exist. Our job is to disturb the consciences of the so-called Catholic elite."

No one said anything for a few moments, and soon the talk moved on to other subjects. Kate, tense and nervous, kept quiet. *After all,* she thought, *I'd better keep quiet until I know what I'm talking about.*

After the meeting, Señora Montoya and Alejandro left, but the nuns stayed on to share the spaghetti dinner Marta had brought over. Father Jack brought out a bottle of red wine, and Sister Josepha nodded as the pastor held the bottle over her glass. Jeanne winked at Kate as she filled a glass to the brim and passed it to her.

After supper they sang a few Christmas carols, and Kate heard Tom's voice over the others, slightly off key. She felt his eyes on her whenever she glanced his way, but he didn't speak to her the rest of the evening.

On the way home Sister Josepha and Jeanne Marie shook their heads in mock despair at Tom's tirade during the meeting. Jeanne Marie said, "Boy, do I get tired of hearing him put down our work."

Kate felt more confused than ever. To her companions, Tom Lynch was a wild man. Yet his arguments made sense to her. If these experienced missionaries couldn't agree on what they should be doing, how was she supposed to know?

She fell asleep thinking of Tom and wondering who had given him the lovely blue shirt.

So it had begun. Kate can't remember exactly when she admitted to herself what was happening. She remembers only an inexplicable happiness suffusing her work as she taught her classes, met with the women who came in the afternoons to learn to read in Spanish, and occasionally drove out in the *campo* with Jeanne Marie on a sick call. She came to love the austere early mornings as she walked across the courtyard from the convent to join the other nuns in the church for Lauds and meditation. The sky was just lightening, the air cold and clean against her face. Every sensation seemed sharper, more penetrating in those days. Precisely at six the bell of the sacristy struck, and she looked up to see which priest was celebrating Mass that day. When it was Father Jack, Kate would feel calm relief.

On the mornings when Tom Lynch's tall form strode into the sanctuary and bowed deeply in front of the altar, she concentrated on her missal in front of her, allowing herself only an occasional glimpse at him. He recited the words of the Mass in Spanish intently, gravely, as if every word were crucial and precious. Only in his sermons would humor flash. Then he would come down from the sanctuary and stand among them, urging the few people there to come forward to discuss the readings.

His sermons were actually conversations; Kate admired the way he could get people to express their thoughts about the gospel of the day. Tom would ask what they thought Jesus meant when he said that the kingdom of God is within you, or that one should render to Caesar the things that are Caesar's, but render to God the things that are God's. Often Alejandro would speak up, and so would the novice, Magdalena, passionately and at length. Kate rarely dared to speak, unsure of her Spanish.

Kate found herself looking forward to chance encounters with Tom around the parish. She would look up hopefully when a door opened in a classroom. Once he had come upon her when she was sitting on the floor with the women in Magdalena's weaving group. The young novice from Lima had organized a group who met twice a week to weave caps and sweaters, which they could sell in the marketplace. Formerly the women worked alone at home or in small groups in the *campo*, but Magdalena thought they would enjoy coming together in the large clean parish hall to chatter and exchange news. After Magdalena's group grew from four to sixteen or so, Kate decided that she would learn to weave, and she joined the group when she could.

The women seemed delighted to teach her, guiding her awkward fingers with rough dry hands that deftly wove the red, yellow, purple, and blue yarn and wool.

One day while sitting on the floor, she noticed dark, muddy boots and black trousers next to her. "What's this?" Tom asked in English. "The new one is going native on us."

She flushed. So what if the women couldn't understand? It was rude to speak in English, and joking about going native seemed uncharacteristically insensitive of him. She answered in clear Spanish so that the other women would hear: "It's just that women are always busy being useful, unlike men who seem to have time to stand around watching others work."

After several moments of shocked silence, the women tittered, their hands covering their mouths. Tom grinned at Kate and walked around to greet each woman and admire her work. *Honestly*, Kate thought, *the man must have been a politician in another life. He could surely turn on the charm when he felt like it.* She noticed that he sat for a long time next to normally quiet Magdalena, who talked earnestly to him in a low voice.

Suddenly Father Tom looked at Kate. "What are the two of you doing after this meeting?" he asked. Kate looked at Magdalena, who shrugged.

"I was just going to catch up on some letter writing before dinner. Why?" Kate asked.

"I'd like you both to ride out to Villa Maria with me. It's a small isolated enclave of a few families about an hour from here. I need to talk to the men, and Magdalena could check on the women and children who need medical attention."

Magdalena nodded, and headed for the clinic to gather some supplies and her first-aid bag.

But why did Father Tom want her to come along? She didn't speak Aymara, and they would not have a translator. Just then Tom turned to her, with a big grin on his face. She felt a blush rise to her cheeks, and turned away to find some paper, pencils, and crayons as well as some hard candy to take to the children. It felt as if he could read her mind.

A half hour later Kate climbed into the back seat of the jeep with the supplies while Sister Magdalena sat in front with Father Tom. The young Peruvian nun was animated as she chattered on in Spanish, laughing often at the priest's remarks. Her recent dark mood had lifted. Kate couldn't hear what they were saying over the noise of the engine, but as she watched them she found herself smiling. She settled back, gazing through the dusty windshield at the dirt road wandering through green fields dotted with yellow wildflowers. She had to keep reminding herself that it was spring here in the Southern hemisphere. Her world had been turned upside down. Gray hills undulated ahead of them, at times allowing a glimpse of the severe, snow-covered peaks of the Andes in the distance. Above, puffy white clouds bloomed in a sky so blue it was blinding.

They passed a woman driving her sheep through the field. Her face was hidden beneath the brim of a man's hat, and her red petticoat peeked beneath a full brown skirt that swayed as she walked. It looked as though she had a baby hidden in the striped blanket slung over her shoulder. Kate tried to imagine her life. How far did she have to walk to get home? Did she have food or water with her on her journey? How often did she have to stop to nurse the baby? She realized she knew nothing about this woman's life.

Finally they came to a group of five huts in the middle of a field, no trees, no grass, just a dusty yard near the road. When Tom pulled up in front, several men emerged from one of the huts, shyly pulling off their hats to greet him. The priest jumped out, embracing each one, slapping them on the back as he joked with them in Aymara. Soon two more men came out, followed by the women and children. The men headed with Father Tom to one of the huts. Magdalena and Kate went with the women and children into an adjacent hut. It was dark and smoky in the room, and it took Kate several moments to adjust to the dimness.

At first Kate thought these women must be the little children's grandmothers. Their faces were lined with age and sun and some had teeth missing. But when one of the women began nursing her baby, Kate realized these were young mothers, aged by their lives in the harsh climate of the Altiplano. Magdalena, using her newly acquired Aymara skills, explained to the women that she would listen to their hearts, and more importantly, listen to their stories and concerns. Meanwhile Kate took the seven little ones to a corner of the hut, sat on a stool while the children squatted on the dirt floor around her. They looked expectantly at the bags she carried. She gave out the paper, the new pencils, and the wildly colored Crayolas. Frustrated at not being able to speak to them, she smiled encouragingly as they began to draw and color right there on the floor, their dark eyes shining at her in the gloom. She understood a few words once in a while, and thought bitterly of her useless degree in English literature. Why hadn't she studied Aymara as well as Spanish at the language school? She was out of her depth here.

From the nearby hut, Kate could hear Tom's light tenor voice rising and falling, blended with the men's quiet deep tones and muffled laughter. Finally the priest's tall form appeared in the doorway, and he stooped as he entered the room, grabbing the bags of candy Kate had brought. Squealing, the children gathered around him, waiting excitedly for him to offer each one a fist full of peppermints and lemon drops.

"*Gracias, padrecito*," they shouted, smiling at the two of them. They hugged the priest's knees and he bent to be eye level with them. Over their heads, Tom grinned at Kate.

They said their goodbyes, and Kate noticed the sun was going down as they headed back to the jeep.

"Okay, candy lady, you ride shotgun this time and let Magdalena rest in the back seat," Father Tom ordered.

Magdalena climbed in and was soon resting her head on the window, her eyes closed in fatigue. Dusk was coming on quickly, and the sun's slanted rays lit up the fields with a rich golden light.

"So, Sister Mary of the candies, what did you think of the little group at Villa Maria?" Tom kept his eyes on the road.

Kate turned to him and tried to keep her voice from trembling. "Oh, I felt so useless! I wish I'd studied nursing so at least I could do something concrete like Magdalena and Jeanne Marie. What good is knowing Keats or Wordworth up here? Without a translator, I'm helpless."

Tom drove on a few minutes in silence and finally glanced at her. "Give yourself a break, Sister. You've only been here a few weeks. Today you brought laughter and spring time . . ." His voice trailed off.

Kate examined his hawk-like profile. "What were you talking to the men about?"

"Oh, we were trying to come up with some ideas for growing new crops here, exploring different ways of using the land, maybe even getting the regional government to sponsor some new methods."

Kate knew nothing of farming, she realized, but she could learn about the local government. She would read. She'd go to the American Embassy the next time she was in Lima and check out some book on agriculture. She was good at studying.

Now darkness was complete. The jeep's headlights traced the rocky road ahead. Tom's cigarette glowed. He drove fast, carelessly. She felt his gaze on her often, conscious of his body so close to hers. What could she say? *That I'm out of my depth here in this upside down universe? That I can't speak the language? That worst of all, I'm falling for you?* In the distance, Kate saw the new moon rising above the dark shadows of the mountains. She prayed for help. Then she felt Tom's hand on her arm.

"Would you like a drag of my cigarette?"

"Sure," she murmured, hoping Magdalena was asleep. She put the cigarette in her mouth. It tasted of him. She inhaled, and when she handed it back, he held her gaze. Then watching her, he put the cigarette to his lips and took a long draw. She did not look away. They drove back to Juliaca, the silence between them heavy, riding through the night on this darkling edge of the world.

# Chapter Five

Much to Kate's surprise, she wasn't homesick during her first Christmas in Peru. In the convent back home she always felt a stab of loneliness on Christmas Eve, so she expected a severe case of homesickness here so faraway.

Nochebuena was celebrated with Midnight Mass, just as it was at home. The sisters had spent the afternoon of December 24 decorating the old colonial church. Since there were no evergreens to be found, Alejandro and some of the men carried branches of eucalyptus trees into the church, and the nuns arranged them around the altar and stuck dozens of small white candles they had fixed in tinfoil holders among the branches. Jeanne Marie unwrapped the figures of the crib scene and placed them carefully in front of the altar. Kate was moved when she observed that the carved figures of Mary and Joseph and the shepherds were Aymara. The familiar scene looked so natural here in the Altiplano with the young poncho-clad mother bending over her tightly swaddled child and the sheep hovering nearby. She could almost feel their breath, warm and sweet.

As midnight approached, the four sisters lit the candles on the high altar. Kate watched Alejandro lift up Tito to pull the thick rope to the bell in the tower. After the ringing of the bell, they turned out all the lights as people from the *campo* began trickling into the church. By the time the two priests entered wearing glowing white and gold vestments, the church was packed with people, all dressed in their best feast-day clothes. The men wore red and blue knit caps, and brilliant woven tunics over their best white shirts. The women wore carefully brushed bowler hats, and their braids shone in the candlelight. All was still. No baby cried. In the darkness, a flute begin to play. Then reed pipes and a drum joined in, and a plangent music filled the church—Inca music played on a high plain at the top of a lonely world under the cold clear stars of Christmas.

She listened to Tom's heavily accented Spanish as he read the gospel of John:

> When all things began, the Word already was. The Word dwelt with God, and what God was, the Word was. The Word, then, was with God at the beginning, and through him all things came to be; no single thing was created without him. All that came to be was alive with his life, and that life was the light of men. The light shines on in the dark, and the darkness has never mastered it. . . . So the Word became flesh; he came to dwell among us, and we saw his glory, such glory as befits the Father's only Son, full of grace and truth.

Yes, she thought, *flesh.* God became flesh. That was the great truth. She clung to this God who had once become human, like her. Into the dense midnight of the Andes, the Light was coming. It was coming into Africa and India, China and Japan. All over Europe on this night people were hurrying to lighted churches, lifting their tired hopeful faces to the light. In the cities of America, well-dressed crowds, their stomachs full after the Christmas Eve dinner, were filling pews in warm, well-lit churches, waiting for the good news. Kate saw the world on this night, hushed and expectant, hungry for the light. And here, in a small forgotten speck of the world, the lights of the church came on, one by one, and the silent people there were bathed in light.

After Mass, Kate knelt for a while, watching people line up before the crib. They unwrapped their bundles and put down their offerings—corn and potatoes, wool, necklaces, even bottles of *chicha*—for the *niño* Jesus. Then they filed out into the cold Andean night. Marta and Alejandro walked out together, Tito slumped in his father's arms.

At the door of the church the two priests greeted the parishioners, the vapor of their breath rising and disappearing in the frosty air. Father Jack grabbed Kate in a bear hug and thumped her on the back. "*Feliz Navidad*, Sister. Happy first Christmas in Juliaca." His breath was warm, and he was sweating in spite of the cold.

Then she faced Tom. He took both of her icy hands in his. "Merry Christmas, Kate," he whispered.

She looked into his eyes, unable to speak at hearing her name on his lips. She moved away to let others greet him, hoping he had not seen the trembling of her lips.

Later, as she read Christmas cards from home she had been hoarding for weeks to stave off Christmas-day homesickness, she felt the warmth of Tom's hands. She was not sad at all. There was no other place she'd rather be on this night.

# Chapter Six

*A*fter the beauty of Christmas, January had been a let-down for Kate. It rained much of each day as great storms rolled over the mountains and swept across the plains. Lightning forked down from the mountains, and thunder crashed in rumbling waves. Some days the fog and mist never lifted. But Kate knew that the weather bothered her less than the prospect of Tom's imminent departure. She had been alarmed by the pang she felt when Jeanne Marie said he would be going down to Lima for R & R.

"R & R?" Kate said. "I didn't know priests got that."

"Oh yes," Jeanne Marie laughed. "Maryknoll owns a house near the beach north of Lima called Casa Mariana. They use it for retreats, but it's also available for their guys when they need to recuperate from the altitude. It must be nice," she sighed. "No one ever thinks nuns need to recuperate."

They were in the clinic where Jeanne Marie was finishing up her paperwork for the day. Kate was folding diapers, and as she looked out the window she noticed that the rain had changed to snow. She ran to the window. "Oh, it's beautiful. I didn't know it snowed here in Juliaca." The flakes were still delicately small, but as she watched they thickened until eventually the courtyard disappeared in a whirl of white.

Jeanne Marie joined her at the window. "Darn it! We have a catechists' meeting tonight. I'd rather sit by the fire and read a mystery. Would you mind bringing those diapers and bandages over to the house and finishing them tonight? You don't have to go to the meeting."

Kate noticed the droop of Jeanne Marie's shoulders. Kate was tired, too, and looked forward to a quiet evening. Her mother had sent her a few records for Christmas, and she could listen to them while folding clothes.

After supper and Vespers in the living room, Josepha and Jeanne Marie put on their cloaks and gloves; when they opened the front-parlor door, a gust of wind blew snow into the room. Alone now, Kate put on her new Horowitz recording of Liszt's "Nocturne," thinking it would be just right for this snowy night. As the first quiet chords filled the room, she finished washing the dishes, her sleeves rolled up and a blue-checked apron covering her white habit. Magdalena had gone up to bed early, complaining of a headache. They were all worried about the novice, for she had seemed sullen and withdrawn lately. Something was wrong. Just as Kate thought that she should go check on her and offer her a cup of tea, she heard a knock on the door. She opened the door, and Tom Lynch stood framed by a swirling mass of white, a red muffler wrapped around his neck his only concession to the blizzard.

"Hello." He stood awkwardly in the doorway, hunched against the cold.

"Come in. What an awful night." Kate stepped back as he entered the small parlor, brushing off snow from his hair and jacket. Kate smelled the cold on him. She hesitated, wondering if they should sit in the formal parlor.

"I thought I smelled wood smoke from the chimney. You wouldn't keep a traveler away from your hearth on a night like this, now, would ye?" Not quite meeting her eyes, he laid on the brogue thickly. Kate laughed, and led him into the living room, where Tom headed straight for the fireplace. He stood rubbing his hands while she went to hang up her apron. "Am I interrupting anything? Were you busy?"

"No, I was just going to fold some things for the clinic. Josepha and Jeanne Marie are at a meeting and Magdalena went to bed early." He still didn't meet her eyes, and his unexpected shyness brought out the hostess in her. "Look, you sit there in the big chair by the fire, and I'll make some tea." She went swiftly to the kitchen and turned on the gas under the kettle. Her hands shook as she spooned tea into the pot. *He's never done this before, just dropped by.*

When she came back into the room, he was looking at the record album. For the first time he looked directly at her, his eyes dark and serious. "The music is lovely. I didn't realize how much I missed it. Jack plays his Elvis records, but that's about the extent of our culture over there."

Kate laughed, thinking of the pastor listening to Elvis Presley in the mountains of Peru. "Sit down, Father. I'll get the tea."

"For God's sake, Kate, my name's Tom."

"Okay then, sit down, Tom, and I'll serve you your tea."

"Much better." He looked up at her and pulled a small silver flask out of his pocket. "A gift from my father. He used to take this to the Galway racecourse on a nippy afternoon. How about a drop of Irish whiskey in our tea?"

"Oh, you go ahead. But none for me, thanks." She was aware she sounded like someone's prudish aunt. But come to think of it, none of her aunts would ever have passed up a splash of whiskey.

"Come on, Kate, it's not good for a man to drink alone, and I don't feel like going to the bar in town tonight."

Kate wondered if he did go into town to drink, watching him as he poured a generous dollop into each cup of tea.

"Nice," he said as he looked at her over his cup. "Very nice." The fire crackled and music filled the silence between them.

Kate was kneeling on the Inca rug in front of the coffee table, folding each small diaper carefully. Uncomfortable with their silence, Kate searched for something to say. "Did you say Galway? My mother's people came from there. The name was O'Flaherty."

Tom threw back his head and laughed. "I might have known." He watched her puzzled face and laughed again. "There's a legend in Galway that at one time there was a huge sign at the city gates that read 'Beware the scourge of the O'Flaherty's.' They were a fierce clan that swept down on the city from time to time to wreak mayhem. So, you're an O'Flaherty. Tell me some more about yourself."

Kate relaxed a little and told him about St. Louis and her family and growing up in America. She kept glancing up to see if he were bored, but every time his blue eyes were fixed upon her. Once he got up to poke the fading fire, and she admired the athletic grace of his body and the ease with which he wielded the heavy iron poker.

"And you? Did you grow up on a farm in Ireland?" She had finished folding by now, and had settled into the chair opposite his in front of the fireplace. Without thinking, she tucked her legs underneath her, and stared into the fire to hide from Tom the pleasure she knew must be on her face.

"Oh, no. I'm a city boy, or at least a town boy. We lived in Salthill, a few miles outside of Galway. There's a boardwalk there on the beach. It's a place where tourists come in the summer to catch the rare Irish sun."

"I've never lived near the sea," Kate said. "In fact, my first glimpse of the sea was in Lima. The sisters took me to the beach at Herradura one day, and it felt so strange to stand in the sand and feel it shift from under my feet as the waves went back out. I didn't like it at first."

"Ah well, you have to push out beyond those breaking waves and into the deep waters. Then the sea holds you and plays with you." He held her glance for a long moment before looking into the fire. "I miss it sometimes, the sounds of it crashing along the rocks. It's so quiet up here."

"Is your family still there?" Kate was determined to prevent another silence.

"My parents are. They live in a bungalow they inherited from my mother's father. My sister Mary Grace got married a few years ago, and her husband dragged her off to Dublin where he teaches. They have a little son now, named after me. I've never seen him." He looked up suddenly. "You know, you remind me a little of my sister. You have that same kind of feistiness. We almost killed each other a few times growing up." His smile lit up his dark face. Kate felt let down by the thought that she reminded Tom of his sister.

He went on. "I was always outside as a kid, fishing, playing football—that's soccer to you Americans. But then I discovered books. My mother's brother has a small bookstore on Middle Street in town. It's called Charlie Byrne's Bookshop." He looked at her as if she should recognize the name. "Anyway, Charlie sells second-hand books, mostly Irish literature, but all the old classics, too. It's a dusty, out-of-the-way little shop where you can hole up for a rainy afternoon and read until your eyes ache. So, when I wasn't outside running around with my hooligan friends, my mother could always find me there in the afternoon or on Saturdays. When I was older I went to work for Charlie, and then went to University College to study literature."

"Is that in Dublin?"

"No, right there in Galway. But I was restless. My father was pushing me to join the Army, like him."

"I didn't know Ireland had an army."

"Ha—that's the one thing the Irish have been best at: fighting. My father was a teenager during the Troubles and ran messages for the IRA. Anyway, the main thing he does now is patrol the border between Northern Ireland and the South. But I had another idea in my head for my future. I wanted to be a priest, but not a priest who stayed at home in Ireland and listened to old ladies' confessions and played golf in Blackrock every Monday. I wanted to go far away, to be a missionary. So I played with the idea all the years I was at the university."

He stopped and glanced at Kate. Her tea was cold beside her. She knew his was, too, but to get up now would break the mood.

"The only thing that stopped me then, quite frankly, was that I wasn't sure I could give up women. Hell, I'm still not sure I can," he laughed.

"Women in general, or a particular woman?" Kate kept her tone light, teasing.

"There was one woman—a real woman, not a girl. A married woman at that." He looked at her. "Now I've shocked you, I see."

Kate shook her head. She hadn't reacted so much to the admission he'd fallen for a married woman as to the pain she'd seen in his eyes. Why was he telling her this? She waited.

"Oh, there's not much to tell. She was the wife of one of my professors, at least ten or twelve years older than I. She was elegant and sophisticated, and I think she enjoyed having poor sex-starved students lusting after her. I thought it was love for a long time, and would sit in my room reading Yeats' poems to Maud Gonne and thinking about her." He shook his head.

"I love Yeats," Kate said softly.

Tom recited:

When you are old and grey and full of sleep,
And nodding by the fire, take down this book,
And slowly read, and dream of the soft look
Your eyes had once, and of their shadows deep.

How many loved your moments of glad grace,
And loved your beauty with love false or true,
But one man loved the pilgrim soul in you,
And loved the sorrows of your changing face.

Tom broke off suddenly, and Kate looked away to hide the tears that had surprised her. Gazing across the room at her, he said with an edge of bitterness, "I seem always to be longing for something I can't have."

She sat unmoving for a minute. Then she rose and deliberately broke the mood by saying with false cheer, "I'll get us some more tea. Keep going with your story. When did you finally go to the seminary?"

But Tom had risen, too, and was heading for the door. "Oh, I went to Maynooth right after I got my degree. After four years there I was ordained, and spent a couple of years in Kerry. For the past seven years, I've been on loan to Maryknoll. I'm hoping they've forgotten about me back home. This life suits me—at least for now."

Kate walked with him to the door. As he put on his jacket and tied the muffler around his neck, his eyes shone down at her. "Here's your cloak, Kate. Walk outside with me a bit in the snow."

She turned around so he could place it on her shoulders. For a moment nothing happened. Just as she started to turn around to see what was wrong, she felt his face close to her own. He said nothing, but placed the cloak firmly on her shoulders. They stepped outside into the snow-covered courtyard.

No flakes fell now. A million stars hung uncommonly near in the black sky. Conscious of her joy as she walked beside him, she wanted the earth to halt its spin toward dawn. No words passed between them.

Suddenly lights from a jeep caught them in its glare, and they froze. It was Alejandro, and now Kate, squinting, could see Jeanne Marie sitting next to him.

"There's been an accident. A man from the village has dropped his child in the ditch and the baby drowned. He was drunk, and now he's crying, begging for the priest to come and baptize the child." Jeanne's voice was exasperated but urgent.

"Damn," Tom muttered under his breath. "The baby's dead. I can't baptize it, Jeanne. It's not magic you know."

Alejandro said nothing. He waited while the priest and nun stared at each other. Finally, Tom spoke.

"Okay, I'll come and see what I can do. It just makes me so mad to get these calls after something terrible has happened."

"Can I come, too?" pleaded Kate.

"No, there's nothing you can do." Tom had already jumped in the jeep, squeezing in next to Jeanne Marie.

"Tell Josepha what's happened. I left her in the parish hall." Jeanne's voice had faded as the jeep roared off, making ugly black tracks in the snow.

Kate walked back to the convent alone, and for the first time that night felt the cold air penetrate to her very bones.

# Chapter Seven

Two weeks after that night, Tom left for Lima. They saw each other briefly at odd moments, but he seemed distant and preoccupied. In his absence, Kate's world had gone gray and cheerless. At last, she'd admitted the truth to herself: she was in love with him. One of her worst moments came when, reliving the night of his visit, she realized that when Jeanne had told them about the death of the baby she had felt no compassion, no pity for the baby, only anger that their time together had been interrupted. What was happening to her? She begged God during meditation to help her get over this crush; if she called it a crush, it wasn't serious.

She prayed and meditated, taught her classes, visited the sick, laughed and joked with the small group of teenagers from town who came to the weekly youth group. But in a terrible literal sense her heart was not in these things. She was discovering the tyranny of love, that awful dependence on a look, a smile, a gesture. She hated feeling this way. But suddenly she would feel a surge of happiness during her work, thinking of his smile, the deep tones of his voice.

She kept repeating to herself St. Thomas Aquinas' definition of love: "To love is to will the good of the other." If she loved Tom Lynch, she wouldn't hurt him. That was the question, wasn't it? What was good for this man? She decided at last that she could never tell him how she felt. She would enjoy seeing him, talking to him, knowing that he existed in the world. Then one of them would be transferred away and that would be that. He was a priest forever. She could not damage that and still claim she loved him. At night she wound her rosary though her fingers and tried not to remember his hands on her shoulders as he'd helped her with her cloak that night.

By February, Kate found herself more at home in the world of Santa Catalina. She had grown to love little Tito and spent time reading to him from a few small children's books she'd found. He sat sprawled on her lap in the garden after lunch while she read to him *Anibal Busca Aventuras*. She inhaled the dust and sweat of his hair, combing it with her fingers. She loved the shape of his bottom in her lap, the feeling of his head against her breast as he sucked his thumb while she read to him.

Now when she walked with Marta to the market, the vendors called out her name. "*Buenos días*, Madrecita Catalina." Alejandro, Tito's father, was still a mystery to her. She often wondered what he was thinking. He worked so closely with the priests and nuns; he saw them when they were short-tempered and grouchy and when they made big mistakes in understanding the people. When she tried talking to him about his hopes for the future, he would usually smile shyly and say only that he was very happy working with the *padres* and hoped his son would grow up to be educated. Once he taught her a word in Aymara, *chaskanawi*, and she loved saying it over and over, its consonants exploding on her tongue. It meant "girl with stars in her eyes."

So, one day at lunch when she glimpsed the letter addressed to her in heavy black ink with the Lima postmark on the buffet in the dining room, it felt like a disturbance, a threat to the precarious peace she had achieved.

"Hey, that looks like Father Tom's writing," said Jeanne Marie looking over Kate's shoulder at the letter. Sister Josepha looked at Kate and rang the bell for grace, saving Kate from having to respond. Kate left the letter on the buffet, and then, after she finished the dishes, she slipped it into her pocket and went upstairs to her room.

Her heart was thundering, and she knew it wasn't the altitude this time. She tore open the thin airmail paper, ripping a piece of the letter in her eagerness.

*Dear Kate,*

*I have started this letter to you many times and then torn it up in disgust at my inability to say what I need to say to you. In case you hadn't noticed, I've fallen in love with you. . . .*

Kate stopped reading and took several gulps of air. Her cheeks flamed.

*It wasn't anything I planned to do, and I can only say that I tried hard to deny it to myself. But those mornings in church I'd see you sitting there so calmly, staring up at me while I nattered on in my sermon, laughing at the jokes no one else even knew I was making—that's what really did it.*

*You are like springtime, young and lovely and breathing hope into me when I've felt so dry and stale. I've begun to see the world through your eyes; you make it new and fresh for me. This is getting really incoherent, I know. Then the snowy night when I came to the convent, hoping you'd be alone and you were. When I held your cloak for you I had to force myself not to take you in my arms. Oh Kate, this is impossible.*

*I've had time to think it through a bit here in Lima. I don't want to hurt you, and I think I could, badly. You see, I still want to be a priest. It's the deepest core of who I am, and even though it is a frustrating, foolish, at times even*

*God-forsaken life, it's the life I vowed. And you are a wonder-*
*ful nun. You make it seem easy to be happy, and I've met very*
*few nuns who did that. So what do we do? I will stay away*
*from you. It's the only way to avoid hurting you and sullying*
*something true and pure. But always know that I love you.*

*I thought of asking for a transfer, maybe to Bolivia. But*
*I think now that I can handle this if I just don't see you alone*
*or look for excuses to be with you.*

*God bless you, Kate. This is the hardest God-damned*
*letter I've ever had to write.*

*Forgive me,*
*Tom*

Kate read the letter several times. Each time her happiness
exploded, and then she'd be terrified by his words. He loved her.
She had never known such sweetness as those words evoked.
Why then was he taking it away? She paced around the small
room until she felt she would burst.

Grabbing the letter, she stuffed it in her pocket and ran
down the steps, stopping briefly in the kitchen to tell Marta she
was going out for a walk and would be back in time for her class
at two o'clock. The gate creaked open and soon she was out in
the street, walking fast past the taxi stand, down the main street
of Juliaca, past the market. She was light and dizzy, and the sun
shone like diamonds through the leaves of the eucalyptus trees.

Their love couldn't be wrong. People couldn't help it if
they really loved each other, could they? She remembered old
Father Finn, the chaplain in the novitiate who taught them moral
theology. "Feelings are never wrong," he would thunder. "We
can't help our feelings any more than we can help what color
eyes we have. It's what we do with our feelings that matters."
Well, what would she do with these feelings? Kate knew she loved
Tom in every sense. She wanted him to hold her and kiss her,
make love to her. Just thinking of it made her melt in a strange

new heat of longing. But she forced these thoughts away. That they could not have. But she would not give up this love, not when she had just found what it was she'd been hungry for all this time. They would have to work out a way to love as a man and a woman without having sex.

She would write and tell him this. After all, he couldn't just decide everything. "I will stay away from you," he had said. Didn't she have a say in all this? Now she felt angry that he dared to make decision unilaterally. He thought she was young and innocent, too naive to understand what was needed here. She'd write back tonight. But he loved her, that's all that mattered. She softly chanted it as she hurried along the dusty road and while she climbed the steps of the square and returned to the convent.

That night, after the sisters had prayed Compline together in the living room, Kate sat for a while in front of the fire. One by one the others went up to bed. Kate assured Sister Josepha that she would dampen the fire and put the screen in place before she went to bed. The older nun stood looking down at her for several seconds. "Is everything all right, Sister? You look a little flushed tonight."

Kate stared up at her for a moment and then felt a foolish smile spread across her face. "I'm fine, Sister. I just wanted to sit here for a few minutes and enjoy the last bit of the fire." The older nun turned away, and Kate watched her walk stiffly out of the room. Josepha seemed tired tonight, elderly somehow. Had she ever loved a man? wondered Kate. She felt sorry now for anyone who hadn't known this joy.

When she finally went upstairs to her room, she looked at her face for a long time in the small mirror over her night stand. The black veil outlined the white wimple that framed her face. Her eyebrows were dark, much darker than her light brown hair. Her eyes were luminous tonight, the blue so deep that it almost seemed black. Her usually pale face was flushed and her mouth curved in a small smile. She felt both pretty and cherished. Then she laughed at herself, remembering the novice mistress' warnings against vanity. She hadn't thought about her looks for a long time.

She sat at her small desk and read Tom's letter once again. It sounded more desolate this time. What did he mean by saying he felt dry and stale? She began to realize she didn't know him very well. But there would be time for that, she hoped. Time to sit together and talk about their lives. She wrote:

*Dearest Tom,*

*Your letter today flooded me with happiness. I love you, too, as you must have guessed. I finally admitted it to myself after the night you sat with me in front of the fire. But I thought I would never get to say those words to you, much less read them from you to me. I thought I would have to bury this love deep within, and now it feels so wonderful to say it to you. I know you want to be a priest—it's part of what I loved in you first. And I have wanted to be a nun for many years, ever since I was a little girl.*

*So here's the question, and please don't think I am too young to understand the problem. I'm twenty-five, and most women by now are married. Can a man and woman who are in love with each other keep that love on a non-sexual plane? It sounds like a risky exercise, I admit. Maybe I'm fooling myself or maybe women really are different from men in these things. But I want to love you, talk to you, enjoy being around you, and still keep my vow of celibacy and respect yours. Could this work?*

*Tom, you made me so happy today. Don't take that gift away now by "staying away" from me. We'll just have to find a new way of loving. We can't undo what's happened between us. I love you. When are you coming back?*
*Kate*

She would mail the letter tomorrow after lunch; she'd have to pretend she needed to go downtown for something. She felt a twinge of guilt at the deception. Was this the beginning of leading a life of lies? Then she wondered at the boldness of her letter. Had she been too frank? The ground was shifting beneath her, and she was learning quickly how to keep her balance as she navigated the split.

That night Kate's dreams were troubled. She felt smothered, as if something was gagging her. She awoke drenched in sweat, panting for air in the small dark room. She slid out of bed to her knees. "Oh, please," she prayed, "please help me." She waited for a long time, but there was no answer.

# Chapter Eight

### Friday, June 26, 1964

⁓

Kate wakes to the smell of coffee brewing in Peter's kitchen. She jumps up, confused by this unfamiliar room, and lights the kerosene lamp on the dresser. She fumbles into her habit, still stained from her travels of the day before, but dry now and warm. Kissing each part as she puts it on, her lips move automatically to say the prayer that accompanies each piece. She pulls the cincture around her waist, and whispers, "Guard me this day from the fire of temptation."

Back in the convent in Juliaca, Sister Josepha would be rising, too, in the dark dawn. She would be sad, worried, maybe even angry at her as she went all alone into the empty mission chapel for Lauds and meditation. Kate whispers the words of the morning hymn as she pins her black veil to the starched headpiece: ". . . that He from harm may keep us free/In all the deeds this day shall see." Would He keep her from harm? It was to avoid harm that she was running away. She had become afraid of her own desire. "Forgive me," she whispers, looking into the mirror that reflects back the nun she has once more become.

Kate finds Peter Grinnell in the kitchen, and he barely looks her way as he piles sandwiches into a bag. "Glad you're up," he grunts. "There's hot water for tea in the kettle on the stove, some oranges and bread over there on the table. I'll be loading the jeep."

Kate nods, feeling shy now in the daylight. He had been different last night, friendlier. She supposes he is nervous about taking her into Arequipa, or perhaps he is just bored at the thought of a long ride through the mountains with a neurotic run-away nun. She hurries through her breakfast as his tall, blue-jeaned form passes in and out of the kitchen, loading his suitcases, boxes of notebooks, and camera into the jeep.

When she joins him in the courtyard at the back of the house where his jeep is parked, he mutters, "I find it incredible that you dashed off with no coat or jacket . . . or whatever you nuns wear," and shoves at her a navy-blue jacket lined with alpaca fur.

Kate murmurs her thanks and clumsily pulls the jacket on over her habit, lifting her veil free of the collar. The air, fine and crisp, smells of frost and reminds her of a winter morning in St. Louis.

She thinks with a pang of her parents. When she left them at the airport a year ago, they were proud, and yet she saw the worry in their eyes. Walking with her onto the tarmac on the way to the plane, her father somehow sprinted ahead of her up the stairs; then he stuck his head in the door to ask the stewardess to watch over his daughter. The tall blond looked surprised to see a nun get on the plane for Miami. She probably expected a twelve-year-old. Kate's mother wrote later that every time she tried to tell someone about her departure, she would break down in tears. Yet the night before she left, they were cheerful and joking in the Irish way of disguising sadness.

Peter helps her climb up into the jeep; then he swings in on his side in one easy movement. The jeep coughs and sputters, but in a few minutes they are out on the road, heading for Puno and then southwest to Arequipa. The sun is just rising, gilding the blue mountains with rose, sending glancing rays into the great Lake in the distance. They follow the curve of the shoreline in silence.

Soon they are on the outskirts of Puno, already bustling with trucks, herds of llamas being driven to market, and groups of women in brilliant colors, their polleras—great full skirts with petticoats—bouncing as they walk, reminding Kate of the crinolines she and her friends had all worn in the 1950s under their full cotton skirts. Many women have babies wrapped tightly in striped mantles slung firmly on their backs. Peter navigates the busy streets quickly, leaning mercilessly on his horn to warn any careless pedestrian of the danger to their life. Kate hopes no one from the Maryknoll house is out at this hour.

There are five nuns here, she knows, and a big house for the Maryknoll priests, a central place for the many men working out in the campo. The priests and nuns from Santa Catalina drive into Puno once a month for team meetings, usually followed by dinner. Last month the nuns had cooked a big pot of spaghetti; someone had saved a few bottles of cheap red wine, so the Americans and the British, along with a few German and French missionaries, had a boisterous supper.

A young priest she didn't know got out his guitar, and soon the center house sounded like a college dorm. They sang *Blowin' in the Wind, If I Had a Hammer*, and much later in the evening, *Moon River.* Kate saw that after a few months on the Altiplano these evenings helped them endure the profound loneliness and frustration they all felt in a culture that was so opaque, so impenetrable. If they acted silly and got a bit tipsy, it was to let out their pent-up frustration. Now, riding in the front seat next to this Englishman, Kate doesn't want to see anyone who knows her. How would she explain what she is doing? As Peter negotiates the winding turns that would lead them through the Andes, Kate looks at him. Last night he had seemed cynical about the work the missionaries were doing. What, then, was he doing up here? She supposes he is observing, studying, cataloging in the dispassionate way of the scientist. He wouldn't be trying to change things.

As if he can sense her scrutiny, Peter turns toward her and grins, "I thought I ought to be quiet for a while in case you were in some sort of contemplative state."

Kate blushes a little, realizing that she hasn't really thought much about prayer this morning. But to pray now would be to open her mind to the reasons for her flight, to Tom.

"I just thought I should be quiet so you could concentrate on your driving. These cliffs terrify me," she smiles, relieved at his joke.

As they ascend a steep grade, Kate gazes out the window at the deep valleys opening before them. The road is dusty and very narrow. The rule is that the vehicle climbing has the right of way, since two cars or trucks can't pass each other on the narrow curves. To alert oncoming cars, drivers sound their horns in warning when approaching turns.

"Tell me about yourself," Kate says. "I'm afraid I did most of the talking last night."

Peter draws on his cigarette. "Not much to tell, really. I was born in Surrey; my father was in the RAF, shot down over Berlin toward the end of the war. I was fourteen; my sister was twelve. I went on to Cambridge to read history and then got interested in anthropology. I did some field work in Egypt, then back to Cambridge for another degree, and finally I was given a research position there."

"Why Peru?" It seems safer to keep talking about him.

"I've been interested in Peru since I was a child and read *The Bridge of San Luis Rey.* So here I am."

"You never married?"

"No, but there were a couple of close calls."

"What about your mother? You haven't mentioned her."

"I can't stand my mother." He looks over to see how she takes this.

Kate is shocked; she has never heard any grown-up say this, she realizes. Most people forgave their parents as they got older. Kate has been exasperated by her parents, sometimes embarrassed by her father's explosive bursts of anger, but loving them was natural, like breathing or sleeping. She doesn't know what to say, so falls silent, watching the road dip and curve.

"She's a selfish, whining bitch," he continued. "Sorry. Anyway, let's talk about you and why you're here, shall we?"

"Do you mean here in this jeep or here in Peru?"

He laughs. "Let me guess. You came to Peru to help the people here liberate themselves from the oppression they've suffered under since the Spanish conquistadors."

Kate decides to ignore his laughter. "Well, something like that. Actually I think I'm just beginning to discover day by day why I'm here. Last week a couple of teenagers asked me if I had any American records. So I set up our old phonograph in the hall and made some Kool-Aid and we sat around and tried to talk to each other. One boy told me how he'd like to go to the city to school. Their parents won't let them go out walking with each other. They asked me questions about my family and how I could bear to leave them to come so far away. They wondered why I don't have any children." Kate raises her chin defiantly. "I think for one thing I can show them another way to be a woman, that women can do something else besides work the fields and bear children."

Peter grins. "Somehow I never thought of nuns as feminists. Aren't you interested in proselytizing? You know, don't you, that your Dominican habit could have bad associations for the people up here?" Kate watches him without saying anything. "The Incas were betrayed by Pizarro and his men in Cajamarca. Do you remember the story?"

"Yes, but why would my habit have bad associations?"

"The Spaniards came with a Dominican priest, Vicente de Valverde. On the night of July 26, after Atahualpa had kept his promise and filled a room with the treasure of his kingdom, the Spaniards led him out and tied him to the stake. Friar Vicente gave him a crash course in Christianity, and encouraged him to convert so that he could be hanged as a Christian rather than be burned at the stake as a heathen."

Peter laughs as he sees Kate wince; she hasn't heard that part of the story. Well, she isn't going to defend the mentality of that long-ago Dominican. She'd try another tack.

"Do you think Peru was better off before the Spaniards came?"

Peter's eyes light up. He looks away from the road for a moment to see if her question was sincere. "In some ways, yes. Under the Incas, Peru had a totally organic society. Religion and work were unified. People worked the land in cooperatives, and no one was hungry. The earth was the mother, Pachamama. Lake Titicaca was female also, and the people made offerings to her." Peter lights another cigarette, and Kate finds the smell familiar, reassuring.

He squints at the rising sun, the cigarette hanging from his lips as he continues. "Divers have found boxes with gold and silver statues buried in the silt. Some of the Aymara around Juliaca believe that the Lake is the wife of the mountain, Illampu-Ancohuma. They believe that the Lake is the source of the sun as well as of man himself."

Kate thinks back to the outing on the Lake, the way Raul hurried them into port when the storm came up. Maybe she should have studied anthropology before coming here.

Peter is driving faster now, taking the turns recklessly. "The really interesting thing is how the indigenous people got Christianity mixed in with their own belief system. An old Aymara man told me once, 'God is very distant. We must deal with his mountains, the intermediaries.'"

Kate nods. "Yes, Father Tom is always saying that this mixture of beliefs is what makes it so hard to work up here. Faith and superstition are all entwined." She hopes he hasn't noticed the slight tremor in her voice when she said the name of the priest.

"Ah, superstition, is it?" Peter looks at her with amusement.

She sighs. To him all religion is superstition, she supposes. "I admit, it's pretty hard to make a sympathetic case for Christianity when you think about what the Spaniards did here. In a way, I think our being here, living among the Aymara people in these desolate towns and villages, is a way of atoning for the past." She pauses, but Peter is silent, taking a drag on his cigarette. She continues: "You know, I spent a few weeks in Lima before I went to language school. I loved the people there. They were easy and friendly. But up here, the people are different. Much harder to get to know."

"Why should you be surprised at that? First of all, you don't speak their language. Some of the people you met in Lima are middle class, more European, more like you. You didn't encounter the otherness of Peru until you came here." He glances over at her. "Who is this Father Tom?"

"A priest I work with. He's from Ireland." She looks out the window, hoping he won't ask any more questions about Tom.

He glances at his watch. "We're almost halfway there. Why don't we look for a place to stop and eat lunch?"

They have entered a break in the mountains and are passing through a wide grassy valley. A silver thread of river winds through it, bordered by fields of bright green alfalfa. Overhead the sky is the same hard brilliant blue as the mountains. They spot a small shack with a tattered *chicha* flag flapping smartly above the door. Rusty tables have been set out in the shade of a few trees.

Peter parks the jeep and tells her to wait in the car. After a few minutes inside the shack, he emerges into the sunlight and motions for her to join him. She brings the lunch he had packed that morning, and they sit across from one another at a small table.

A balding, heavy-set man brings out two tall glasses of *chicha*. He bows slightly. "*Buenas tardes, madre,*" he murmurs, not looking at her directly. Kate feels her face flush. What does the man think, seeing a nun having lunch with this gringo in blue jeans? She hopes he is simply glad for the customers, and not especially surprised at anything these foreigners do.

The sun is warm on their backs, and Kate can already feel the heavier air of the lower altitude. They don't speak much, listening mainly to the hum of the insects in the cypress branches above them. Few cars pass on the road, and the air is still.

Peter sits smoking and watches as Kate cuts into an apple and hands a piece to him. "Isn't there a biblical scene something like this?" he grins, his face boyish despite the lines. Confused, Kate realizes that she likes his teasing. It has a comfortable normalcy after weeks of overheated tension. Nothing has felt real to her lately.

Hours later, when they reach Arequipa the sun is setting. "That's Misti," Peter says, pointing out a conical peak covered with snow, gleaming in the last rays of the sun. "Arequipa has the best climate in Peru, an eternal spring."

She wonders if Peter has someone he's going to see here, someone special. For the first time today she begins to worry; she can't expect him to take care of her. Peter glances over at her. "I'm just going to run in here and make a phone call. I think I know a Peace Corps worker you could stay with for a couple of days." Without waiting for a response from her, he jumps out of the jeep.

As he disappears into the small *farmacia*, Kate knows what she will do. For a moment she looks hesitantly at the navy blue jacket Peter loaned her that morning; then she snatches it up and climbs down from the jeep. Rapidly, she crosses the street and tries to blend into the throngs of workers headed toward the bus stop at the Plaza de Armas. Aware that her habit makes her conspicuous, she has to find somewhere to hide from Peter. He will probably try to find her.

She crosses the Plaza de Armas, passing a three-tiered fountain that splashes water on her white habit, and turns down a side street into an old colonial section of the city. Sunlight glares on the white streets, blinding her. Suddenly she is in front of an old mansion, its coat of arms carved in the porous volcanic stone. From iron gates, great puma heads stare at her, serpents writhing from their mouths. Beneath the serpents are carved *ccantu*, the sacred flower of the Incas. The gates are locked.

Finally she comes to a square with benches in the shade of scrub oak trees. A statue of St. Francis opens his arms to the people hurrying past. She sees a church with an intricately carved door. A perfect hiding place.

She pushes open the door and steps over the high wooden portal. The church smells of must and incense. Candles flicker in front of various statues; hundreds more burn in front of a tall Virgin Mary. Her cape is blue velvet; her veil is scarlet. Necklaces and rings cascade from her neck, glittering in the candlelight.

Someone would probably lock the door after dark; she can stay here tonight if no one sees her. Kate sinks to her knees in a side pew, folding the jacket beneath her arms. Feeling a slight bulge in the pocket, she pulls out a note wrapped around a wad of *soles*.

> *Sister Mountain Spirit,*
> *Just in case you decide to bolt, this may help you get wherever in hell you are going. Good luck in your flight. I'll be worried until I know you are safe.*
> *Best,*
> *Peter*

So, he had suspected she would run away. "Thank you, forgive me," she whispers in the darkness of the church. She is asking to be forgiven a lot these days.

Kate gazes up at the altar, so distant in the settling gloom. A candle burns in the sanctuary lamp, signaling the presence of Christ in the Blessed Sacrament. She stares at the altar a long time. *I'm not running from You. Only from myself. I just need to figure things out.* She slumps against the pew, her face buried in her hands. What is happening to her? First she was a runaway, now a thief. Well, not really a thief, maybe. After all, the Englishman had offered her the jacket. Suddenly she wants to tell Tom about her night in the stranger's house. They would laugh about it. Tom would tell her not to worry about the jacket; the British had been stealing from the Irish for centuries.

Only two weeks ago she and Tom had been riding together to Juli to look at a new well the people were putting in. Alejandro was driving, and the pastor, Father Jack, sat in front while she and Tom squeezed together in the back. The men joked and laughed as Alejandro taught them some of the more imaginative curses of the Aymara. Kate had looked out the window in a daze, conscious of nothing but Tom's face so close to hers. Often he would turn and look into her eyes, and Kate had to turn away from what she saw in his. As they drove into town he passed a piece of paper to her, neatly folded into a small square.

Now, in the darkening church, Kate reaches into her pocket and pulls out the note she has read so many times. It is a poem, copied in block print.

**BE STILL AS YOU ARE BEAUTIFUL**
Be still as you are beautiful
Be silent as the rose;
Through miles of starlit countryside
Unspoken worship flows
To reach you in your loveless room

From lonely men whom daylight gave
The blessing of your passing face
Impenetrably grave.

A white owl in the lichened wood
Is circling silently,
More secret and more silent yet
Must be your love to me.
Thus, while about my dreaming head
Your soul in ceaseless vigil goes,
Be still as you are beautiful
Be silent as the rose.

Underneath he had scrawled:

*You won't have heard of this poem. It's by Patrick Macdonogh,
who died a few years ago. I heard him read it in my uncle's
bookstore in Galway. I hoped someday I would meet the woman
I could give it to. Tom*

That day had passed in a haze. She had trailed after the
priests as they met with the village elders, trying to understand the
brief exchanges in Aymara. Alejandro stood next to her for a while
during the meeting, whispering to her in Spanish what the men
were saying. Then the group walked through the dusty streets to the
edge of town where the new well was being dug. Now the women
and children joined them, and Kate was surrounded by small children tugging at her habit, vying for the chance to hold her hands.

She walked fast, and then would suddenly stop and send
the two little ones clinging to her crashing harmlessly into each
other. Squealing with excitement, they begged her to do it again.
"*Otra vez, madrecita, otra vez.*" It was a trick her father used to do
with her brother and her when they were little. Her heart ached,
but she couldn't tell if it was the altitude or not.

When they got to the newly dug well, Father Jack took out a small plastic bottle of holy water from the pocket of his windbreaker. He blessed the well, and all the people made the sign of the cross. Then he walked among the group, sprinkling them with holy water. The drops glistened in the sun like thousands of sequins.

Then Tom began to speak, slowly and deliberately, so that Alejandro could translate. Tom acknowledged their initiative in getting the prefect of Juliaca to come out and consider their need for a well. When they worked together they had power—power to change their lives, to make a better future for their children. The day of the passive *campesino* was past. It was time for them to reclaim the ways of their ancestors, a people who did not know hunger and want.

Kate had watched the impassive faces of the people as Tom's voice rose. Their eyes were fixed on the young Irish priest with his hawk nose and cold blue eyes. When he finished, they clapped politely, and the men came up one by one to shake his hand. In Aymara, he joked and laughed with them, his smile dazzling in the noonday brightness.

Now in the empty chapel, Kate no longer hears the sounds of traffic outside. She spreads the jacket inside-out on the pew and lies down, burying her face in the fur. It smells of Peter's cigarette smoke and eucalyptus of the Altiplano. But incense hangs in the air, too, and as she drifts off to sleep she is back in St. Roch's, a little girl trying to stay awake during benediction as the choir sings the *Pange Lingua*.

# Chapter Nine

*K*ate knew she was supposed to be a nun since she was in eighth grade, but she hid this secret all throughout high school. To be a nun was the dream of many girls in St. Louis in the 1940s and '50s, but it was not Kate's dream. She dreamed of being a ballerina.

Once, she remembered, Bishop McCarthy visited their seventh grade classroom to examine them for the sacrament of Confirmation. His long black cassock bordered in scarlet braid, he was a small, almost bald man with wire-rimmed glasses that made his blue eyes look glassy and unnaturally large.

After a brief question and (carefully rehearsed) answer session, the bishop began to speak softly about vocations: "Now you see, boys and girls, the word *vocation* comes from the Latin word *vocare*, meaning to call. Some select few of you are being called by God to a very special life, that of a priest or a sister. You must listen very closely for this call. God does not come in the rushing wind, as the prophet Isaiah says, but in a still small voice." He stopped to let this sink in, and then raised his voice dramatically. "Now how many of you girls think that God might be calling you?"

He looked into each of their eyes, his gaze traveling slowly around the room. Almost every girl's hand shot up, with no hesitation. Kate noticed that among the girls, only she and Gracie Gilmartin, who was a tomboy and swore a lot, had not raised their hands.

"And what about you, young lady?"

The bishop focused on Kate, and she stood up as Sister had taught them to do when called on by the bishop. "Actually, Bishop, I've been thinking about becoming a ballerina."

The boys behind her snickered.

"And what is your name, my dear?"

She couldn't tell if the bishop's tight smile was one of amusement or annoyance. "Mary Katherine O'Neill, your Excellency."

"Well, Mary Katherine O'Neill, you'll be just the one to enter, I'll wager," he said with a slight smile, nodding his head to Sister Mary Joan sitting on the edge of her seat in the back of the room.

Kate dismissed this—to her—ominous prediction. Although the nuns' lives were mysterious and thus seductive, she knew she was too vain to become one of them. She spent many hours standing on the marble-topped coffee table in the living room watching herself swirl and curtsy in the red-gold mirror over the sofa. Sometimes she would sit for hours at her mother's old dressing table with its large central mirror flanked by two swinging mirrors. If she positioned the mirrors just right, she could see an endless series of Kates. Once she read a whole scene from *Romeo and Juliet* into that mirror, watching her face in the multitude of reflections until it grew too small to see.

Kate couldn't remember when she began to notice the grace of the nuns' habits as they glided down the long polished halls of St. Roch's. The habit of her teachers, the Sisters of St. Joseph, had a medieval elegance that was becoming on even the plainest among them. Their long black wool habits with wide sleeves, when rolled back, revealed silky net sleevelets that covered their pale arms; white wimples framed their faces, and thin, diaphanous black veils fluttered behind them as they rushed to catch up with their uniformed charges scampering to recess.

Many mornings as Kate arrived at St. Roch's on her bike, Sister Mary Theresa, the convent cook, would smile and wave to her from the porch she was sweeping. A round, saucy woman, she swept briskly with her sleeves rolled back and her long habit pinned up beneath her blue and white checked apron.

They were old friends. One day, when Kate was in second grade, she forgot her lunch. Sister Cornelia, her teacher, sent her over to the convent where Sister Theresa bounced cheerfully around her neat kitchen, fixing her a lunch of the daintiest ham salad sandwich, slices of apple, and homemade oatmeal cookies full of raisins. After Sister went off to look for a holy card to give her, Kate wandered into the back hall and stared up at the narrow staircase that led to the second floor. If she could only go up to see their bedrooms! They were called cells, she knew, which lent a mysterious, penitential air to that part of the convent labeled "cloister," where only the nuns were allowed to enter.

Sister Helene, the eighth-grade teacher, was Kate's favorite, and ever since fifth grade Kate had been waiting to have her as a teacher, hoping Sister wouldn't be transferred. This nun was tall, athletic, and young, with thin, perfectly arched black eyebrows like the wings of a blackbird framing her dark eyes and a heart-stopping smile. When she looked at you it was as if you were the only one in her life. Sister played softball with the girls at recess, lifting up her habit and running hard when she smacked the ball against the back fence, laughing and flushed when she scored a run. All the girls agreed that she had a wonderful figure hidden beneath that habit.

Her past, hinted at in bits and pieces, was exotic. She hadn't entered the convent right after high school as most girls did, but had gone to St. Louis University and majored in theater. She told the class about the time she directed and starred in Synge's *Riders to the Sea*—and when they read the play aloud in class, the throb of emotion in her low voice thrilled them.

One Friday afternoon in the spring of Kate's eighth-grade year, Sister Helene called Kate aside and asked her if she would have time to go with her downtown on Saturday, since she had a doctor's appointment and none of the other sisters had time to accompany her. Kate knew that nuns never went out alone, but always in pairs, like sedate penguins. Kate wondered what the nuns thought might happen to them on the quiet, leafy streets of St. Louis, but she was thrilled at the invitation—a whole afternoon by herself with Sister. Maybe she would ask Sister about being a nun, maybe even confess that she, too, was thinking seriously about entering the convent.

Kate dressed carefully, choosing and discarding many combinations until she settled on a freshly ironed white cotton blouse with a Peter Pan collar, her long, gored green-and-black plaid skirt, and her Bass Weejuns with shiny pennies tucked in the flaps. In the bright sun, she walked the few blocks to St. Roch's, swinging her purse, noticing the lacy shadows the new leaves cast on the sidewalk, tasting the incredible sweetness of life.

Sister had dressed with care, too, for she had on a longer, finer veil than usual, and her black oxford shoes were new and highly polished. She and Kate chattered all the way to the bus stop on Forest Park, and Kate felt proud when they got on the bus together and all eyes swiveled to the young nun and the girl.

During Sister's doctor appointment, Kate sat in the waiting room, wondering if nuns took off their clothes when they went to the doctor. She leafed through some outdated *TIME* magazines. She wished there were copies of *LIFE* or *National Geographic* with pictures of bare-breasted women in grass skirts, but before long Sister emerged and told Kate they would go over to St. Louis University and have lunch there in the lounge for nuns.

Its walls lined with oak bookcases, the lounge was an austere room with long tables for studying and a few creaky sofas—*For what?* she'd wondered. *Did nuns ever put their feet up on a sofa and read a novel until they dozed off?*

After a lunch of sandwiches and fruit, which Sister Helene had produced magically out of her large black briefcase, the nun opened a beautiful small leather-bound book with gold-edged pages. "I'm going to say my breviary now," she told Kate. "You can go exploring in the building, if you want. There's a chapel down at the end of the hall if you'd like to make a visit."

Kate walked carefully on the polished marble floor of the long hall, dimly lit by weak spring sunlight. A door opened and a tall young priest, his cassock swirling around his long legs, rushed out. Through the half-opened door Kate smelled pipe smoke and heard the quiet murmur of men's voices and the rustling of newspapers.

At the end of the hall Kate saw two dark-maroon leather doors crowned by a half-moon stained-glass window depicting a bearded youthful Christ with a lamb on his shoulders. She pulled open one of the heavy doors and tiptoed in, afraid to disturb the calm of the chapel. The only worshiper was a young man kneeling in a front pew, his head in his hands. Startled, she realized it was Tony Martino, a boy from the neighborhood who had been away at college for the last few years. She remembered that there had been talk in the neighborhood of his entering the priesthood. She sat very still, watching him. The sun glinted on the gold of the altar, and above it the stained-glass windows gleamed like rubies and sapphires.

What was he praying about? Was he struggling with God? Was he resisting his vocation? Suddenly that word tolled like a bell—*vocation*. Yes, she had a vocation. God was calling her to be a nun. The realization was a blow, and she felt it, low and hard, in her stomach. There was no sweetness in the revelation, no great rush of love for Christ. Yet, at thirteen, she knew that her life had changed. Stunned, she left the chapel where Tony Martino prayed on in silence.

From then on, through high school, the certainty of her call never wavered. She told no one about it, except Sister Helene. To others, her family and friends, it would sound weird, she knew.

Like many of the graduates of St. Roch's, she went on to Mercy High School in University City. Wearing navy blue skirts and white blouses with smartly turned-up collars, Kate and her friends rode the bus down Skinker to Olive then walked two blocks to school, hugging their books tightly to their chests. Boys in big-finned cars screeched past them, yelling mild obscenities to the girls' delight.

At their co-ed high school, the brothers and the nuns were demanding, strict teachers with no patience for what they called nonsense. The most serious discipline problems were smoking in the bathrooms, writing notes to each other during class, or worst of all, playing hooky to spend a day by the waterfall in Forest Park. Kate hated her math classes, loved English and history, and was surprised by the praise she received for her part in the freshman production of *The Merchant of Venice*. During her junior year she got the lead in *The Crucible*, and for a few weeks thought longingly about life on the stage.

But she kept her eyes on the nuns, watching them carefully. Kate cried bitterly when she saw *The Nun's Story*. Audrey Hepburn made a graceful nun, but Kate didn't recognize any of the funny, opinionated, very human nuns she knew among those stiff, cold nuns she saw on the screen. That summer, when her mother's friends found out she was going to the convent, they asked her how she could stand it if the life was anything like the movie.

She waved her hand airily in dismissal. "Oh, that movie was about European nuns. They're very old-fashioned."

Kate's vocation had one close call in the summer between her junior and senior year of high school. His name was Bill, and he was a sophomore at the University of Missouri in Columbia. He played soccer with Kate's older brother Dan; Kate was often aware of his eyes following her when she walked by the den where the boys were sprawled on the sofa and floor, sweaty and raucous after a practice.

One day she lay sun-bathing in the back yard with her mother's copy of *Kristin Lavransdatter* and a glass of iced tea. Little drops of perspiration trickled between her breasts. When she raised her head from her book, she noticed Bill standing on the back porch, staring at her. Feeling his gaze on her skin, Kate nervously replaced the straps of her white bathing suit on her shoulders. Bill grinned slowly from the shade of the porch.

"Little Katie's all growed up, I see," he drawled, trying to achieve a leer on his youthful Midwestern face.

"Shut up, Wigmore," she said, pretending indifference.

"No, seriously, Kate. I've been noticing you this summer. Let's go to Talayna's for spaghetti tonight. Then maybe we'll drive over to the Muny and sit in the free seats at the opera. I think it's *The King and I.*"

She squinted up at him, shading her eyes with her hand, trying to see if he was serious. Well, why not? She wasn't in the convent yet. She'd better see what she'd be missing.

Bill picked her up at seven and was unusually shy and respectful to her parents, who had been surprised when she'd told them Bill had asked her out. She felt a rush of pleasure walking into Talayna's with him—the crowd was older, with many students from nearby Washington University. Bill had two beers before their dinner arrived. The waiter hadn't even carded him. She sipped her Coke, realizing that the white sundress and delicate sandals she wore were too prissy for this crowd.

It was 8:30 by the time Bill headed his old yellow Chevy Nova into the park. Through the open windows Kate smelled freshly cut grass in the humid evening air. On the radio, the Everly Brothers' "Bye Bye Love" played.

Instead of heading toward the Muny, Bill swung the car up towards the Art Museum. He parked in a tree-lined circle atop the steep hill that sloped down to the lake, quiet and luminous, the dusk filled with the hum of cicadas.

"We used to come sleigh-riding here when we were kids," Kate whispered, trying to make conversation. He didn't seem to have heard what she said, for he sat slumped against the window, half turned away from her.

"Are you cold?" he asked suddenly.

She laughed. "Cold? It's August—how could I be cold?"

Suddenly he pulled her toward him. The first kiss was very gentle—perfect. His lips were soft and full and he smelled of Old Spice. The next time he kissed her, she put her hands on his shoulders and was startled by their solidity. Their kisses became longer, more insistent. Her head flung back on the vinyl seat, Kate felt crushed beneath him.

At last he drew back. His voice seemed to come from far away. "We'd better head home, Katie. I guess I won't be able to think of you as Dan's little sister anymore." She couldn't read his expression in the darkness.

He walked her up to the porch of her house. Lights glowed through the screen door, and she knew her parents were sitting in the living room. She kissed him quickly, and shoved him gently toward the steps.

"You'd better go on—or my dad will be after you. He's pretty suspicious about guys. He must have been terrible himself." She was amazed at herself. Where had this new-found cocky assurance come from?

Bill nodded, tongue-tied, and walked slowly to his car, jingling his keys.

That first date was their last, for they had moved too fast. Kate was afraid—more of herself than of Bill. Although she didn't even know Bill, much less love him, she'd been quite moved by his ardor, his groans and sighs breathed into her hair, his lips on her neck. And she, pierced by his kisses, had felt gates opening within her she hadn't known were closed. That night, Kate felt, she had been under a spell, an enchantment.

But she shook it off, and gradually Bill stopped calling. But her memory of that night lingered, disturbing yet seductive. She returned to it often at odd moments.

# $\mathscr{C}$hapter Ten

*St. Thomas Aquinas Convent*
*Box 55*
*Chesterfield, Missouri*
*May 2, 1957*

*Dear Mary Katherine,*
*I am writing in response to your letter of application into the community and am most happy to tell you that your application has been accepted. We were only waiting to receive the two letters of reference. Both Monsignor FitzGibbons and Sister Helene wrote glowing letters of recommendation for you. The religious life is not for everyone, and it requires a great degree of maturity and dedication. All the sisters in the community will be praying for you and the twenty-seven other prospective postulants as you ready yourselves for the great step you will take at the end of the summer.*

*Your entrance day has been set for Saturday, August 29, between 1:00 and 3:00 p.m. Please come to the back entrance to the novitiate so that you may unload your things easily. Your family may accompany you that afternoon, but all farewells must be said by 3:00 p.m. If you have any questions, please feel free to contact Sister Mary Margaret, the mistress of postulants.*

*Finally, we ask that you bring one hundred dollars as your dowry on entrance day. This money is kept in trust for you the whole time you are in the community so that, if you ever leave religious life, you will have some money to begin your life in the world again. I have also enclosed a list of clothing and supplies you will need to bring.*

*God bless you, Mary Katherine. I am looking forward to getting to know my new spiritual daughters. As Jesus said to Mary, sitting at his feet, "You have chosen the better part."*
*Yours in Christ,*
*Mother Marie Clare, O.P.*

## Clothing and Supplies

six white cotton undershirts
six pairs of white cotton underpants
eight pairs of black cotton stockings
two pairs of black nylon stockings
one dozen white linen handkerchiefs
one black sweater
two pairs of black lace-up oxford shoes
one pair of black gloves
two dozen cloth sanitary napkins (diapers)
two long white nightgowns
brush, comb, toothbrush
shampoo and toothpaste
hand lotion
stationery

*Holmes House*

*Mizzou*

*Crazy Kate,*

*You will fall over dead to get a letter from me, your beloved brother, but I can't believe what Mom just told me. She said you are going to be a nun! Kate, have you lost your mind? I thought you were happy to be long gone from the clutches of the nuns at Mercy this year and anxious to get out into the big bad world of college. Don't get me wrong, Kate. I know there are decent nuns, and some of them even have a sense of humor. Remember the time I formed the Hate Sister Jean Marie Club? She showed up at our meeting in the McCarthy's backyard with two six-packs of root beer and we almost died of embarrassment. Anyway, the point is I just have never thought of you in those terms. I always saw you as an actress or a politician—somebody out there in the world influencing people. And you're not totally ugly, either, so why would you want to put on all those medieval robes and hide away in some backwater convent?*

*Think about it, Kate. We only get one life, you know. And not to get pious on you, but my theory is that we can serve God better by being active in the world not running away from it. Please write and say it isn't so!*

*Love, Dan*

St. Brendan's School
Pontiac, Michigan
June 5, 1957

Dear Kate,

I was delighted to receive the announcement of your graduation and really thrilled when I read the news about your
entrance into the Dominicans. Of course I am not hurt that
you are going there and not coming to us, the CSJ's. What
difference does it make? We are all doing the Lord's work, at
least I hope we are. The Dominicans are an ancient teaching
order, as you know, and I can just see you someday in your
white habit teaching away.

Kate, just a few words about the next couple of years.
If the Dominican Novitiate is anything like ours was, these
next weeks are going to be very difficult. Somehow all novice
mistresses think of themselves as God's drill instructors,
whose purpose is to try by fire the raw recruits they find
before them. My three years in the novitiate were the hardest, but I was determined that they were not going to scare
me out of my desire to be a nun. The rule of silence will
be especially hard for you, and I know your bouncy ways
will be a target for the decorum patrol. On a deeper level,
you will get desperately homesick. The once a month letter
we got would send me weeping to the chapel many a lonely
Sunday afternoon.

But there will be beautiful times, too. You'll learn to love
the quiet of early morning, the beauty of the chant as it soars
up into the eaves of the chapel, and if you are lucky, you'll
grow to love some of your fellow postulants.

Anyway, what I'm trying to say is that things loosen up
considerably once you get sent out on mission, so don't despair
these first few months. Write and tell me how you're getting
on. They will open all incoming letters, and you won't be

*allowed to seal those you send, but I think this was usually just a formality.*

*To be a bride of Christ is a demanding role, but you've got what it takes, Kate.*

*With great affection from your old teacher,*
*Sister Helene*

*The Admiral*
*11 North Fourth Street*
*St. Louis, Missouri*
*July 25, 1957*

*Dear Miss O'Neill:*

*It is with real regret that I accept your resignation from the position of dining room hostess that you filled so well. You were dependable, cheerful, and were able to deal with difficult customers, even those who all too often were intoxicated, tactfully and graciously. In fact, I had been thinking of promoting you to a higher-paying position in the company, manager of the entire restaurant floor of the boat. So, if your plans should happen to change, please don't hesitate to apply again.*

*Best regards to your father, and tell him that we haven't seen his Irish face down here in a long time, so perhaps he's grown too grand for the lads from the old neighborhood.*

*Yours truly,*

*Thomas J. O'Callahan,, General Manager*

*On a warm September night*

*My dear Katie,*

*Your mother has gone to bed, Maggie is out with her friends at St. Louis U. High's first soccer game of the season, so your old dad is all alone and realizing how much he misses you. Ever since the day you met me at the door when I came home from the Pacific, we've been good pals. Oh, I know there were many times in these last few years that you didn't think I was your friend at all, but even when we had our (shouting) differences, I think you knew deep down that I loved you and wanted only the best for you. You must know how proud I am that you're going to be a nun and serve God with all your heart and soul. Your mother was really opposed to your entrance this year, but I think I had a small hand in persuading her to let you follow your call.*

*Did I ever tell you that at one time I wanted to be a priest? You'll laugh, but I was actually pretty serious about it in the eighth grade. My Aunt Mamie, though, got in some fuss with Father O'Flaherty and decided that she wouldn't allow me to enter the seminary. Later, of course, I met your mother and that made celibacy seem like a pretty impossible life. But now you are fulfilling my never forgotten dream in a way.*

*God bless you, my girl. Someday I'm going to drive out to the Motherhouse and see if I can catch a glimpse of you when you're sweeping the front walks. It's much too long to wait until visiting day to see you.*

*Love always, Dad*

*our house*

*Hi Sis,*

*Mother is making me write this letter before I can go any-where, so that's why I'm writing. Don't get any mushy ideas that your little sister misses you, or anything like that. Oh, before I forget, thanks a million for your enamel jewelry box, the pearls, and the gold charm bracelet. I'm still a little bummed out that you gave Carol all the rest of your goodies, even if as you say, it was mostly junk.*

*Well, have fun in the convent (Ha Ha!) and I guess I'll be there on visiting day. Do we have to stay four whole hours???!!!*

*Love and all that stuff,*
*Maggie*

*Fort Leonard Wood, MO*
*Sept. 15, 1957*

*Dear Kate,*

*I know you'll be surprised to hear from me, but I just got a gossipy letter from my mother giving me all the news from home, and I was shocked to hear that you have entered the convent. I don't know if they even let you get letters from guys, but here goes anyway. I guess you can see from the address that I'm in the army. I didn't finish my last year at Mizzou—I don't know why exactly. The whole college scene just seemed pointless and silly after a while. So here I am, in training for God knows what mess our country will get involved in. Lots of guys think it will be fighting Communists somewhere, but we'll see.*

*I'm sitting here trying to picture your life in the convent. Kate, why did you do it? I never figured you for the type. You know, after that one night we went out you never seemed to want to see me again, and I couldn't figure out what I had done. I thought we got along just great! Oh, hell, oops I mean heck, now I'll never have a chance with you again. This letter isn't turning out the way I'd planned, so I guess I'll just sign off. Pray for all of us. Can nuns write to soldiers?*
*A voice from the past,*
*Bill Wigmore*

*Home*
*Sunday night*

*Darling,*

*You've been gone two weeks now and the house seems too quiet without you. I caught Dad sitting in your room, just looking around blankly late the other night. Maggie says she loves being an only child, but secretly I think she misses having you around if only because Dad and I can now focus all our (unwanted) attention on her.*

*I can't wait for our first Visiting Day. We'll be there at one o'clock sharp. I'm just sorry Dan won't be there. He and Kevin drove up to Columbia yesterday to move into their new place. They found rooms in a big old Victorian house not too far from campus and not too expensive either.*

*Do you need anything when we come? Grandma wants to come, too, so I guess the whole bunch of us will be there. God bless—*

*Your loving,*
*Mom*

# Chapter Eleven

**August 29, 1957**

---

Entrance Day! Finally it came. Waking in her flowered bedroom that morning with Maggie sprawled in the twin bed across from her, Kate's first sight was the black trunk piled with black and white clothes. The only splash of color was the pink bottle of Desert Flower Hand Lotion.

Kate yawned and stretched. Her parents had taken her downtown the night before for dinner and dancing on the Admiral. Under the stars her father had held her close. She could feel his breath on her cheek as he gazed down at her. She hummed along to "Unchained Melody": "Time goes by so slowly, and time can do so much . . ."

"Katie," he whispered, "you can always come home. We'll always have a bed for you."

"But Dad, I thought you were happy for me."

For once there was no witty remark. Her father just tightened his arm around her waist.

Sunday afternoon was heavy with an oncoming storm. As the O'Neill's station wagon pulled away from the curb, Kate looked back and watched the brick house of her childhood recede in the shade of the elm trees lining the street. The storm broke loose as they got on the highway, forcing her father to pull over for a few minutes. He cursed under his breath. Maggie announced that surely this was a sign that they should just turn around and forget the whole convent thing. Nobody said anything after that.

Finally the station wagon pulled up to the back entrance of the novitiate, and Kate's family spilled out as her father unloaded the black trunk Kate had packed so carefully with her black and white trousseau. Three other girls from her high school were entering with her, and Kate was relieved to see their faces amid the chattering nervous group of girls. Each new postulant had been assigned a senior novice as a "guardian angel" who would be a guide and confidante for a few weeks until she could get her bearings in this alien world.

As they all stood around uncertainly in the large entrance hall, Kate saw a tall novice gliding toward her with a smile. She realized it was Joan Schmidt, a girl from Mercy High School who had graduated two years before. Her brother Eddie had been in Kate's class.

"Hi, Kate," she said, putting her arm around Kate's shoulder. "I'm Sister Gabriela now. Welcome to the novitiate. I'm so glad I get to be your guardian angel." She greeted Kate's parents and told them she would give them a little tour while Kate and all the other new postulants went upstairs to the dormitories to change.

In a daze, Kate followed the other girls up the wide mahogany staircase, its steps worn by the tread of hundreds of girls over the years. They came to a wide hall with dormitories of six beds each on either side. Kate saw her name on the door of St. Joseph's dormitory and found her cell, the first one on the right, next to the door. Each cell was marked by iron rods from which hung white sheets, now neatly tied back, but which at night were drawn, isolating the girls from each other's sight, but they were still able to hear the sighs, occasional giggles, and sometimes sobs of each other. A narrow iron bed with a thin white coverlet, a small four-drawer stand with a pitcher and bowl on it, and a single wooden chair were the only furnishings.

All the other girls were pulling the curtains around their beds, so Kate did, too. Then she changed into her postulant uniform, which had been hung from the iron rod near her bed. As she fastened the snaps of her black cotton blouse, she noticed that her fingers were trembling. Then she pulled on the pleated black wool skirt and black cotton stockings. When she lifted her new black leather oxfords out of the tissue paper, she remembered the little old gray-haired lady in Famous Barr who had admired them.

"Ooh," she had trilled, "those look so comfortable. I need a pair just like them."

When Kate told her friends the story later she had laughingly admitted that it was the one time all summer when she'd had serious second thoughts about her decision. But now she was excited. She couldn't wait to go down and show her family how she looked. As she hurried to pull back the curtains and join the other giggling, chattering girls heading downstairs, she realized there was no mirror in her cell. Sister Gabriela was waiting for her, and as she helped Kate fasten on the stiff white collar and cuffs, she smiled.

"You'll wear this outfit for three weeks," she said. "Then on the third Sunday, you'll receive the cape and veil of the postulant."

"When do we get the real habit and white veil, like you?"

"Oh, that's a whole year away, not until next July 25, the feast of St. James, if you make it that far," she said with a grin. "Okay, let's go. Your parents want to see you, and the bell will be ringing in a few minutes for the end of visiting."

As Kate came downstairs, she caught sight of her parents and Maggie in the crowd of families waiting in the foyer below. She twirled before them. "Well, how do I look?"

Then she saw their faces. Her mother's set smile could not quite hide the pain in her eyes. Her father for once said nothing and looked nervously away. Only Maggie seemed herself, and as they hugged goodbye, she whispered, "Better you than me, kiddo." Kate felt tears forming, and could not even whisper that last goodbye as the heavy convent door shut behind her family.

Kate followed the novices into a long line forming in the cloister walk. On her right was a carefully tended square courtyard garden with roses and zinnias and petunias, beside a flagstone path. The afternoon shadows were lengthening across the grass and the ivy-covered walls of the chapel opposite. Then the long line of novices and postulants filed into the chapel, cool after the heat of the August afternoon. As Kate's eyes grew accustomed to the dimness, she saw that the chapel was filled with a hundred or so black-veiled nuns, all rising as the organ intoned the music for Vespers, the evening song. Suddenly light flooded the church, and Kate gazed down the long aisle to the gold and white altar that lay at the heart of the convent, the altar of sacrifice.

Those first weeks in the convent were strange yet exciting. Kate felt as if she were living in a foreign country whose language and customs she was struggling to learn. Each minute of the day, the postulants followed a strict routine in the old monastic tradition of prayer and work. Kate was awakened each morning in the dark at 4:45 a.m. by the irritatingly cheerful voice of her guardian angel Sister Gabriela, the novice assigned to their dorm: "Life is short; death is certain. God alone knows the hour of death." With this scary thought Kate would be jolted out of some dream and struggle to her feet to bathe her face and hands in the basin of water on her night stand, brush her teeth, and dress quickly, all the while trying to remember the sequence of morning prayers the other sleepy girls were reciting around her. Then it was down to the cloister walk to wait for the little silver bell that Sister Mary Margaret, the postulant mistress, would ring when all were assembled to signal the postulants and novices to file into the chapel for the first hour of the Divine Office, Lauds. Silent meditation followed. Kate would begin to meditate on a scene from the Gospel, say the one with Jesus and the woman at the well, and fifteen minutes later would find herself fantasizing about swimming in a lake with her friends from high school.

After a half hour, Father Finn, the chaplain, came to the altar to say Mass. There were rumors that the Father was a shell-shocked veteran of World War II, and Kate wondered about his story. The only man living among all these women, he became for her a comforting presence, and she was happy to see him on his walks through the grounds, smoking his pipe, his old Irish setter padding stiffly behind him.

Kate wasn't used to going to Mass daily, but it soon became her favorite part of the day. When the nuns sang the Gregorian Chant, the singing rose like silver in the echoing chapel. At times high and ethereal, their voices would suddenly sweep low and passionate so that Kate trembled at the intensity. She felt like crying for happiness sometimes and would whisper her thanks to the image of the handsome resurrected Christ on the cross above the altar. This was no man of sorrows, suffering and gruesome, but a splendidly dressed bridegroom, and they were all his brides.

Once when a group of the postulants were scrubbing the floor, they began to laugh about being brides of Christ. JoAnn, older and more cynical than the others, said she felt more like Cinderella at the moment, and Kate snickered and wondered aloud, "Well, does that make Jesus a bigamist?" At this they all laughed helplessly, wiping their tears on their blue-and-white checked aprons until Sister Mary Margaret appeared in the doorway.

After a quick silent breakfast of hot cereal and a roll, the postulants and novices scattered to make their beds and do their chores before class started at eight. Their studies were interrupted at nine to pray Terce, and fifteen minutes later the postulants and novices were all back in class until Sext at noon. After a brief spiritual reading at lunch, Sister rang the bell permitting them to talk freely for the first time all day. Their eager young voices would rise in a great clash of laughter and teasing until Sister tapped the bell, "Sisters, let's remember to speak in ladylike tones."

Kate thought that Sister Mary Margaret's idea of ladylike came from a Victorian novel, but in general the postulant mistress was friendly and understanding. According to the novices' gossip, this was Sister's first year in the newly designed job of postulant mistress. Previously, the whole novitiate had been under the strict reign of Sister Mary Paul, the tall, bent mistress of novices, whose piercing blue eyes struck fear into the heart of every postulant.

After lunch, which was more what the girls from the country called dinner—a heavy meal of soup and homemade bread, a salad, a main course of roast beef or chicken, vegetables, and some tasty little custard for dessert—the postulants would pour out into the backyard to sit under the trees or walk up into the orchard, happy to be free for a while in the apple-filled air of autumn. Too soon the bell rang for afternoon classes.

Once a week they would have instructions with Sister in their study hall. Sister Mary Margaret led them through each chapter of the Holy Rule of the Order, which had been handed down from St. Dominic himself. A study period followed, during which Kate often nodded over her algebra assignment, then Vespers in the chapel, and then another hour of recreation, spent sewing in their upstairs community room, or playing pinochle on feast days and Sundays. Kate's mother played bridge, but pinochle! Kate had never heard of it. Sister Mary Margaret scolded her for not paying attention when she and Kate were partners one night. Kate saw that the nun was deadly serious about the game and decided not to volunteer to be her partner again.

When the bell rang for Compline, the girls filed into chapel for the last prayer of the day, their chant books heavy in their hands, smothering yawns. The last song was always a hymn to Our Lady, and when the voices of the nuns died away, deep night silence muffled the convent like a blanket of snow.

Kate hadn't seen the point of all this silence, having been raised in an Irish family where everyone gabbed on from morning until night. The postulants often played tricks on each other in the darkness of the dormitories, short-sheeting beds and mixing up dresser drawers. They would stuff sheets in their mouths to stifle laughter when the unsuspecting victim discovered the prank and swore softly in the dark.

Some of the postulants were a few years older than Kate. They had already been to college or had worked, so were more sophisticated than she. Because several girls were in the throes of nicotine withdrawal during their first weeks, Sister Mary Margaret supplied them with hard candy to help them over the hump. Gradually friendships formed as the girls got to know one another. Kate found herself drawn to several of the older girls whose wisecracks undermined the rules and formalities of daily life in the novitiate. The six-inch rule was particularly funny to them all. Signs, neatly lettered, were posted everywhere. The water in the bathtub was not to exceed six inches; the windows could be raised only six inches.

Kate's world was shrinking. She lived in a cocoon of women, free to wander around the convent property, up into the orchard or woods, but she saw no other people for days at a time. Kate found herself delighting in watching the nine-year-old altar boys as they brushed back their hair and winked at each other during Father's daily homily. There was no radio or television, and worst of all for Kate, no daily newspaper. The great world beyond shrank into a dim memory.

Sometimes her memories returned with vivid poignancy. One Saturday night Kate had gone to bed after a long day of housework (Saturday morning was entirely devoted to major housecleaning), choir practice, and instructions. Finally, starting at eight o'clock, the nuns spent an hour and a half in chapel singing Matins. Sister Mary Margaret told them to offer up these prayers for all the sins that were being committed in the world on a Saturday night. Several postulants grinned knowingly.

Although it was October, the windows were open in the dormitory, as it had been a particularly warm day. Kate heard a car go by with the radio blaring loudly. She tried to identify the song, when a girl's laughter rose ethereally in the humid night. The car sped off, and the silence of the country echoed in the sudden stillness. She pictured herself in that car. That's where she belonged, she thought. She was eighteen. What was she doing in bed at ten o'clock on a Saturday night? She tried to sleep, but tears ran down her cheeks, wetting the pillow.

Most days she was cheerful. She loved her classes, especially English. She had discovered the poetry of Gerard Manley Hopkins and would wander out to sit under a tree during Saturday afternoon study period when she should have been working on her algebra, and memorize his poems: "Elect'd Silence sing to me . . ." Hopkins' struggle to give himself over to the Divine Lover helped her see the way to surrender the world.

Sundays were Kate's favorite time. As the external world receded, she felt her internal world expand. Kate remembered the rainy November Sunday she found Thomas Merton's *The Seven Storey Mountain* in the library. She had curled up in a big chair in one of the empty front parlors used only for visitors and was startled several hours later when the bell rang for Sext. Kate was mesmerized by Merton's early life—the loss of his mother, his travels all over with his artist father. Reading about his years of desperate adolescent loneliness, and his drinking and chasing girls, took her far away from the convent for a few hours, yet brought her closer to an obscure understanding of what was supposed to happen to her. She read in *The Seven Storey*

*Mountain* of Merton's delight when he discovered the way of life of the Trappists, and she copied the passage into her notebook: "What wonderful happiness there was, then, in the world. There were still men on this miserable, noisy, cruel earth, who tasted the marvelous joy of silence and solitude, who dwelt in forgotten mountain cells, in secluded monasteries, where the news and desires and appetites and conflicts of the world no longer reached them."

Yes, Kate thought, this, too, is what she would learn: to give up everything for Christ, to be stripped of her old self in order to be reborn. As she headed to chapel that Sunday afternoon, she knew that her journey had begun in earnest.

Eleven months later, on July 25, the feast of St. James, Kate awakened to the sound of the novices singing, "Behold the bridegroom cometh." It was the day she and her classmates would receive the full habit of the Dominican sisters, but with the white veil of a novice instead of the black veil of the professed sisters, those who had taken vows. Drenched in sweat on this summer morning, Kate stripped to her waist and sponged off her body, the water cool and delicious on her skin. She touched her short hair—hair that had been cut yesterday in preparation for the veil she would receive today. Some of the girls had wept to see the long blond and brown waves drift to the floor as old Sister Madeline, the convent barber, wielded her sharp scissors. The nun, bent and worn, clucked and hissed at them to be still, insisting that God would be pleased with the sacrifice of their beauty.

Kate stood next to her good friend Cookie, and they laughed at the drama taking place before them. Neither had long hair, so the short cut would not be much different from their usual style. Kate couldn't wait to receive the habit and finally begin to feel like a real nun.

After breakfast, the girls gathered in the community room, where they dressed in long white gowns and veils for the ceremony. From somewhere boxes of powder had appeared mysteriously, with names like *My Sin*, *Arpege*, and *Je Reviens* embossed in gold. Kate stood very still in her underwear as her guardian angel, Sister Gabriela, dusted her with the powder; soon she saw clouds of it floating around the room, and the scent of jasmine and honeysuckle rose in the heat.

"This is so you don't sweat all over the gown," Sister Gabriela whispered. "They use these gowns every year, you know, and they have to be sent to the cleaners in town." Then she slipped the gown over Kate's head and tied the wide sash tightly around her waist.

All the postulants had been badly disappointed when they saw their gowns, which were nothing like the wedding gowns they were supposed to suggest. More like angel costumes from a school play, the gowns were made of cheap imitation satin belted at the waist, with wide butterfly sleeves. The tall, thin girls looked fairly graceful, but short, chubby Marilyn Becker looked more like a Kewpie doll. Oh well, they weren't supposed to be vain anymore, so what did it matter? Finally the long net veil was secured to her hair with bobby pins, and a wreath of real carnations and baby's breath crowned the veil.

The heavy, spicy odor of the carnations made Kate think suddenly of her senior prom and how it felt to be dancing with Eddie Macon as he held her too close, his body pressing against her.

She shook off the thought as they all lined up and filed slowly into the chapel. Kate knew that her parents, along with Dan and Maggie and even some of her girlfriends, were somewhere in the church, but the whole scene swam before her eyes as the postulants glided to the altar past their families, past the professed nuns, the novices, and up into the sanctuary, crowded with priests, where the towering wide figure of Cardinal Cody himself, dressed in gold vestments, his miter gleaming in the lights, waited for them.

After reciting together the ritual request for the habit of the order, the postulants filed out a side door into the long hall off the kitchen leading to the chapel. Chairs had been placed for each of them with their new white habits and veils carefully folded over the backs. Kate's hands trembled as she took off the bridal veil, the gown, and the long slip. As she pulled the long white habit of the Dominicans over her head she tried to remember the prayer she was supposed to say. Standing by a window that looked out into the courtyard garden, she watched a few sparrows splashing with abandon in the bird bath, and it seemed suddenly that time stood still and that she could never move on from this point. Soon unseen hands were helping her fasten the starchy white wimple that covered her hair, and pin the fine white wool veil to her headdress.

When Kate looked around she was startled. All the girls had disappeared; in their place was a row of look-alike, somber young nuns, their hands tucked beneath their scapulars, their eyes shining with wonder at the enormity of their transformation.

Later when the families gathered in the shade of giant elm trees out on the lawn, the new novices chattered and laughed as they opened their presents. When her father and Dan decided to find a spot for a smoke, Kate found a moment to look at her mother, pretty and young in her flowered summer dress.

She smiled into Kate's eyes and took her hand, surprising Kate, for her mother was usually cool, reserved. "Well, Katie, you're finally the nun you've been longing to be. I must confess, though, that when we saw all of you coming down the aisle you looked more like ghosts than brides. I wanted to cry!"

Kate laughed and then realized that she felt like crying, too. Somehow the play-acting days were done, she knew, and these next two years would be the real test of her grit, her determination to stick it out.

That first year of the novitiate was a blur, her time spent in the laundry, with the huge vats of bleach and the hot hiss of the mangle as the novices pressed the nuns' veils. In the afternoons, they would be sent up to the apple orchard where they walked among the trees fragrant with blossoms in the spring and heavy with fruit in the late summer days. She was a city girl, but found to her surprise how much she loved being in the fields and orchards of the convent grounds.

The novices took turns working in the kitchen, and the month she was assigned to the kitchen was a disaster for Kate. As she and the three other new novices reported for the first day of their month of kitchen duty, Sister Emmeline, the crabby sixty-year-old head cook, sat dejectedly at her small desk in the corner of the kitchen. She surveyed them with a great sigh: "Humph. Not a farm girl among you, I suppose. College girls . . . lots of book learning and not an ounce of common sense, I can tell already. I don't know how in the world I'm supposed to run a decent kitchen when they send me four green novices every month to train. I just get them broken in, and four new ones show up. Come on, I'll show you how to get the potatoes started for tonight." With that she hobbled off, her white apron immaculate, her walk unsteady and arthritic.

Kate bridled at the injustice of the nun. Why, Sister Emmeline didn't even know them. Wasn't that her job, to train them? And what was all that stuff about college girls? Kate supposed the cook sister was just jealous that she didn't get to go to college. Kate wondered if she would be able to hold her tongue. Sister was always after her—about the way she stood with her hand on her hip as she stirred the great pot of soup; nagging her about the way she didn't pin her veil back neatly, instead letting it hang down so that it got in the way when she chopped the onions and celery for the soup. Kate was also a careless dishwasher, Sister Emmeline pointed out, as she rejected bowls with traces of dried food that Kate had missed.

The final humiliation occurred one Saturday morning when Kate was in charge of getting all the food dished into serving bowls, placing them in the large warmer and then, ten minutes later, handing the bowls to the novices who were serving tables. The food was, of course, still supposed to be steaming hot. Sister yelled at her to get a move on; the nuns were already filing in from chapel and Kate hadn't even started dishing out the food. Nervously, she grabbed the huge iron pot of mashed potatoes and looked around for a place on the counter to put it. In desperation, she swung the pot up on the high serving wagon and stared up at it, realizing that she couldn't reach the potatoes to spoon them out.

At that Sister Emmeline flew across the kitchen with a great cry and whacked Kate soundly on the back, right between her shoulders. "Get out," she cried. "I can't stand it another minute. You don't have the sense God gave you!"

Kate tore off her apron and rushed through the scullery, tears streaming down her face, while astonished new postulants watched in disbelief.

Kate ran down the hall to the chapel, pushed open the swinging doors with all her might, and threw herself down in the pew nearest the altar. She sobbed until her rough linen handkerchief was soaked; then she sat down and stared up at the risen Christ over the altar. How dare Sister hit her! Wasn't she supposed to be in control of her temper? And why was she always finding fault with her? Kate was not used to being bad at anything. She wasn't great at sports, but she was a decent softball player and a good swimmer. But in Sister Emmeline's kitchen she couldn't do anything right.

It wasn't much better in the sewing room. Three times she had to make over a simple blue-and-white checked apron, until finally Sister Carol Ann grabbed it away from her, muttering in exasperation that she would do it herself, since it was such torture to watch her mangle the job.

The class in Gregorian Chant was a relief for Kate, for she loved to sing and was beginning to appreciate the contemplative nature of this music. But she didn't understand yet how she was supposed to contemplate while Father Jean LeBeau scowled at them over half-moon glasses, making great, frantic swoops in the air as he tried to get the novices to follow his rhythm.

Le Beau was a Benedictine monk from France. For some years he had been teaching at Washington University in St. Louis while living with Father Finn in the solid two-story brick rectory on the grounds of the Dominican Convent. As payment for room and board, Le Beau taught the advanced piano pupils among the young nuns and directed the chant. Short and graceful, he had a heavy French accent that was a source of mimicry for the more gifted actresses among the novices, at least when they were out of Sister Mary Paul's earshot. He drove them hard during chant rehearsal, often keeping them well over the allotted hour.

Once he had hurt Kate's pride badly as he walked around the room while the novices struggled through the Introit for the first Sunday of Advent: "*Ad te levavi, anima mea.*" Although the music was soulful, intense, almost introspective, Kate sang with all her might, hoping Father would notice her clear if untrained soprano and choose her for the *schola*, the special small group that led the nuns' singing and took all the difficult parts.

As he walked by her, his hands behind his back, he stopped suddenly and glared at her: "Shut up, big mouth!" he cried. "Blend, blend your voice with the others in a seamless flow!" Afterwards, her cheeks had burned for an hour.

But there was humor and tenderness in the man, too. One day he startled them all by asking if they knew how to dance. After a few murmured assents, he took the hand of a pretty dark-eyed novice and led her to the front of the room. Then, humming a waltz, the priest grabbed her around the waist and swirled her around and around while Reverend Mother and Sister Mary Paul looked on unsmiling. All the novices clapped; Kate wished that she had been the one chosen.

Once on a damp gloomy Monday afternoon in November, Father LeBeau was trying to teach them a particularly difficult motet by Palestrina. Suddenly he motioned for them to stop. He leaned against the tall stool he sat on during practice, slipped his hands in the sleeves of his Benedictine habit, and silently regarded the twenty-four young novices before him. Finally he asked with amazement: "Why, what's the matter? I feel as if I am at a funeral." When no one answered, he walked around among them, lifting a chin here and there to look into eyes that shied away from his. "Ah," he said softly. "I think I know what it is. Yesterday you had a visiting day. It was your last one until Easter. Christmas is coming. You will not see the dear parents for a long, long time. Is that it?"

Several novices nodded. Kate kept her head held high, vowing she would show no tears. Father went on in the same unnaturally soft tone. "Well, you go on to the chapel when I dismiss you. Go sit and stare at the crucifix and tell Him you want to go home. Do you think He wanted to stay on the cross?"

The novices sat in silence as he packed up his books and swept out of the room. One by one they filed out, most of them heading for the chapel. Kate went out to the courtyard and sat on the single step leading into the garden. She hugged her knees and thought about the awful analogy Father had made between their lives and Christ hanging on the cross. Maybe he was talking about himself, she thought; at nineteen she was not ready to face long-term suffering.

Gradually Kate realized that she was not the only first-year novice having difficulties. One by one their number was dwindling. She would wake in the morning and see someone's bed still made up from the day before. Then she would know that a novice had left the community and that they would probably never see her again. Kate hated the hugger-mugger secrecy of it all, as if it were shameful to leave.

She grumbled bitterly to her friend, Sister Francesca, as they took a long Wednesday afternoon hike through the brown, lifeless, early-January fields of dried cornstalks. They were supposed to stay with the group but had lagged behind to talk.

Francesca pulled her black shawl tightly around her shoulders and looked at Kate. "Were you surprised that Lucy was gone when you saw her bed this morning?" Lucy was a girl Kate had known in high school, and although not best friends, they had always been close, sharing news from home after visiting days.

Kate thought several moments before replying. "Not really, I guess. She had seemed so glum lately. About a month ago she told me that she'd gone to Sister Mary Paul to tell her she was thinking about leaving. Sister had asked her to wait and pray about it for a while. But she and that postulant called Anna had become great friends. I used to see them meeting secretly in odd corners, whispering intensely. When Anna left two weeks ago, I had a bad feeling about Lucy."

Francesca faced her, a grim smile on her face. "Well, guess what? The rumor is that Lucy didn't really leave with permission—she escaped!"

"But why? We're all free to leave whenever we want to!" Kate strode more quickly now, not wanting to hear this.

"Evidently Sister Mary Paul kept urging her to stay. Lucy and Anna were thick, so when Anna left, Lucy arranged for her to come back with a car in two weeks. Then when we were all at Vespers, Lucy changed into a skirt and blouse she had in her trunk since her entrance, stuffed her habit into a laundry basket, and slipped out the front door to meet Anna."

Francesca stared into the distance, kicking at the rows of dirt beneath her feet. Kate felt sick. The story was sad. If Lucy didn't want to be a nun, why couldn't she just tell them all? Why did she have to sneak out in the night, like a prisoner escaping her guards? She was a runaway!

Finally, with a fierce pull at the shawl that kept slipping off her shoulders, Kate said, "I'm going to ask Sister Mary Paul about this today during instructions. We need to get this out in the open. All this secrecy makes us feel a hundred times worse about people leaving than the truth ever would."

Francesca struggled to keep up as Kate strode ahead. "She's not going to like it," Francesca warned Kate.

Kate knew that her friend thought she was too outspoken and enjoyed stirring up rebellions occasionally in the regimented world of the cloister. But Kate didn't care; this secrecy was like a worm gnawing away at her sense of certainty in her vocation.

That afternoon Sister Mary Paul, apparently anticipating the approaching rumble of discontent, was unusually frank in making the announcement. "Sisters," she began, "I know you are all very saddened by the departure of one of your classmates, Sister Mary Lucy. The circumstances of her leaving were . . . irregular, and I can only say that we have been in touch with her parents as well as her pastor at St. Roch's, and I would like you all to pray for Sister in what must be a very difficult time." She looked slowly around the room. "Are there any questions?"

Kate raised her hand immediately, but Sister looked past her, trying to see if anyone else had something to say. Finally, she nodded at Kate.

"Sister, we . . . that is, I was wondering why we never get to say goodbye to someone who leaves. You're always encouraging us to think of each other as sisters and to love each other. It just seems so cold to have someone hustled off in secrecy without time to say a word to anyone. Of course, I'm not talking only about Sister Mary Lucy," she amended, seeing Sister Mary Paul's face darken.

"Yes, I'm sure it does seem cold, as you say, Sister Mary Katherine. It hurts us all when someone decides to leave. But my responsibility is to protect and encourage those of you who are choosing to stay. I do not want you influenced by someone who is questioning and doubting our whole way of life. Do you understand?"

"Yes, Sister, but I don't agree."

There was a long moment of silence while Sister Mary Paul's cheeks flushed and Kate held her gaze. No one moved until finally, from the back of the room, Kate heard someone murmur, "I don't agree either."

"Neither do I." The comments were coming now from all over.

Sister Mary Paul got up stiffly and rested her hand on the table in front of her.

"Well, my dears, you must realize by now that religious orders are not democracies." She smiled tightly and left the room. Kate realized that her victory was hollow and would probably cost her in some way.

That's why she was astonished later that afternoon. Hurrying to chapel for None, she almost bumped into Sister Mary Paul and Reverend Mother in Our Lady's Chapel, huddled in conversation. Though their voices were low, Kate sensed they were talking about Sister Lucy's flight. Meaning to slip past them quietly, Kate was startled when the novice mistress reached out and grabbed her arm, holding her lightly as she said kindly, more so than ever before: "I was talking to your pastor, Father Peters, this morning about . . . well about Sister Lucy, actually. He asked me how you were doing. I told him to send me ten more just like you."

Both Reverend Mother and Sister Mary Paul gazed at Kate with mingled affection and amusement. Kate was dumbstruck. Sister liked her! Since the day Kate became a novice, Sister Mary Paul had seemed constantly irritated by her, chiding her for her bouncy, undignified way of walking, her careless handwriting, her stream of chatter during silent time.

Kate mumbled hurried thanks and ducked quickly into her pew in chapel. She was distracted during the chanting of the office by what the novice mistress had said. Kate thought she understood now the psychology used by the novice mistress in forming young nuns. Constant, intense criticism, which, if it could be borne with reasonably good grace, would be the refining fire that would separate the gold from baser metals, or something like that, she thought, realizing at once the arrogance of her analogy. She didn't agree with this theory of education, but it was an immense relief to know that despite all her carping, Sister Mary Paul thought she would make a good nun. But wouldn't it be better, more effective, to show encouragement, affection, even love to all these struggling young women?

Suddenly Kate thought of her mother. What she gave Kate was what she missed sorely here—that deep, unshakable love that lay beneath the normal nagging of a teenager's mother. Love had been like air at home. Nobody talked about it, but it was always there, invisible, indispensable. Now she was living at a rarefied altitude; the air was thinner here. The question was, could she survive in this atmosphere?

Without having answered that question, Kate knelt two years later on the feast of St. Dominic, August 3, and pronounced her first vows: "I, Sister Mary Katherine, vow and promise to Almighty God, and to you Reverend Mother, that I will live for three years in poverty, chastity, and obedience." She unpinned the white veil of the novice from her headdress, and in its place pinned the black veil of the professed nun. Dry-eyed and calm, Kate had whispered as they filed back into the chapel, "If You want me to do this, You'll have to help me. I have a feeling it's not going to be easy."

# Chapter Twelve

## Saturday, June 27, 1964

*In the dark church, Kate awakes, panicked. Feeling the woolen jacket beneath her, she remembers Peter. She thinks sickly of the trouble she caused him. Thank God he left her the money! How will she be able to repay him? She pictures the nuns and priests in Juliaca. By now they would have radioed Sister Jeanne Marie who was still in Bolivia with the Poor Clare nuns after her retreat there. She would be the calmest, trying to reassure the others about Kate, but secretly furious at her for causing all the commotion.

Sister Josepha would be angry and deeply worried. At sixty-two, Josepha was an ascetic, committed missionary, scornful of creature comforts and of the younger nuns' questioning of their mission in the Altiplano. Her fair, serene Slavic features were straight out of a painting by Van Eyck, Kate had thought the first time she'd seen her. Her eyes were light blue, fringed by pale, almost invisible lashes, and her hands were as large and red as a farm wife's. She bustled around the parish with a brisk, no-nonsense approach to doing good. Self-doubt didn't seem to be a part of her makeup, and she had a hard time disguising her impatience when it surfaced in others.

One afternoon when they'd been working together in the small sacristy polishing the gold chalices and patens, Kate tried to talk to Sister Josepha about Tom Lynch. It was a cold, rainy April day, and Kate's mood reflected the weather. She was desperate to open up to someone.

Suddenly, Kate put down the chalice she was polishing and turned to Sister Josepha with a sob. "I've really got to talk to you."

The older nun's pale blue eyes regarded her serenely. She continued to rub the chalice briskly as she waited for Kate to go on. "Why, Sister, what is it?"

"I think . . . no, I have fallen in love with someone. I've tried so hard to fight it. I've prayed, I've asked God to help me through this, but nothing seems to work."

Sister Josepha did not look at her, but smiled slightly as she buffed the golden chalice. "Why, Sister, surely you're not surprised at being human? Men and women fall in love all the time. Remember, our feelings are never sinful; we can't help them. It's what we do with them that matters." At this she put down the chalice and looked directly at Kate. "May I ask who is the object of your feelings?"

In Sister's tone was a hint of laughter; Kate flushed. How could her superior make light of what was to her a source of agony?

"It's Father Tom." Kate's tightly clenched fists rested on the wooden work table. In the silence that followed her admission, she did not look to see the other nun's reaction.

Sister Josepha broke the silence in the sacristy by clearing her throat and saying dryly: "I confess, I never would have guessed him."

"Why not?" Kate was eager now to talk about Tom.

"Father is—how shall I put this—rather distant; even cynical, I might add. He's a good priest, extremely dedicated to the people. But there's a wall around him. I always thought he had little use for nuns. I believe he finds us slightly ridiculous." The older nun turned to face Kate squarely. "Look, dear, you know what you have vowed. You're still in temporary vows, so this experience of struggle is healthy. But in the end only you can decide. I will pray each day for you." As she gazed at Kate, her eyes softened. "I'd hate to lose you, Sister. You have a magnetic personality that draws others to you. This is God's gift, and I hope you decide to continue to use it in His service." Brusquely, she gathered up the chalices and placed them in the cupboard. She locked the small doors and hooked the large circle of keys on her cincture, unconsciously giving them a little house-wifely pat.

Kate knew she was dismissed. Well, at least she had finally told someone. Sister Josepha didn't refer to their conversation again, but two nights later Kate found a book on her bed, *The Gift of Chastity*, when she turned on the light after evening prayers. *Great, a book to give me all the answers. I'd probably do better to re-read* Anna Karenina. Books had always been her great treasure, but somehow Kate knew the answer to her dilemma would not be found in a book.

Now in the quiet of the still-dark church Kate gazes at the far-away altar. It is decorated in the ornate, baroque style that Spaniards loved. The sanctuary lamp gleams steadily, suspended in a silver wheel above a side altar of the Virgin. She kneels, burying her face in her hands. Startled by the creak of a door, she looks up and sees an old man in a long black cassock shuffle in from a side entrance near the altar. With great effort he lights the six tall candles on either side of the altar. One by one the flames catch, flicker weakly, and then settle into a steady glowing flame. The old man works slowly, stopping often to cough, to adjust his robe. Finally, he heads down the aisle, swinging a brass circlet of keys at his side. Kate waits for him to notice her, and tries to think what she will say. But with a great rasping of sliding bolts and squeaking of wood he unlocks the wooden doors, and for an instant the strong morning sun illuminates millions of dust motes in the air.

One by one people enter. Thin, elegant ladies in black mantillas, women with babies on their backs, a few businessmen, all cross themselves on the threshold and head for a statue to light a candle or whisper prayers to their favorite among God's saints. Mass would begin soon, she thinks; she better leave before the priest notices her, an out-of-place American nun.

Kate genuflects quickly and steps out into the freshness of the morning, her mouth dry and stale, her body stiff from the hard bench she slept on. She follows two women carrying baskets down a side street and soon comes to the open-air market. She buys two hard rolls, a banana, and a cup of coffee, and then sits on a bench in a nearby square to eat her breakfast. Carefully she folds the precious *soles* Peter has left her and tucks them securely in the deep pocket sewn into the skirt of her habit.

After her breakfast she rinses her mouth in the fountain nearby. The water, smelling of copper, has a metallic taste. Uncertain what to do now, she looks around the square and notices a bus rumbling by, covered with dust, packed with *campesinos*. It must have just come in from the mountains. She stops a group of schoolboys, their brown packs strapped to their backs. They are dressed in the short white coverall jackets worn by public-school children.

"*Con permiso, niños. Me pueden dirigir a la estación de autobus?*"

"Oh yes, *madre*." They grin, obviously happy to use their hard-won English. "The bus is over there. Yes, over there," they point excitedly to the far corner of the plaza.

"Thank you," she smiles, not wanting to leave these boys with ruddy faces and dark, shining eyes.

"Yourrr welcome," they shout in chorus. They make Kate homesick. They remind Kate of her old neighborhood and the kids of St. Roch's. How in the world has she landed here? She is Kate O'Neill, Tim and Mary's daughter. She quickens her pace and holds up her head as if she knows where she is going.

As Kate rounds the corner of the square she sees the bus station, teeming with families, the women swaying in their wide skirts, carrying bundles easily with their babies tucked neatly in the scarlet-and-tangerine and green-and-yellow shawls slung around their backs. With small knitted caps tied firmly under their chins, the babies stare wide-eyed at the commotion around them. There are middle-class businessmen, schoolteachers, and across the room, a tall, thin young man with long hair tied back in a ponytail, dressed in jeans and sandals. *He must be Peace Corps,* Kate thinks, as he nods unsmilingly at her.

She stares at the blackboard with the destinations and times written in chalk. She could go east to Vitor, then north to Nazca, Ica, Pisco, Chilca, Callao, and finally Lima. Or she could head west, back into the highlands.

She steps up to the cashier's window and asks for a ticket to Lima. The thin, mustachioed man looks up when he hears her American accent.

"*Ida y vuelta?*" he asks.

"*Ida, no más,*" she answers faintly. One way. She would not be returning. She counts out the *soles* carefully, and slips the now much smaller roll deep in the pocket of her habit. She looks around for the bathroom, hoping her period has not begun. In the grimy stall she is reassured for now. She splashes water on her face and scrubs her hands. She doesn't dare drink this water.

She takes a seat next to an Aymara family. The husband moves down the long bench to make room. The children gaze at her and whisper something in Aymara to their mother. Both the woman and her husband laugh, and the man whispers to Kate, "The children say you are *una muñeca*, with blue eyes." Kate laughs.

Finally, at nine thirty, the bus for Lima pulls up in front of the station, half full of passengers from the Altiplano. Shouting over the crowd, the driver herds the waiting passengers toward the bus, and they surge forward, clutching parcels and boxes. Kate, without baggage, arrives first and takes the third seat on the right behind the driver. Two women get on the bus chattering in high-pitched voices, giggling and swaying down the aisle, and Kate realizes they have been drinking. She is surprised, for in the mountains the women are serious and dignified, even when their men are falling down drunk at a carnival. One wide woman in a bowler hat squeezes in next to Kate, plumps herself down with a great sigh, and arranges her many parcels beneath the seat. By the time the bus pulls out of the courtyard, the woman is asleep.

Kate stares out the window at the elegant neighborhood the bus is passing through. They travel down a wide, tree-shaded street, on both sides of which are high walls with massive wooden gates. Once in a while Kate glimpses a villa, its white walls gleaming in the sun, scarlet bougainvillea spilling over wrought-iron balconies. Kate hasn't seen this part of Peru, the world of great wealth, in which, she imagines, sons were sent to Brown and daughters to Vassar, and women shopped in Miami, Paris, and New York, and men deposited their money in Swiss banks, safe from the dangerous currents of Peruvian politics. Kate has heard Tom and the other priests talk about privileged children, products of exclusive schools run by the Jesuits and the Religious of the Sacred Heart. Surely they had been exposed to the teachings of the Church on social justice, but the consciences of many of the rich remained serenely undisturbed by their fine Catholic educations. No wonder many missionaries followed with great interest Che Guevara's recent attempt to arouse the Bolivian peasants to join the struggle for change.

She remembers how one Sunday Tom had read out the gospel of St. Matthew to the impassive faces of their small congregation, with a handful of middle-class families sitting in the front at Santa Catalina. "'Lord, when was it that we saw you hungry or thirsty or a stranger or naked or ill or in prison, and did nothing for you?' And he will answer, 'I tell you this: anything you did not do for one of these however humble, you did not do for me.' And they will go away into eternal punishment, but the righteous into eternal life.'"

The engine groans in low gear as they climb the final mountain range before descending to the coast and the Pan-American highway that leads north to the capital. Suddenly Kate hears the brakes grind, and the driver, swearing slowly and methodically under his breath, stops the bus. When Kate notices a line of soldiers stretched across the highway, she thinks there must have been an accident. Then she hears a few people mutter, "*Contrabando*," and she realizes this is a blockade to search for smuggled goods. According to Father Jack, the border patrol at Desaguadero between Peru and Bolivia is notoriously sloppy as well as greedy; Bolivian goods were constantly being smuggled in and traded at the extensive black market in Lima.

The driver leaps from his seat and flings open the door. He is met by two serious young soldiers who demand his papers, oblivious to his strenuous complaints. Then one of the soldiers boards the bus. Stooping a little as he peers in, he barks the orders: all Peruvian citizens are to get off the bus with their baggage and have their papers ready to be inspected. Kate feels her throat go dry and she sits very still, remembering her passport in the drawer of her desk in Juliaca. She glances at the Peace Corps worker who is pulling his papers from his knapsack. Suddenly the woman next to Kate wakes. She leans over Kate to peer out the window at the soldiers, and her breath reeks of *chicha*, warm and intimate on Kate's face. Swiftly she bends down to a small bundle at her feet and slides it under Kate's seat.

She speaks directly to Kate for the first time, her face smooth and brown and untroubled. "*Madrecita, por favor, ayúdame.* Guard these things for me. The soldiers will not search you, for you are a foreigner." In a graceful motion, surprising in one her size, she hoists the other bags on her back. By the time Kate starts to protest, the woman is already down the steps of the bus.

Kate bends down and unwraps the package enough to see twelve bottles of Bolivian beer. She straightens up and keeps her eyes fixed on the cut-out picture of the Sacred Heart that the conductor has tacked up over the steering wheel. Trying to look as if she is deep in prayer, Kate reflects that if ever she needed to pray it is now, for she has become not only a fugitive but a smuggler. Oh God! How her father would enjoy this story—if she lived to tell it. The officers— finished with the Peruvians— are talking and gesturing toward the bus with the two lone Americans still on it.

In a few minutes another officer of the Guardia Civil boards the bus and heads straight for the Peace Corps worker. Short, with shiny straight black hair and intense dark eyes, the officer asks to see his passport. His voice is polite but cold. After a careful inspection, he asks the American to stand up and open his bags for a "routine check." The Peace Corps worker does as he is asked and even tries a few friendly words to defuse the tension, but the officer is businesslike, unsmiling. Watching his compact, powerful body, Kate feels a prickle on the back of her neck.

He turns to her next, removing his hat. "*Por favor, señorita, su pasaporte.*" It is a demand, not a request. Kate knows that by calling her *señorita* he is deliberately ignoring the fact that she is a nun. This makes her apprehensive. His accent is not that of the Altiplano, but she hasn't been in Peru long enough to place it.

"I don't have it with me, officer. Since I was traveling within the country, I didn't think I would need it. I am Sister Mary Katherine from the Dominican nuns in Juliaca."

"Stand up, please." His eyes slide down her body in the practiced, almost involuntary way of Latin men, and then she notices him staring at the smudged dirt on the front of her white scapular. He gestures toward the brown paper package, half hidden by her long skirt. "What's in the bag?"

Kate freezes. If she tells the truth she will implicate the woman. But how can she explain twelve bottles of Bolivian beer?

"The package isn't mine. I think there's beer in it."

The officer's eyes are expressionless. "Then to whom does this package belong?" he asks in Spanish with exaggerated politeness.

Kate looks directly into eyes almost on a level with her own. "I don't know," she says evenly, trying to keep a tremor out of her voice.

At that he wheels around and barks out a command, all pretense of politeness gone. "Follow me. We're taking you in for questioning." Then he stops and comes back to the seat where she still stands, unable to move. With a lithe movement he reaches down and picks up the package, holding it away from his body as if it were garbage.

Kate follows him then, and as she steps off the bus into the harsh sun the people move back in silence as the officer strides to his jeep. He motions for her to get in the back, and then quietly gives orders to his men. Another soldier hops into the driver's seat, and in a moment they are speeding down the treacherous mountain road, back toward Arequipa.

As in a dream, Kate watches the deep blue of the mountains as they appear and disappear above the hairpin turns in the road. They drive fast, the driver honking his horn at each curve to warn any approaching car or truck. By now it is almost noon, and the sun directly overhead is hot. Descending through shade and sun, the winding curves, Kate feels nausea rise in her. Finally they come to a tin hut with a Peruvian flag, slightly faded, hanging over the door at an angle. Two mangy black dogs drowse in the dirt.

While the driver helps Kate out, his superior is already striding toward the first building. As Kate and the driver enter the hut, the officer is speaking gruffly to a heavy soldier who is eating a plate of sausage and rice, a bottle of beer at his elbow, at the only desk in the small front room. The soldier wipes his mouth and stands up.

The officer motions for Kate to follow him. She enters a large room with several windows looking upon jagged mountains. Surprised by the clean, orderly air of the place, Kate tries not to stare. Books on crude, homemade bookshelves line the walls from top to bottom. A few pieces of pottery adorn the shelves, and leaning against one wall on a low bookcase is a framed print of Diego Rivera's *The Flower Seller*. Kate recognizes it because she had once cut this same picture out of a calendar and hung it on the wall of her sixth-grade classroom at St. Rita's. She stands by the lieutenant's desk watching him as he moves restlessly around the room, loosening his collar and rolling up his sleeves. He seems almost to have forgotten her when he suddenly goes to the door and asks the man in the next room to bring them two bottles of Orange Crush. Finally he tells Kate to sit down. He sits in his desk chair, facing her.

"I am Lieutenant Roberto Vargas, in charge of a small patrol here that does routine checks on buses and trucks for smuggling. However, it is very seldom that I encounter such an interesting case as I have today." For the first time his face relaxes and a glint of humor shines in his eyes. But his face turns serious, and he speaks in slow, clear Spanish as if she were a child. "I am afraid, reverend sister, that there is something very irregular about your situation. Perhaps you would like to clarify everything for me?"

Hesitating, Kate tries to sift through the facts; she'd tell him just enough truth but not too much. His eyes focus intently on her face, and Kate struggles to breathe in the stifling room.

"First of all," she begins, "the beer beneath my seat wasn't mine. It was put there by someone sitting next to me, and I did not want to cause her trouble." She watches him to see if he accepts this. His face remains impassive.

"Go on," he nods.

"I left Juliaca rather suddenly," Kate says in halting Spanish. "I had some problems and I needed to get away for a little while. So I hitched a ride to Arequipa."

"With whom?" Vargas watches her.

"With an Englishman from Cambridge University, Peter Grinnell."

Vargas's eyes widen, and he asks her to spell the name for him, writing it down carefully on a scrap of paper. "So where is this Englishman now?" Vargas looks faintly incredulous.

"I . . . I don't know. He was staying on in Arequipa for a few days, and then going back to England for vacation."

A knock on the door, and the fat sergeant with pockmarked skin brings in two Orange Crushes and two cloudy drinking glasses. Glancing insolently at Kate, he puts the sodas on the desk in front of his superior, and adjusts the pistol hanging carelessly from a belt around his bulging middle.

"*Algo más, teniente?*"

He looks hopefully at Vargas, who nods no without a word. Carefully, the lieutenant pours the orange soda into a glass and places it before Kate; then he pours one for himself and sips delicately, deliberately. He nods at Kate to drink; when she tastes the sweetness of the childish orange drink she feels unexpected tears. What is she doing here? Vargas looks at her and then away. Has he seen the sudden weakness his small kind act had aroused? As if reading her mind, he changes the tone of the interrogation.

Vargas gets up and walks around the room. "I would like to ask you something that I have often wondered about when I see the American priests and nuns and even Peace Corps workers coming to our country. Why are you here? Aren't there problems in your own country? Last year your president was assassinated, and everyday I read in *El Comercio* of the growing tensions between the blacks and whites in America. There are riots in your cities, no?"

Stalling for time, Kate takes a gulp of soda. How can she answer his question? It was one she'd asked herself hundreds of times since she had come to Peru. She decides to be frank with her inquisitor. "Yes, there are many serious problems in my country. Before I came to Peru I was teaching in a school in a poor area of St. Louis. The school had just combined two segregated schools into one. You understand that in America, until very recently, white children and black children did not go to the same schools?" She's chattering, she knows, hoping to distract him, to win him.

He nods.

"The black children and parents were unhappy that their school had been closed, and the whites felt the same. Everyday there were fights, lots of name calling, and almost unbearable tension. Many days I would go into the bathroom and cry, where the students couldn't see me, because I got so tired of all the hatred." She looks up to see him watching her closely. His glass is untouched on the desk, a white stain spreading on the wood beneath it from the moisture.

She hesitates, thinking what to say next, wishing her Spanish were better. "Little by little my students began to listen to each other. I made them read a book called *Black Boy* by Richard Wright."

Vargas says nothing, his eyes flat.

"It tells the story of a young black boy growing up in the South. At first the students hated reading it, but then they began arguing about it, shouting at each other, writing about their feelings when they read it. A slow change came over the classroom during the year. For the first time the white children began to see how it would feel to be a black child in America. And the black students saw white children really listening to them and trying to understand what they were saying." Breathless now from the effort of the Spanish, Kate admits in a weak voice, "It was a very small change."

Vargas gets up from his chair and paces around the room. "But you still haven't answered my question: Why have you come here? You must see that your presence here seems patronizing to us. Peru has a very old and very complicated civilization and history. Missionaries have been coming here since the time of the Inca Conquest."

Kate winces, expecting another attack.

Vargas continues without looking at her, walking back and forth like a college professor giving a lecture. "Have you read anything by José Mariátegui?" he asks suddenly. When Kate shakes her head no, he goes over to a bookshelf and pulls out a slim volume. "He has a wonderful essay in here on the Catholic Church's genius in adapting itself to the customs and beliefs of the people it tries to convert. He gives credit to the early missionaries of Peru who brought not only dogma but seeds, vines, tools." Changing the subject, the lieutenant looks at her directly. "What did you study in school? Theology?"

"Well, yes, but my major field was British and American literature."

"Ah, Wordsworth, Keats. Do you like Faulkner?"

"No, not really."

"To me he is the greatest American novelist. You should read him if you want a picture of a decaying, crumbling feudal society." Vargas smiles, a half-embarrassed look flitting across his face. "I am sorry. I do not often have the chance to speak of these things."

He sits down across from her. His voice is urgent, low. "I am an incarnation of my country. My father was a *campesino*, a peasant who worked on a great hacienda near Arequipa. My mother was the daughter of the owner. They had known each other since childhood. They fell in love, and when I was born my father was whipped within an inch of his life and sent packing with his wounds untended. My mother never saw him again. She ran away and disappeared into Lima, where she worked as a seamstress in Rimac. She educated me in good schools, but for years I never knew the story of my birth. She is dead now, and I despise the system and the class that has made me a divided man. Peru must change, and I will do whatever it takes to bring about this change." His face has a hard, steely set as he looks across the table at Kate. "But we *ourselves* will bring about this change."

Kate says nothing. Everything he has said echoes the doubts she has begun to feel about what she and the other nuns and priests were doing here in Peru. He stares down at the notes he had taken when she had told him about her journey. "Now I'm going to have to get on the radio and place a call to Juliaca. I must verify your story."

"Please." Kate's voice is hoarse. "I really want to get to Lima before nightfall."

Avoiding her eyes, the lieutenant stands up, makes a slight stiff bow, and leaves the room. In a few minutes, she hears the squawking of the radio and some rapid two-way Spanish. After ten minutes Vargas stands in the doorway. "The Guardia in Juliaca have sent a messenger to the Maryknoll priests there. They will be calling here in a few minutes. You may speak with them after I do."

Helplessly, Kate searches for something she can say. She has been foolish and thoughtless. She has run away blindly as an animal would, to avoid pain. Now she can hear Vargas talking to the pastor, Father Jack Higgins. Although the priest has a deep and simple faith, a boundless enthusiasm for the work, the pastor also has the dirtiest mouth of any priest she has ever known. Sister Josepha had tried to reassure her that this was simply his way of getting rid of tension, but Kate still flinched at the onslaught of his language. He will be furious now.

After several minutes of polite, carefully phrased inquiries on both sides, Lt. Vargas motions for Kate to sit in front of the radio and speak to the pastor. The voice of Father Jack Higgins sputters in the small room:

"God dammit, sister Mary Katherine, what in the . . . frigging hell are you doing?" He is making an effort to control himself, she knows, since he is on the public airwaves.

Kate holds the microphone close to her mouth, trying to keep her voice steady. "I'm really sorry, Father, I just had to get away. I'm fine, really I am. Don't worry."

"How in the hell did you get that far? Josepha says she doesn't think you have any money. Over."

The stilted radio conversation is frustrating, especially with Vargas and his sergeant sitting there. She doesn't know how much English they understand. "Oh, it's a long story. Tell the sisters I'm fine. I'm going to Lima and I'll write them as soon as I get there. I'm sorry for all the trouble. Over."

"Trouble! That's an understatement, missy. Tom's been out in the jeep all night scouring the countryside for one small baby nun who doesn't know her ass from a hole in the ground. Jesus Christ, Kate, I'm about ready to fire off a letter to your Mother Superior telling her to recall you immediately."

Kate glances at Vargas. Was that a ghost of a grin? Oh Lord, let him not understand English.

"Yes, Father, I understand perfectly. Over." Kate hopes her docile tone will mollify him. She hands the microphone back to Vargas who soon signs off with a curt expression of reassurance about her safety.

He looks at her somberly for a few moments. "I'm going to warn you, Sister, that what you are doing, traveling alone like this, is very dangerous. You have no identification; not every *guardia* is interested in an intellectual debate with a young, blue-eyed American nun. Do you understand me?"

Kate flushes at his implication and catches, too, the note of restrained gallantry. He is not joking, she knows. Her naiveté, she feels, only gives him further proof of her presumption in thinking that she is helping his people.

He looks at his watch. "The night bus leaves for Nazca

and Lima at 7:00 p.m. The sergeant will take you to the station up the road and wait with you there until it arrives. Then you are on your own."

Kate stands to thank him and holds out her hand to shake his when he grasps it suddenly and brings it just beneath his lips; then, with a quick, ceremonial bow over it, he abruptly releases her hand.

"I'm very grateful for your kindness, Lieutenant. *Muy agredicida*. I will think about what you said."

Kate turns away and climbs into the jeep. When she looks back, Vargas is watching her from the door of the small police station, fondling absently the ears of a black dog that has sidled up to him.

# Chapter Thirteen

Without a word, the sergeant drives Kate to the bus station in Vitor. He parks the jeep, and, with a grunt, heaves himself out of the seat. It is dusk now, and the town's few lights blink forlornly in a bar and one store lining the main street. Kate follows him across the street where, from an open door, the plaintive music of the mountains mingles with the hectic music of the coast. *It must be Saturday night*, she thinks, as she watches small bunches of drunken men lurch down the street, their arms around one another, their voices loud and slurred. She sees few women.

With a slight nod of his head the sergeant indicates the bus station; then he swaggers across the street to the bar.

Alone again, Kate feels dizzy. She's had nothing to eat since breakfast. She grips the jacket. The money Peter had given her would be gone as soon as she bought another ticket to Lima. Then what?

As she enters the bus station, she sees an Aymara couple slumped against each other, fast asleep. Three young girls, carefully made up and dressed in wool skirts and bright shiny blouses, their good shoes stored carefully in mesh shopping bags at their side, sit laughing together in a corner of the cramped room. They look at Kate in surprise and stop talking, watching her as she steps up to the ticket window. She counts out the few remaining *soles* and then asks the tired-looking clerk where she could find a place to wash her hands and go to the bathroom.

"*Sí, sí, madrecita. Hay servicios atrás,*" he motions vaguely toward the back of the building.

Kate finds an overgrown garden in the back. She sees a small outhouse and, as she walks closer, she hears a steady stream of urine, as if from a horse, splashing into a hole. The door slams, and a slight, dark man with a cane lurches past her in silence. Kate holds her breath as she enters the falling down shed. In the solid blackness the stench is unbearable; Kate gropes her way to the wooden hole, holding the skirts of her habit out of the unseen muck.

She closes her eyes, trying not to breathe. For a moment she thinks she will faint. There is no water to wash with and, of course, no toilet paper. *Well, what did you expect? This is the way the poor live. You thought your life was austere when you entered the convent and took a vow of poverty, but now you are beginning to see what real poverty is.* The jeering voices of Peter and the sergeant mingle in her mind. Reaching into the deep pocket of her habit, she finds her handkerchief. She tears it in half and carefully puts one part back in her pocket, thinking she might need it later. Using the other half to wipe herself, she then peers at the white cloth to see if her period has started. *Please, God, no, not that.* She throws the scrap of cloth into the dark hole beneath her. She hurries out, and in the garden breathes in the cold night air. The moon is rising over the tops of the few eucalyptus trees, coating everything with silver. She stops for a moment, lifting her face to the beauty of the night.

Hearing a truck backfire in the street, Kate panics and runs. She cannot miss the bus. When she sees that no one in the station has moved, she crosses the street and enters the only open store. The woman behind the counter is startled; Kate realizes she must look like a grimy, bedraggled ghost in the harsh light of the single bulb hanging from the ceiling.

"*Por favor, señora*, do you have a place where I might wash my hands? I have been traveling all day."

"Oh, *madrecita*, of course. You can come into my little room here in the back." The woman is kind, and leads Kate into a small room with three beds pushed together in one corner. In the gloom, Kate can see three or perhaps four pairs of eyes staring out at her from under the covers. "You should all be asleep by now," the woman whispers as she leads Kate to a small sink in the corner; she hands her a clean white towel, embroidered with tiny blue cornflowers. Kate examines this salute to beauty, and feels her eyes fill. She is dangerously close to hysteria. Pushing back her veil and headdress, she splashes cold water on her face. Her scalp itches under her veil, and she smells of sweat. She rolls up her sleeves to wash her arms, and gratefully scrubs her hands in the cool running water.

As she leaves the room she looks over at the children in the bed, their white teeth gleaming in the darkness. The woman at the counter glances at Kate as she emerges from the bedroom. Kate smiles at her. "*Mil gracias, señora*, that felt wonderful. Could I please have three bananas and an orange?" Looking around the shop, she feels in her pocket for the last four *soles*. "Also, I would like a wedge of cheese, two *pancitos*, and two bottles of Coca-Cola."

Above the racks of Coke is a faded poster of a smiling blond, blue-eyed American girl, dressed in a skirt and sweater and black-and-white saddle shoes, perched on the hood of a car with a Coke in her carefully manicured hand.

The woman follows Kate's eyes to the poster and begins to laugh softly. "She looks a little like you, *madre, no es cierto?*" She continues to laugh as she opens the bottle of Coca-Cola carefully; she wraps the rest of Kate's purchases in clean brown paper and ties the package tightly with string. "*Buen viaje, madre*, have a good trip." Kate feels her watching her as she crosses the street. She wonders if the the woman was laughing at her naivete.

Now it is dark. Kate stands under a swinging light bulb, waiting for the bus to the city.

Finally, the bus rolls into the station, already half full with passengers from Arequipa. As Kate climbs on, on she notices two young, fair-haired women in the second seat behind the driver snuggled fast asleep under their sleeping bags. She makes her way to the back to an empty double seat by the window.

The town slides away as the bus pulls into the winding mountain roads that will take them down to the coast. Kate gingerly holds the open Coke. Finally she takes a long swig; the sweet warm soda tastes of America and of a summer afternoon at Sportsman's Park. She devours the cheese and one of the rolls, then a banana, and sits back to savor each section of the orange. When she looks out the window she can see nothing except the reflection of her pale face. Although the motion of the bus seems to lull the rest of the passengers, Kate feels despair settle in like an unwelcome, talkative guest.

How has she gotten into this mess? She is an O'Neill from St. Louis, Missouri. This wraith-like creature with a smudged face and hollow eyes staring at her from the window is no one she recognizes. Hurtling through the night to an unplanned destination, she feels loneliness seep in like fog. No one knows where she is; no one around her knows her name, her history. It is hard to conjure up images of her mother, her father, in this blackness. Even Tom's face, so desired, has become a shadowy image, dimly seen in an old mirror. A terrifying chasm looms before her. What if she is truly alone? What if God is only a word the poor and frightened of the universe use to comfort themselves in moments of cold fear—a word repeated in vain, like the cry of a sobbing child who's lost and can't find her mother?

Doubt is a stranger to Kate, and she struggles against its pull. She tries to think about Tom, of these last few months when he has somehow become the center of her universe. But now in the darkness she sees. She has fallen into idolatry. She has made him the reason for her existence. Again her thoughts race back to the early days.

The euphoria of knowing she was loved had yielded quickly to anxiety. After those first letters admitting their love for each other, the next two weeks had dragged by. Kate found herself going to the dining room early before lunch, looking for a letter with Tom's thick scrawl on the envelope. She hated the way her stomach dropped each day when there was no letter for her on the buffet. One Sunday the three nuns sat talking together after lunch.

"I think what this group needs is a little excursion," said Sister Josepha, wiping her mouth neatly on the napkin while looking across the table at Jeanne Marie and Kate. The mood in the convent the past week had been somber. Sister Magdalena had left the community the week before. Moody and withdrawn for weeks, she had burst into tears one evening at supper and rushed away from the table. Later, in a tearful session, she blurted out how unhappy she was, how much she missed her family and friends. Kate watched as she shredded her delicate handkerchief in her hands, her eyes shining with relief at having at last said the truth.

Magdalena had looked at the three American nuns pleadingly. "The thing is, I feel so guilty abandoning you. These are my people, and yet I feel as if I am on the moon. I feel so strange up here."

Jeanne Marie interrupted, her voice calm, matter of fact. "Now there's nothing to feel guilty about. You gave this life a wonderful effort."

"When will you be going?" Kate asked.

Sister Josepha answered for her. "Father Jack is going down to Arequipa on Thursday. She'll go with him that far, and then her mother and father will meet her there and take her home." Kate knew that Josepha was crushed. It was her dream to build up a small Dominican community of Peruvian nuns. There were other Dominicans in Peru, but they were the old European orders, tucked away in their houses in Lima or Arequipa.

Magdalena, intelligent and lively, had seemed like the perfect first candidate for a new community of native Peruvian sisters. The daughter of a teacher, she had been at the University of San Marcos for two years studying philosophy. She was idealistic and passionate about her country. But Kate wondered if the nuns had done the right thing in bringing her up to the Altiplano so soon. She had been in the order for only two years; it might have been better to have left her in Lima. Learning to be a nun was hard enough in the best of circumstances. She thought of her own long years in the novitiate, yet here in the Altiplano she was still as confused and uncertain about her vocation as a homesick postulant.

After Compline that night, Kate had gone to Magdalena's room. She knocked softly and whispered through the closed door, "May I come in?"

Magdalena was in her nightgown, and Kate was startled at her shiny black hair. It reached almost to her shoulders. She saw Kate staring at it and laughed softly. "As you can see, I've been planning my exit for some time."

Kate grabbed her and hugged her. "I'll really miss you." They sat on the bed together whispering like two girls at a slumber party.

The young woman stared at Kate. "Catalina, how do you stand it? You are intelligent. You could be anything."

Kate met her gaze. "Pray for me, Magdalena. And be happy—God wants you to be yourself." She found she could say little more; after another embrace, she left the room quietly.

Magdalena had left at dawn with Father Jack on a windy, rainy morning in late January. The three nuns had stood aimlessly in the courtyard for a while after the jeep disappeared through the gates of Santa Catalina. Without a word they'd cleaned Magdalena's room and stored her freshly washed linens away, ready for the next time they had a guest.

So to Kate, Sister Josepha's suggestion they take a holiday came as a welcome relief. The superior had a definite plan in mind. "Next week is the Festival de la Virgen de la Candelaria in Copacabana. Sister Mary Katherine, you haven't seen a real Peruvian festival since you've been up here. I suggest we drive over to Puno, and then go on to Copacabana and rent a room in a little *pension* there for one night. I think we can afford it."

"Well, I hope so," laughed Jeanne Marie. "Last year it was only two dollars for a room with a communal bath."

Sister Josepha got up to clear the table. "Anyway, no one will be working or coming to school in Juliaca next week. They'll all be at the fiesta."

Kate was grateful for the promise of a diversion. It would take her mind off Tom, she hoped.

After breakfast on Thursday the nuns loaded their canvas bags into the jeep and waved goodbye to Marta and Tito in the courtyard. Alejandro had been fussing around the jeep for an hour, checking and re-checking the tires and the oil. He frowned as Jeanne Marie with a grin gunned the engine.

"*Con mucho cuidado,*" he warned. "The roads are dusty now. You have to sound your horn when you go around a curve."

Jeanne nodded and backed up, shifted gears, and pulled out of the courtyard.

"*Despacio!*" Alejandro's voice echoed in the silent early-morning streets. Kate and Jeanne laughed together.

"I bet you were a holy terror before you entered," said Kate, looking at Jeanne, eager and intent on her driving. She had the window open, and her veil flapped in the wind. Sister Josepha sat in back, knitting a small navy blue sweater for Tito. Kate called back to her superior over the roar of the engine. "Sister, I don't think I've ever seen you idle for two minutes."

Josepha put down her knitting with a rueful laugh. "The thing is," she said shaking her head, "I feel guilty when I'm not busy. That's my German background, I suppose." She took up her knitting again.

"Well, I'm glad I'm Irish then," shouted Kate. Her heart lifted as the jeep sped over the plains toward the Lake. The morning was fresh and clear, and the sun glinted on the mountains in the distance. As they passed through a strangely quiet Puno, Kate wondered if the townspeople were on the way to Copacabana, too. After a while she saw terraces on the hills, and then a huddle of huts around a central square.

"This is Chucuito, an old colonial town," Jeanne said. "Next we'll go through Juli."

Sister Josepha turned to Kate and shouted over the noise of the engine. "Did you know that the Jesuits came to Juli in the sixteenth century? They set up a training center for missionaries going to the remote regions of the Altiplano. They used the Inca's system of organization as their model. They were so influential that the Spaniards kicked them out in the late seventeenth century."

"Why?" Kate wished she had studied more Latin American history before coming here.

"Oh, I think they were worried by how effective the Jesuits were in organizing the *campesinos*, teaching them good methods of farming. The big landowners got nervous, I guess, and they put pressure on the government in Madrid to expel the Jesuits. Since then, very few priests have worked in these parts."

"When the Jesuits were expelled from South America, the people quickly reverted to their ancient faith," said Jeanne.

Kate was silent for a long time. She wondered if the people ever really accepted the beliefs of the missionaries. But then she remembered Christmas, and the reverence of the people as they came from far-away villages to celebrate the birth of el Niño Jesus. The old church had vibrated with faith that night—or was it longing? Maybe they were the same.

They stopped in Juli to eat the picnic lunch Marta had packed for them, and Josepha led Kate past the church of San

Pedro to a strange thatch-roofed building with ornately carved double doors. "That's the House of the Inquisition."

They stared at the building. Kate had studied the history of the Catholic Church. Much of it was ugly, like an open sore on the face of a beautiful woman.

Sister Josepha seemed to read her thoughts. "According to Father Tom, the Inquisition in Peru during colonial times tried cases of worldliness and corruption among the local clergy."

Kate wondered if those cases included priests who fell in love with nuns. At times she felt terrified at what was happening to her and Tom. As her mother would say, they were skating on thin ice. Then she would laugh at her fears, telling herself that nothing had happened yet. But something would, she knew. It was one thing to bravely declare her love and resolve in a letter. But Tom would be back, his eyes gleaming at her. She would have to work side by side with him, pretending a cool indifference to his every move. She forced herself to focus on Josepha's lecture.

"The indigenous people, by the way, were not considered suitable persons to be judged by the same standards as the Spanish Catholics."

"Lucky for them," muttered Jeanne Marie. They turned away then, repelled by the place.

By two o'clock they had reached Copacabana after following the great curve of Lake Titicaca, blue and remote in its purity. The roads were crowded with buses, old cars, and people on foot, all heading for the shrine of the Virgin on her feast day.

After the austerity of the plains, Kate was startled at her first view of the town. It was sunny and welcoming, its buildings of adobe and red tile an oasis of color. The streets were wide and well paved, and a holiday bustle hummed in the thin mountain air.

"This is one of the big feasts, the celebration of the Purification of the Virgin. Wait till you see her image in the Cathedral," Sister Jeanne Marie said.

Suddenly she slammed on the brakes and motioned to two young boys who were walking their bikes along the busy street. *"Por favor, muchachos. Nos pueden decir donde está la Residencia Patria?"* They waited while the boys conferred importantly in whispers. *"Sí, madrecita. Está por allá. Por la esquina."* The taller of the two waved his arm vaguely in the direction of the next corner on the left. The other boy nodded his head, and Jeanne thanked them.

Kate realized how happy she felt to be on the road, in a new place. The world of Juliaca was still strange to her after two months. She felt a constant strain as she tried to understand the new world she was in. Now for a few days she could play the part of the tourist. Best of all, there was nothing here to remind her of Tom.

They found the small *pension* on the Plaza 2 de Febrero. Everything in this town revolved around the great dark Virgin; even the streets were named for her feast day.

The three nuns entered a tiny vestibule and waited until their eyes became accustomed to the darkness. They finally made out a gray-haired woman, all in black, standing behind a desk, waiting for them in silence.

In her heavy Midwestern US accent, Sister Josepha negotiated in Spanish for a double room with access to a hot shower. The *señora* insisted that the only time there would be hot water would be between two and four in the afternoon. They were finally given the key to a room that turned out to be wide and clean, with four single beds lined up against one wall. The two windows looked out over the plaza. In the distance gleamed Lake Titicaca.

Kate stood at the window, watching a group of *campesinos* below struggling to put on the feather headdresses of their costumes. From above they looked like a flock of nervous birds as their feathers swayed and shone in the brightness of the afternoon sun. She could hear bands playing all over town. The music of a flute soared over the drums, and the chords of the charango increased the tempo. From further away came sounds of tubas and horns.

They joined the crowds in the streets and made their way to the plaza and the shrine of Copacabana. The wide cobble-stoned plaza was thronged with people in their feast-day best. No one paid much attention to the three American nuns in their long white habits. The Dominicans had come here in the 1600s, Josepha explained, so their habits fit in with the colonial atmosphere. They stopped in front of a Moorish-looking arch. Through the arch Kate could see three tall wooden crosses against the blue sky where huge clouds mushroomed in the distance. The white cathedral was outlined against the dark, distant peaks of the Andes. Jeanne Marie wanted to take a picture, and posed Josepha and Kate in front of the arch.

They passed through the arch, crossed the wide courtyard, and entered the cathedral. From brilliant sunshine they stepped into a vaulted dark space, chilled by stone never warmed by the sun. To the left of the altar, Kate noticed the towering pulpit carved in the ornate, heavy style so loved by the Spaniards. But who had carved this? It must have been the native people, taught by the craftsmen from the old world. What had they thought as they'd hewn out these cherubs surrounded by fruit and leaves? As she stared she saw a small carved serpent peeking from under a vine. His fixed smile made her shudder. The candle in the sanctuary lamp glowed through the silver filigree of its frame. Kate hurried to catch up with the other two nuns in front of the high altar.

Towering above the gold and jewels of the altar was the black Madonna, encased in glass. Remote and young, the image stared out over the heads of the pilgrims who came to honor the Mother of God. Everyone was on their knees now, except Kate. She stood stubbornly, gazing at the carved face above her. It's just an image, she thought. She watched the faces of the people around her. They wept, they murmured, they lifted their arms, pleading with the young Virgin to succor them. Their great trust moved her. She too sank to her knees and began to repeat the Litany of the Blessed Mother she had prayed only a few Mays ago as a teenager in the church at St. Roch's. "Mystical Rose, Star of the Sea, Tower of Ivory, House of Gold, Ark of the Covenant, Star of David, pray for us . . ."

When she looked up at last she saw Sister Josepha still on her knees beside her, her eyes shut tightly, her mouth whispering the Hail Mary as she clutched her worn rosary beads. Jeanne was not there. Kate rose and genuflected in front of the altar and maneuvered through the crowds streaming in to the back of the church, where she found Jeanne reading an inscription on a small stone. She looked up as Kate came near, and read aloud. "The statue of the Virgin de la Candelaria was carved in the late 1570s by the Inca artist Francisco Yupanqui, grandson of the Inca Tupac Yupanqui."

Again, this confusing mixture of Catholicism and the ancient religions of Peru. The town had been a shrine for the Inca before the arrival of the Spaniards. It had been built in honor of the sun god and his children Manco Capac and Mama Ocllo. In the sixteenth century, after the presentation to the town of the statue of the Virgin, miracles occurred. Soon the people were streaming in from the countryside to honor the Virgin. The cathedral had arisen from the faith of the pilgrims. All this devotion to a statue was foreign to Kate. It bordered on idolatry.

"Come on, Kate. Let's go see the dancing. This church is freezing," Jeanne whispered to her as she grabbed her elbow and moved Kate out the door and into the sunshine.

Kate was grateful for Jeanne Marie. Her mind was decidedly unmystical. Practical and brisk, she worked hard, yawned her way through early morning prayer, and shrugged at long discussions on the meaning of existence. She didn't struggle with her life; it seemed to Kate, she relished her work. She was outraged only by human stupidity and cruelty. The body was her field of expertise, yet through her touch she repaired spirits as well as the bodies of her patients. Kate wished she had studied nursing. At least then she could be sure she was doing some good.

As they waited in front of the cathedral for Sister Josepha to finish her rosary, Kate admired the modest courtyard to the side, a riot of red and purple and yellow flowers. She walked over and bent low to smell the poppies and chrysanthemums. There were wild flowers she had never seen, whose spiked blue and white shafts blended in a lush bed against the wall of the courtyard. Josepha joined them, and cried out at the sight of a garden that rivaled her own. Then she went to see if the small museum was open, hoping to find a caretaker who could give her some seeds. But the place was closed. Everyone had gone to the festival.

Now they were in the street, and the smell of roasting beef reminded Kate of supper. She eyed the *anticuchos* hungrily, watching the man deftly slip the bite-sized chunks of meat on straw skewers while stirring sizzling pieces in the iron skillet on his stand. Kate looked at Sister Josepha. "I'm famished!"


They bought six skewers, and Jeanne looked around for something to drink. There were *chicha* stands on every corner, and men were staggering through the streets after hours of celebrating. After finding a vendor selling sodas, they bought Cokes and sat together on a bench near the main plaza to eat. Kate ate greedily; the meat was spicy and hot. She licked her fingers behind her handkerchief, hoping no one noticed.

Later the three nuns followed the crowds to a small stadium on a hill about twenty minutes outside of the town where rickety wooden bleachers had been set up. The scene reminded Kate of a high-school football game. They watched as group after group of fantastically dressed devil dancers swayed before them. Each town for miles around had a brotherhood of dancers.

Jeanne told Kate how the men worked on their costumes all year, spending their meager funds on spangles and gold trim, which the women sewed into the fine cloth of gold and silk. Devils were everywhere with leering masks, prancing with giant phalluses swinging between their legs. Some dancers wore cartoon masks to portray the Spanish Conquerors beneath helmets of silver and gold. The women, in layers of petticoats called *polleras*, twisted and swung to the incessant beat of the drums and the high whine of the flutes. On their heads were huge feathered hats from which dangled streamers of curly silk ribbons.

A float bearing the Inca was pulled in by a dozen men in bright red costumes. Kate watched one woman, taller and more slender than the others, twirl her handkerchief high in the air, bowing and weaving among the men who surrounded her. As it grew dark, the temperature plunged rapidly, a cool breeze coming off the Lake. Torches were lit, for there was no electricity this far from the town. In the swirling dust the dancing figures took on a red, hazy hue, as if they were performing in a lake of fire. On and on the music played.

By now the dancers were drunk; Kate saw more than one person fall as he danced, and roll out of the way of the others. Sister Josepha stood up abruptly. "I think we've seen enough, Sisters."

Soon the nuns were working their way through the crowds milling around the stadium. A man turned to them as they passed, and Kate saw his penis in his hands. He bowed and greeted them, his urine plunging in a steady stream at their feet.

Later, in their room, Kate stood at the window in her nightgown. Both Josepha and Jeanne Marie were asleep, and someone was snoring softly. Kate gazed at the people in the plaza below. The music was muted, but in the distance she heard the blare of horns. A man and woman staggered together, their arms around each other. They stopped beneath a tree, and in the dim light of the plaza Kate watched their bodies meld into a long passionate kiss. She felt a stirring deep inside, a fierce ache of desire like a clutching hand within. She and Tom should be below in the street, tipsy and happy, on their way home from a dance. She wanted to press against him and feel the length and hardness of his body against hers. But that would never be if they obeyed the rules she had so naively set.

What had Tom thought of her letter? That she was a green girl, like Ophelia, "unsifted in such perilous circumstances"? Green she was at love, she thought as she lay down on the thin mattress and watched the moonlight through the gauze curtains. Outside the music throbbed in the long night of the festival of Copacabana.

# Chapter Fourteen

## Sunday, June 28, 1964

⌛

*T*he bus winds along the coast through fog, twisting like Kate's thoughts. She leans her head against the window, finally dozing in a fitful sleep punctuated by the *huayno* music coming from the driver's portable radio. When she awakes, the gray light of dawn gleams on the Pacific, its waves crashing against the long stretch of beach. Kate drinks in the lonely beauty. Through the dusty windows to her left she glimpses sand dunes, spectral white in the early light. The curves and billows of the dunes swim before her like ghostly whales amidst blowing sand spray from the desert ocean. For all is desert now, all the way up the coast, yet beyond, the ocean stretches to the horizon.

Kate swallows the rest of the Coke she has saved and munches on the last of her roll. Gazing out at the moon-like landscape, she mumbles the words of Lauds, the morning prayer: "Now in the sun's new dawning ray, lowly of heart our God we pray . . ."

By mid-morning, as the highway enters a green valley, the driver shouts: "*La proxima parada, Nazca! Una hora, no más!*"

Passengers begin to grumble. One man shouts, "It's that you have a girlfriend here in town, no?" The driver grins into the rear-view mirror. Soon the passengers are gathering their packages and heading for the nearest restaurant or *chichería*.

When Kate steps off the bus she is startled to see the two American girls—she has forgotten all about them. As she passes them, she smiles and says hello. They look up in surprise, and the short, blond girl holds out her hand.

"Hi, Sister. I'm Diane McKenzie, Peace Corps."

"Sister Mary Katherine. I'm with the Dominican Sisters in Juliaca."

Diane gestures to the other girl, who stands a little to one side, looking on with a stiff half-smile. "And this is my fellow Peace Corps worker, Sheila Ford. We're going to get a bite to eat. If you aren't meeting someone, why don't you join us?" Diane looks around the narrow platform in front of the bus station, which is now nearly empty of passengers.

Kate feels inordinately grateful for the breezy American friendliness of the girl. "Thanks. I'd love to join you."

The three women cross the street and enter the Plaza de Armas. The neat, compact town bustles with tourists. Kate has read about the Nazca Lines, a series of animal figures and geometric shapes drawn across the bleak, stony Pampa de San Jose. She had wanted to see them, but has been too busy to be a tourist.

Now Kate hears German and French all around her. With expensive cameras slung over their shoulders, many of the tourists are dressed in elegant khaki, and Kate smiles at the contrast the American girls present. Diane, short and chubby, is resplendent in a yellow flowered blouse and fuchsia pedal-pushers. Espadrilles laced halfway up her legs, she walks with short swaying steps. She lifts her face to the sun, and, although her eyes are hidden behind a large pair of sequined sunglasses, she radiates cheerfulness.

So far, Sheila has said nothing. Tall and slender, she wears faded jeans and tennis shoes, and carries a poncho made of llama wool. She has a beaded choker around her neck studded with dark blue stones. When she speaks to Kate for the first time, her voice is low, assured. "We're looking for a restaurant called La Canada, near the Hotel Montecarlo. The guys in La Paz told us about it."

Trailing behind the two girls into the small, dimly lit restaurant, Kate is hit by a blast of fast *música criolla*. A few male heads go up as the three women enter. Kate imagines their confusion at seeing a nun with two young *gringas*. Cigarette smoke hangs in the mid-morning air.

The waiter leads them to a table near a window, where Kate sits facing Diane and Sheila. The girls quickly order two beers, then glanced quizzically at Kate.

"*Una limonada*," she says softly to the waiter, thinking of her fast-dwindling *soles*.

As if reading her mind, Diane says briskly, "Hey, Sister, this meal's on us. We're in a good mood because after six months in La Paz we're on R & R. First for a few days at a little resort in Ica, then on to Lima for some fun in the sun—we hope. So let us pay for your lunch. They're supposed to have wonderful ceviche here."

Kate glances hungrily at a nearby table where several businessmen are tucking their napkins under their chins, staring at great plates of rice and shrimp. "Oh, you don't need to do that," begins Kate, but Diane just shakes her head.

Sheila is reading the large, hand-printed menu carefully. "Why don't we start out with Papas a la Huancaína and then have a big bowl of shrimp? It should be really fresh here." She sips her beer, glancing coolly around the busy restaurant.

Kate nods. "Where are you two from?" Suddenly she feels lighter sitting with these two girls, who are about the age of her sister Maggie.

"I grew up in Ann Arbor, Michigan," Diane said. "I went to Catholic schools all my life. I about died when I saw you get off the bus—you reminded me so much of my favorite teacher, Sister Marguerite!" She beams at Kate and finishes the beer, which leaves a white line of foam on her upper lip.

"What are you doing in La Paz?" Kate asks.

"I work with a group of priests and nuns up in Cristo Rey. They're all from St. Louis."

"Oh, I've been there. I'm from St. Louis, too," Kate says, feeling uneasy. Maybe they knew Father Tom.

Diane continues. "Well, anyway, I help the nun in the infirmary giving shots. I visit families in the parish, telling them about the programs we have there. And I also teach an evening course in English at the Instituto Cultural. That's where I met Sheila. The truth is, I don't really have any special skills—that's what I discovered when I came here. I wish now I were a nurse or a farmer." A note of self-doubt has crept into her voice, but she recovers and grins. "And, of course, I came down here hoping to meet some interesting guys."

Kate turns to Sheila. "And what about you?"

Just then their first course arrives. Kate bites into the warm potatoes covered with spicy dressing and sighs with pleasure. She realizes she hasn't had a really good meal in three days, since that first night in Peter's house. She eats too fast, barely savoring each bite.

After a few careful bites, Sheila puts down her fork to answer. "I'm from Boston. My mother's a professor at Harvard, and my father's a partner in a small law firm. Everyone expected me to apply to Harvard, but instead I went to Amherst, in the wilds of western Massachusetts." She picks up her beer, and holds it in front of her face, her eyes narrowing. "I can't say I loved it there. Most kids there were spoiled upper-middle-class kids just like me, but I did have some outstanding teachers. My favorite professor was a fiery woman from Peru. She opened my eyes to the reality of the class struggle in South America."

A small dog limps over to their table. After Kate slips the

mangy creature a crust of bread, it whines and slumps beneath her chair to wait for another bite. Sheila and Diane seem not to have noticed the beggar.

Sheila glances at Kate, then goes on. "I signed up for the Peace Corps the week before graduation, when all my friends were signing contracts for low-level jobs with big corporations. My parents think I'm wasting my time, although secretly I think it gives them a little cachet among their friends to have a daughter doing something so bizarre."

When Sheila flicks back her long, straight brown hair, Kate notices the delicacy of her hands. "So are you working with Diane?"

"Right now I'm teaching English at the Instituto with Diane. That's about all we liberal arts people are good for."

"But she's also keeping a journal," interrupts Diane. "She'll probably write the great Peace Corps novel someday. Okay Sister, it's your turn. We can't wait to hear about your life!" She wriggles eagerly in her chair, a wide grin showing perfect white teeth.

Kate wonders suddenly what her life would have been like if she had not been a nun. Would she have been like the two women before her? This is not a question she has ever let herself ask before, and she is stunned to think it has taken her so long to come to it. "Well, I grew up in St. Louis, went to Catholic schools, and entered the Dominican convent in Chesterfield the summer after my graduation from high school."

Diane stops eating, and gazes at Kate with her fork in mid-air. "Why?"

"Let her finish," Sheila says, lighting a cigarette.

"It's hard to explain. It's what I thought I was supposed to do. Anyway, I majored in English at the convent's junior college and then finished up my last two years at Fontbonne, a small liberal arts women's college in St. Louis. Then I taught for a year at one of the grade schools there."

The waiter removes the plates. Diane asks for another beer, and Kate nods when he asks if she'd like more lemonade. The heat and spicy food have made her thirsty. Sheila stubs out her cigarette and leans back in her chair. "How did you get down here?"

"When I was in the novitiate, they asked us if anyone was interested in being sent to the missions in Latin America or the Philippines. I raised my hand for Latin America. I never really thought about what I would do when I got here." As she says the words, Kate realizes how true they are. What did she think she would be doing down here—a twenty-four-year-old American who barely spoke Spanish and had never traveled before in her life? Kate looks up and finds Sheila staring at her intently. She goes on, "Well, they took me up on my offer. So, about a year ago I came down to Lima, then spent five months in Cochabamba at the Language Institute, and now I'm working in Santa Catalina in Juliaca, with our sisters and the Maryknoll priests."

"Where are you headed now?" Sheila's question hangs in the air.

The two girls smoke quietly, waiting for Kate to explain. Ah, that is the question, isn't it? Where would she head now? Kate raises her eyes. "I don't really know," she whispers finally.

Diane and Sheila look at each other.

"What do you mean?" Diane leans in, lowering her voice.

"I really don't know. I just sort of . . . left. I've been struggling with a problem," Kate says slowly, choosing her words carefully, "and I felt as though I needed to get away, take some time to think it out." Kate looks at them helplessly, aware of how foolish she sounds.

"Do the other nuns know where you are?" Sheila asks, watching her carefully. She seems much more interested in Kate now.

"Not really, although they have a vague idea of the general direction I'm traveling in."

The three women sit in the nearly empty restaurant in silence for a few moments.

Suddenly Diane bursts out: "Wow! A nun on the run! This is so neat! Wasn't there a movie years ago called *I Leap Over the Wall*, or something like that—about a nun who escaped?"

Sheila frowns at Diane. She looks at Kate, "Listen, we're going to stay in Ica for a few days. It's supposed to be lovely. Why don't you share a room with us for a day or two? We've already paid for it. Take a little rest, and then figure out where you're going next."

Feeling tears spring to her eyes, Kate tries to laugh them off. "Oh, just what you wanted on your vacation—a nun tagging along."

"Don't worry. We've both had it with men right now," Diane assures her. "All we want is some warm sand to lie in, a couple of trashy novels, and plenty of beer and wine. Come on, Sister, it'll be fun—sort of an advanced slumber party."

Sheila is inspecting Kate's habit, dusty and smeared from travel. Her eyes travel to the man's jacket Kate is holding, and Kate is sure that she's noticed that she has no luggage. "This would give you time to wash your clothes and freshen up a little," she says casually.

Kate blushes at the thought of how dirty she is. "Okay, I'll stay one night with you—really, I'm very grateful." She swallows hard, thinking of the ticket to Lima in her pocket. Maybe she'd be allowed to use it later. She is becoming more comfortable with not planning everything.

Both women appear immensely relieved, as if they have rescued a dangerous mental patient from the ledge of a skyscraper. Sheila pays the check, talking to the waiter in efficient, clear Spanish. As they leave the restaurant, Kate feels the eyes of the few remaining men on them.

In late afternoon, after a short ride, the bus pulls up at an elegant plaza. Ica. After months in the altitude, Kate is shocked by the hot sun, the dampness of a tropical place. The air is heavy with fragrance. Kate feels she's in a dream. Diane and Sheila hail a taxi, and negotiate with the driver with the air of experienced travelers. Kate wouldn't have known how to do this, she realizes, always having depended on Sister Josepha or Jeanne Marie when traveling.

Diane, sitting in front, turns around. "We're heading for Huacachina, an old resort where rich Peruvians used to come in the 1920s and '30s. It's somewhat shabby now, they tell us, but still a really nice place to relax and swim. There's a lagoon there, so we can do a little sunbathing, too."

Ten minutes later the driver turns into the gates of a long winding drive, lined with ancient dusty trees. Kate wonders if they are olive trees, for the place, so much farther south now near the coast, has a tropical look, an air of indolence and heat. At the end of the drive, a white, two-story villa shimmers in the afternoon glare. An old man, perspiring heavily in a shiny black jacket, opens the door of the cab. He gathers the girls' bags and takes the jacket Kate holds with a swift unobtrusive movement.

"We're in a fairy tale," Diane whispers in a stage voice. Kate follows, wondering whether it's a dream or a nightmare. She feels like a grimy refugee trailing real ladies. They enter a cool, dim foyer with a slowly whirring ceiling fan. The parquet floors are covered here and there with Peruvian rugs, their reds and blues a bit faded. The foyer empties into a long drawing room that overlooks an interior courtyard. Through the open French doors Kate hears the splashing of a fountain, broken now and then by laughter and the clink of glasses.

The woman at the front desk is dark-haired and handsome in the severe Spanish style, her hair pulled back in a smooth bun. Looking past the girls to Kate in her wrinkled habit, she frowns. "*Las señoritas* made reservations for two, isn't that correct?"

Diane steps forward to explain, but Sheila cut her off. "Yes, but now we are three. Will that be convenient?" She looks haughtily at the woman, whose eyes travel down Sheila's jeans to her dusty tennis shoes.

"I suppose that will be all right. Will you need another bed? I can have a cot brought upstairs for you."

"Yes, thank you." Sheila's voice has an edge of privilege, even in Spanish.

Kate notices a slight thaw in the *señora*'s manner. Sheila shows the woman her passport and then signs for all three of them in the large registration book.

"I am Mercedes Reyna, the manager of the Hotel Massone. If you need anything while you are here, I will be glad to be of service." The woman walks around the desk and pulls from her belt a brass key ring with dozens of keys. "You are in number seven." In a raised voice she calls to a boy sweeping the patio beyond the French doors. "Pepe, take the *señoritas'* bags up to the room."

Kate hears soft footsteps behind her, then turns to see a young man carrying the girls' bags. Kate notices with a jolt the clean sculpted lines of his face, the ruddy cheeks, the broad chest typical of men from the sierra. He looks so much like the children of Santa Catalina that she is momentarily confused. Less than twenty-four hours away is a world straight out of the fifteenth century. She's been living in that world nearly a year. It now seems more real to her than the nineteenth-century atmosphere of the Hotel Massone. This world is a fantasy.

She watches Pepe carry their few bags easily up the stairs, half running before them with a serious, purposeful air. He unlocks the door to their room and stands aside; as Kate passes by him she whispers, "*Yuspagara*, thank you," and presses one of her remaining *soles* into his hand.

He looks up at her with a grin. "*Yuspagara, madrecita*," he says as he shuts the door quickly behind him.

Diane is already at the window, pulling back the white cotton curtains. "Look! We can see the lagoon from here. It's gorgeous."

Kate joins her. Beyond the high stucco wall that surrounds the hotel, the lagoon stretches away, a vivid blue-green in the afternoon sun. Diane is already peeling off her blouse and untying her shoes. "I'm going in for a swim. How about you two?"

Sheila looks at Kate, and when their eyes meet, Kate knows she senses her awkwardness. It has been a long time since she has casually undressed in front of anyone. Startled, she remembers Peter, and how she'd undressed in his guest room and sat in his kitchen in his borrowed pajamas. What is happening to her?

Sheila comes to her rescue. "Sister—" she begins.

Kate interrupts. "Look, you might as well call me Kate. It seems a bit formal to keep saying 'Sister' to someone you're sharing a room with."

The girls nod, relieved, she can tell. Sheila continues, "Anyway, Kate, you must be dying to get out of those clothes. I have some extra things here you can probably wear. Go ahead and take a bath and get changed while we go for a swim. Take a nap. Remember, this is a vacation."

After the two leave, carrying towels, straw hats, and magazines, Kate runs water for a bath in the high, claw-footed tub. She unpins her black veil, dusty and creased, and then, with great relief, peels off the headdress she's worn for more than forty-eight hours. Her short hair is matted, sweaty; she runs her fingers through it, grateful for the freedom. Then she quickly steps out of her habit, her underwear, and throws all of it in a heap by the bed. She'll wash her clothes after her bath.

The water smells like copper, and she sinks into its warmth, leans back with her head against the edge of the tub. Suddenly she ducks her head under the water for as long as she can, and comes up with a gasp of pleasure. Then she scrubs her scalp with the lemon soap she found. Bending her knees, she lies back again, letting the soap stay on her hair for a while, and watches the water fall away from her breasts and thighs, still covering her belly. Her body is pale except for the pink nipples and the dark pubic hair.

What was this body for? She holds up her hands, examining them. Yes, she could work with these; she could bandage or paint or write. She could hold a child's hand in hers and help it cross a busy street. Hands were clearly useful. But what about the rest of her body? What were her breasts for? Were they to be forever unseen, unsucked? Would they never swell with milk and feel the fierce tug of a baby's insistent mouth, or the kiss of a lover? Her hands slide across her belly. Her womb—every month the unused rich blood drains out of her, wasted. For a long while she lies still, conscious of her slow breathing, the blood streaming in her veins, the even beat of her heart.

Suddenly she rises with a great splash; she turns the shower on at full force, delighting in the water streaming down her body. She dries off quickly, rubbing her body hard with the thin white towel. Wrapping it around her, she goes to the mirror. Her skin is glowing, alive. She slicks back her hair behind her ears and goes over to the bed where Sheila has left the clothes. She steps into skimpy bikini underpants, a type she's never before worn. As she puts on the lacy bra, she watches herself in the mirror. Not too bad. She's still slim, but her body has rounded, become more generous. She tugs on the shorts and T-shirt. Now she looks like any other pale American tourist, down for a Peruvian vacation.

Having filled the sink with hot, soapy water, she scrubs each piece of her habit, plunging her arms into the hot water up to her elbows and wringing out each piece vigorously. Then she washes the black veil and carefully pats it with a dry towel. She notices a small wooden towel rack in the bathroom and decides she would hang her clothes there to dry, not wanting her habit to be seen flapping in the breeze of the hotel's courtyard. She laughs—feeling light and free in her new costume. Once again she is playing a part, just as she had played dress-up in her grandmother's house. While slipping on the sandals Sheila left for her, she thinks: *I'll enjoy it as long as it lasts.*

When she joins the two girls on the modest beach near the lagoon, they clap and whistle.

"Now that's better," crows Diane. "We'll have to watch you like a hawk. There'll be guys all over you!"

Sheila regards her carefully. Kate suspects that this quiet, thoughtful girl senses the conflict in her, and she feels slightly irritated that she is so transparent. She lies down next to the girls and tries to relax, letting her body mold itself into the warm sand. Soon she dozes off, lulled by the lapping waves of the lagoon.

When Kate awakes the air has turned cool, and the two girls are packing up their things. Back in their room, Sheila loans Kate a long gauzy skirt to wear with the rose T-shirt she has on, and Diane slips a strand of wooden beads around her neck. Standing next to Kate, Diane gazes admiringly at Kate's reflection in the mirror.

The three women go down the polished staircase to dinner, which is served on a veranda overlooking the lagoon. As they walk across to a table with a good view, heads turn, and there is a lull in the conversations. Kate notices that most of the patrons seem to be Peruvians, but their understated elegance speaks of shopping trips to Miami and New York. The waiter who comes over to light the lamp on the table startles Kate, for it is Pepe, dressed in a crisp white shirt and shiny black pants. When he sees her looking intently at him, his eyes widen in recognition.

Sheila looks up at the young man. "I've heard that Ica is famous for its wines. Could you suggest a good one for us tonight?"

Kate admires Sheila's easy way with Spanish. Hers, she feels, is halting, awkward.

"*Rojo o blanco?*" he inquires.

"We'll start with a white wine, I think."

Kate looks at prices nervously. How many bottles are they planning to drink?

"Then I would suggest Tacama's Blanco de Blancos. It's from a winery very near here, about twenty minutes from town."

"Perfect," says Sheila.

Pepe bows and rushes off. Diane suggests that they begin with the Caldo Gallego, and follow it with the Ají de Gallina. Kate is ravenous; when the wine arrives she has to force herself to drink it slowly. It is dry and astringent, with a delicate woodsy taste. Sheila suggests they toast Pepe for his excellent choice. As the sun sinks into the lagoon, they find themselves laughing at everything. A bolero plays from somewhere inside the hotel, "*Bésame, bésame mucho.*" Kate thinks of Tom. Her lips tremble. She looks away from the girls, out to the lagoon. The moon is rising, casting long silver shards onto the water. Is he seeing this same moon tonight and thinking of her? She's been a coward—or worse, a baby.

After Pepe clears away the dishes and brings tiny cups of expresso, Diane puts her elbows on the table and leans toward Kate, staring into her eyes. Kate tries to focus her slightly unsteady gaze. "Sheila and I were discussing you this afternoon, and we feel you're holding out on us. Are you ever going to tell us the story of why you're running away?"

"Well, it's not very original, or even very interesting," Kate looks away.

Diane persists. "Our guess is that there's a man involved."

When Kate nods in an exaggeratedly forlorn way, they all laugh. Even Kate finds that thought hysterically funny tonight in this magical place, so far away from the mission at Santa Catalina. She is grateful when Pepe appears so they can change the subject.

"Did you enjoy the wine?" Pepe asks, smoothing crumbs from the tablecloth with a knife. When they cry out their enthusiasm he smiles slightly. "You ought to visit the winery if you have time. It is about thirty minutes from town in an old hacienda."

Kate hasn't even thought about the next day's activities. How is she going to steal away? She has complicated her flight by joining Diane and Sheila; yet she finds them kind and comforting. They bring back a world she had left years ago, a world of impulse and fun, a world with no commitments.

Pepe lingers at their table, and says, looking at Kate, "I will tell you a true story about this winery that many tourists do not know, nor even many Peruvians, I think. The winery is still irrigated today by a canal that was built by the great Inca Pachacutec. He built it as a gift to Princess Tate, with whom he was in love. According to the legend of my people, it took 40,000 men only ten days to build the canal. It brings cold pure water down from the mountains to make the desert of Ica bloom with grapevines. Pachacutec named the canal Achirana." He stood very still as his words echo in the evening air.

"What does Achirana mean?" Kate feels that Pepe wants her to ask him this.

"It means: 'That which flows cleanly toward that which is beautiful.'"

After he leaves, the girls sit in silence on the veranda. Kate feels the damp air on her bare arms, and the long forgotten sensation of the breeze ruffling her hair. It has been years since she had sat outside bareheaded. A little tipsy, she finds herself longing for Tom. Absently, she listens to Sheila and Diane plan their visit to the winery the next day. She says nothing about leaving. Kate knows she should push on to Lima, but now she wants to see the canal that Pepe had spoken of.

Later, stretched out on her cot under the window in one corner of the spacious bedroom, she falls asleep thinking of flowing water, cool and clean, as waves lap the sand of the lagoon under the chaste moon of Ica.

# Chapter Fifteen

## Monday, June 29, 1964

⁓

*W*aking to the sound of birds twittering outside the window, Kate remembers where she is. Early-morning bird chatter was one of the things she has missed most during her last six months in the Altiplano. Although it is still dark in the room, she can make out the outline of two sprawled bodies in the great *cama matrimonial*, as the *señora* called it. This has been her first good night's sleep since staying at Peter Grinnell's house three days ago.

In the bathroom she finds her habit still damp. She slips on the shirt and skirt she wore the night before and unlocks the door quietly. She'll go to Mass before the girls get up. Yesterday had been Sunday. She's shocked to realize she hasn't even thought of Mass.

No one is in the foyer below, but she hears sounds coming from the hall that leads to the kitchen. She knocks timidly on the swinging door, and pushes it open to see Señora Reyna seated at the long table, sipping her *café con leche*, reading a newspaper. Pepe is bending over the stove, lighting the gas; the smell of strong coffee fills the room.

"*Buenos días, señora,*" she says to woman. "Could you please tell me where the nearest church is with an early Mass?" Kate, dressed in the Peace Corps worker's clothes, waits for a look of surprise or disapproval to appear on the woman's face. Surely she recognizes Kate as the bedraggled nun of yesterday.

The *señora* looks at her for several long moments and then puts down her cup. In silence she rises and walks with Kate down the hall to the front doors. She pulls back the sliding locks and steps out onto the porch to show Kate the direction she should walk to find the church in the village.

Walking down the tree-shaded driveway, Kate breathes in the fragrant morning air, and watches the gray sky turn pink. She turns right at the gate and soon passes some concrete-block houses before entering the main street with its few store windows still shuttered fast. Then she sees the chapel, all white stone, squat and rounded like a massive loaf of bread. She steps over the wooden portal and blinks in the sudden dimness. The two candles on the altar are lit, the priest bent over, mumbling the Confiteor. Kate realizes that not a whisper of the recent changes to the liturgy had reached this remote church. She genuflects and joins the few elderly black-clad women who are the chapel's only worshipers. The priest, too, is old, his shoulders bowed beneath his cream-and-gold embroidered vestment.

She listens carefully to the priest recite the words of the Gospel:

> I baptize you with water for repentance, but he who
> is coming after me
> is mightier than I, whose sandals I am not worthy
> to carry; he will baptize
> you with the Holy Spirit and with fire. His shovel is
> ready in his hand,
> and he will winnow his threshing floor; the wheat
> he will gather into his granary,
> but he will burn the chaff on a fire that can never
> go out.

Water and fire. Both are dangerous. But fire can purify and refine. It can burn away the dross. And water can drown you, or quench your thirst. *Like love*, she thinks. She'd never known its fierceness before now. There was a passage in the scriptures about love, something about how "many waters could not quench love." What was it from? And how could one tell the wheat from the chaff in love? She sinks to her knees, burying her face in her hands.

When she raises her head Mass is over, and she did not go up to receive communion. The parishioners are leaving the chapel. No one glances her way. Kate enjoys the anonymity. Dressed as she is, she does not represent anything other than herself. She has ceased to be a symbol.

She watches as the elderly priest enters the ancient confessional in the shadows of the shrine to the Virgin Mary. No one enters. Footsteps echo as the last old woman shuffles out of the church into the early morning. She'll go to confession, Kate decides. But what will she say? *I love a priest? I'm burning up with desire? I'm sorry for my sins?*

And what about the firm purpose of amendment she is supposed to make? She stumbles over the pew and hurries to the small black door. Inside it is pitch dark, and the smell of incense mingles with the scent of an old man, musty yet sweet. The priest coughs as he slides back the wooden door, leaving only a thin black linen screen between them. He waits, the outline of his face barely visible in the gloom.

"Bless me, Father, for I have sinned," she murmurs. "It has been two weeks since my last confession." Her Spanish is halting, childish. She says nothing.

"Go on, *mujer*. Don't be afraid. God knows all our thoughts and actions."

"Father, I don't know what to say. I'm in love, I love someone I am not supposed to love."

He sighs. "Are you married, my dear?"

"Yes, no . . . I'm a nun."

"Ah, I see. And is the man married?"

He waits. By now Kate is trembling, her voice breaks. "He's a priest," she manages.

Silence. Somehow a coldness has entered the tiny space. "Well, have you done anything?" the voice rasps.

"No. But I want to," she blurts. Now the words come rushing out on her pent up breath. "Father, tell me what to do. I've taken a vow of chastity. Does that mean I can never love a man? How can love ever be wrong?"

"My child, God is love, as the evangelist tells us. But the question is what is this you feel for this man? Can it be love to want to lure him from his promise of celibacy? And what about your vow? You know in your heart what you must do. Renounce. It is the only way to peace. You will look back in the years to come and know that your love for God has been tested by fire and has come through brighter and purer than ever. Now go, and pray the rosary for strength to do what you know is right." Swiftly, the old priest raises his arm and she hears the familiar words: "I absolve you from your sins, in the name of the Father, the Son, and the Holy Spirit." The wooden panel closes with a firm click.

Kate stumbles out into the dim light of the church. He had forgotten to have her say the act of contrition. Could she have said it? "Oh my God, I am heartily sorry for having offended Thee." But was she sorry? She prays the rosary, counting the decades on her fingers. It's Monday, the joyful mysteries: the annunciation, the visitation, the birth of our Lord. Her head sinks down on the smooth wooden pew, she rests her bottom on the seat. Finally, she lifts her head to stare at the tabernacle, the sanctuary light gleams cheerfully in the dark church. *Where are You?* No answer.

As she walks back through the town, she smells baking bread. Children in white smocks dawdle on their way to school, gazing into shop windows. Most of the girls have their hair tightly braided, with shiny black braids hanging down their backs in a single coil. The boys' hair is slicked down, wet and shiny in the early morning. The children's high voices ring out in the quiet streets.

When Kate reaches the hotel, she hears the clatter of dishes from the dining room, where she finds her two companions cradling cups of coffee as they wait in silence to be served breakfast.

Sheila looks up and smiles at Kate. With a tilt of her head towards Diane, Sheila says, "This one has one big headache this morning. How're you feeling?"

"I feel wonderful," Kate says, hoping there is no trace of her tears on her face. "That's the best night's sleep I've had in three days. I'm ready to explore the winery and canal Pepe told us about last night. Are you?"

Diane looks up with a groan, and lights a cigarette. "I don't know," she says sleepily. "I was hoping to crash on the beach again."

Sheila laughs and pulls her arm. "Come on, girl. I've seen you dance for hours after drinking gallons of *chicha* at the village festival. Surely you can manage a little sightseeing today."

"Okay, okay. But you guys make all the arrangements. I'm going to sit in the sun on the veranda for a while.

Diane is dressed in plaid madras shorts and a sleeveless blouse, and she sashays confidently across the room.

By nine o'clock the women are crossing the foyer on their way to tour the winery when Kate hears a querulous voice behind her.

"Otto, I'm not sure I'm up to another day of tromping around in the heat. Wouldn't you rather stay here by the lagoon and read your book?"

The speaker is a dainty, gray-haired woman in her late-sixties, Kate guesses, in a flowered summer dress. A straw hat shades her face. She is looking up at the florid blond man Kate had taken for German or Danish the night before.

"Oh come on, Mother," he says. "We haven't come all this way to sit around swimming pools. We can do that back in California." By this time the couple are aware that their scene is being played out in front of English-speaking women near the front desk. The man walks toward them, holding out his hand. "Good morning, girls," he booms. "I'm Otto Schneider from Fullerton, California, and this is my lovely wife Lucille." He shakes their hands vigorously while Kate notices the way Mrs. Schneider's smile flits across her face and reveals the girl she once was. She seems embarrassed by, yet proud of, her bear-like husband. When the Schneiders hear that the women are planning to visit the Tacoma winery their faces fall.

"Oh what a shame! We're going into Ica this morning to see the textiles in the museum." Mrs. Schneider leans over confidentially to the three women. "I don't think Otto is up to walking around in the sun at midday, especially if he starts sampling all the wine."

Mr. Schneider suggests they all meet later in the day over cocktails and compare notes. Kate is relieved. She's feeling uncomfortable posing as a Peace Corps worker and is reluctant to admit she is a nun. How can she explain being here at a resort with two freewheeling companions?

As their taxi pulls up in front of the hotel, Kate watches the couple from the front porch. The tall, stooped man takes his wife's arm as they go down the steps of the veranda. Kate imagines them on their wedding day some forty years before, he engulfing her in his embrace and she small and shy in his arms. What blows have the years delivered, she wonders, and how have they managed to hang on to each other through them all? Kate thinks of her parents, whose marriage was hardly perfect. They'd had more than a few quarrels, usually over money or the children.

One of Kate's earliest memories is of the night her mother had wept on the phone because her father was late. She and her brother and sister were all dressed up, waiting for their father to come home and take them to Grandma Sullivan's house for dinner. Finally her mother gave up and put them all to bed. Much later Kate awakened to the voices of her parents, an angry, indistinct buzz coming from the lighted kitchen. She padded to the door, and stood watching as her father, his face flushed and happy, kept trying to grab her mother. "It's done now. I've enlisted. I couldn't stand it any longer." Her mother was crying, pushing him away.

Kate found out later that it was the night her father had joined the Marine Corps. He had been gone for four years, and she was six when he came back. She thought she remembered the day he came home, but it could be that she heard the story so often that the memory had been created by the telling. She was alone in the living room on a Sunday afternoon. Her mother was out shopping, and her grandmother was taking a nap. Where was Dan? Kate had her Betty Grable paper dolls spread out on the rose carpet when the doorbell rang. She ran to the door and peeked between the curtains covering the panes of glass. A tall, dark-haired man in a dark-green uniform stood waiting, ominous amid the red begonias in clay pots and the green-and-white cushions of the porch swing. He had a mustache.

Kate backed up slowly and sat still on the sofa. The man rang again, insistently. She edged over to the door and peered through the muslin curtain. Startled, the man stooped down to her level, took off his hat, and yelled: "Katie, open the door. It's me—Daddy."

She opened the door and was swept up in his arms as he whirled her round and round the living room. Her face was crushed against his chest, his ribbons cutting into her cheek. He smelled of pipe smoke. By the time her mother came home she was perched on a big easy chair telling her father, who sat on the floor in front of her, about the trials of kindergarten. His eyes never left her face. Then her mother walked in. They stared at each other in silence. Then they were kissing, and Kate wondered why her mother was crying.

Kate saw now that her parents had gradually melded until they merged into something new. They came through all the arguments, the struggles with money, and were transformed into a faithful, tested, heart-scalded couple. Love grew like vines between them. They could not be separated without destroying each other.

Was that the kind of love she felt for Tom? She realizes that she's never loved anyone like that. As a nun, she was supposed to love everyone. But she never got up in the middle of the night in response to a child's terrified cry nor sat with a discouraged husband to reassure him that she was perfectly satisfied with his salary. She had only herself to worry about. Will she become a selfish, crabby old nun, whining because her toast was soggy, the room too hot? What could be worse than giving up marriage and children to be free to serve many, only to find herself at life's end a shriveled, self-centered old woman who loved no one except herself?

Otto Schneider interrupts Kate's thoughts, shouting at her from the road. "Here comes your bus! Hurry up or you'll miss it."

Kate runs to catch up with Sheila and Diane as a faded orange bus pulls up at the gates to the hotel. The three of them run down the lane, waving to the bus driver. They climb on, laughing and out of breath, to the obvious amusement of the few housewives and workers inside the bus.

Crowding into the long seat at the back of the bus, Sheila sits down with an exaggerated sigh. "Whew! That was a close call. I really wasn't looking forward to spending the day with Otto Schneider. I have a feeling that we'd be lectured on the merits of the good old USA at every turn."

"Oh, they aren't so bad," says Diane. "They kind of remind me of some of my aunts and uncles back home." She looks slyly at Kate. "I wonder how they'd react if they knew that Kate here was really an escaped nun."

"They'd be horrified, I'm sure." Kate smiles at the two women, glad that she didn't have to face the Schneiders' reaction—at least not yet. She is getting dangerously comfortable with living in the moment. Holding up a mesh bag, Kate says, "You'll be happy to know, though, that without this escaped nun's careful planning skills, you two would be starving this afternoon. Pepe told me this morning that people often take a picnic lunch when they tour the winery, so they have something to eat to absorb all the samples they try. He had the cook give us some cheese and fruit and a couple of loaves of bread for our picnic."

"You seem to have made a conquest of Pepe." Sheila peers closely at Kate.

"He reminds me of the kids in Juliaca. He's so quiet and smart."

The women fall silent and watch the desert landscape as the bus churns up clouds of dust in its wake. Twenty minutes later the bus stops in front of a yellow stone arch with "Bodega Tacama" in stucco letters across the front. As the bus door slaps open, the three women are the only passengers to get out. They start down a long eucalyptus-lined drive; Kate breathes in the tangy scent with a pang of memory. She remembers the trip with Sister Jeanne and Tom into Coroico, where the smell of eucalyptus was everywhere. Smelling it now brings back those few hours she spent riding so close to Tom, watching his hands grip the wheel, his sharp profile alert to the dangerous drivers in the city. The thought of him is a knife, clean and small as a scalpel, and for a moment she can't breathe. How far away he seems. Does he hate her now, or worse yet, pity her? She has surely become an embarrassment to him by this time, for Sister Josepha would probably have spoken to him, remembering what Kate had told her in confidence. Well, so what? He loves her; he said it over and over. He laughed at her qualms. Now he will see how serious is her love. He underestimated its force.

As they round a curve in the driveway, Kate sees a green oasis amidst the desert. Off to the left is a yellow stone house, shaded by sycamore trees. On the veranda, geraniums and roses sprout from clay pots, and a wicker shade is half lowered against the late morning sun. Kate sees several empty chairs and a wicker table in one corner, under which three gray cats doze in the shade.

Trucks enter and leave a courtyard ringed by low stone buildings. All around the compound grape vines stretch green and lush in the hot air of the morning. It is not yet harvest; workers are spraying the vines and walking among them to check for insects, Kate imagines. Sheila points to a sign over the nearest building and motions to the others to follow her to the office.

It is cool in the dim office where, from behind a counter, a dark-eyed young woman comes to meet them. "*Buenos días, señoritas.* I am Ana María Castillo, the niece of the owner of the bodega. If you like, I can give you a tour of the winery starting in about ten minutes. We may have a few more visitors, so I'd like to wait, if you don't mind." Her perfect white teeth flash in the dim shadows of the office.

Diane mumbles something about being Peace Corps workers, and Kate sticks out her hand before being introduced. "I'm Kate O'Neill from St. Louis, Missouri."

It feels strange to use her old name, but she likes the sound of it.

By eleven o'clock no one else has arrived, so Ana begins the tour by leading the women across the courtyard and into the first of the low stone buildings. For the next hour and a half they walk through cool labyrinths, oak casks lying in the gloom. In precise English, Ana explains the process of making wine, the great difficulties with the vagaries of the climate, and the even greater difficulty of finding a market outside Ica for their product. "Year after year," she says, "my uncle plods on, hoping for the miracle that will make the wine of Ica famous in the big world beyond."

"Pepe, the waiter at our hotel, recommended your wine." Kate smiles hopefully.

"It is a very good wine," she says, looking at her watch. "I must leave you in the garden in back to do some wine tasting, as I have a luncheon engagement. It has been so good to meet you." Briskly she leads them to a patio on a slight hill with a shaded picnic tables and benches. She produces three bottles, one a deep red wine, the others white. "You can start with these." She smiles. "If you'd like to try any more, just ask the man in that office there."

She rushes off, and in a few minutes Kate hears the sounds of a car starting and tires spinning in the gravel.

"Luncheon engagement, my foot," laughs Diane. "She's going to meet some dreamy Latin lover. Hey, guys, isn't it time to imbibe?" Diane eyes the bottles of wine.

From the edge of the brick patio, Kate gazes at the surrounding fields. "There's one more thing I'd love to see before lunch. Remember the story Pepe told us the other night about the canal that Pachacutec built for his princess?"

Sheila stands beside Kate. They both look out at the sloping fields.

Sheila says, "'Achirana,' he called it. 'That which flows cleanly toward that which is beautiful.' Is that the canal over there?" She points toward a row of small trees that line the field as far as they can see.

The two women start walking toward the trees. Behind them Diane is settled at a picnic table, pouring out three glasses of wine, one from each bottle. She waves and shouts, "I'm staying here to do some research. You two go on and see the sights."

There isn't much to see, Kate realizes. The canal of Pachacutec is merely a quiet tree-lined stream that irrigates the fields.

The sun is directly overhead now, the air hot and still. Cicadas sing, as they do on sunny summer afternoons in St. Louis. Kate turns to Sheila. "Do you ever get homesick?"

"Not much, really. I think my mother is a bit offended by that. How about you?"

"Sometimes. I've been here almost a year now, but life in Peru still feels as if I'm in a play or something. I need to learn more. I wish like you, I had studied Latin American history and culture."

"But doesn't it help living with the other nuns? I mean, don't you feel at home with them?" Before Kate can answer, Sheila goes on. "You know, I've never known a nun before. I'd never even talked to one before I met you."

Kate smiles. "So what do you think?"

"I think something's wrong. I don't think you're happy."

Funny. For many years, during most of the time she had spent in the convent, everyone told her how happy she seemed. "Honey, you look so happy," her mother would say on visiting day, squeezing her tightly. Later, her sixth graders at Holy Angels called her Sister Smiley and confided their secrets to her. Even in language school, in Cochabamba, she overheard one of her teachers, a small Chilean man, describe her to another teacher as "the tall, smiling nun." But one could smile and smile and be a villain, she thinks. Or be unhappy.

"Sorry. I didn't mean to pry," Sheila says. "It was just an observation."

Kate has trouble speaking. Tears well up, and she shakes her head and keeps walking, her eyes down on the dry grass of the field.

Suddenly Sheila stops and begins peeling off her shirt. "I'm going skinny-dipping, Kate. You want to come?"

"Here?" Kate looks around. The fields are empty now, the workers gone to lunch. But they are still not far from the house, and the trees along the canal provide only a lacy curtain. Kate shakes her head no. "You go on. I'll be your bodyguard."

She turns away as Sheila strips quickly and slips into the clear water of the canal. When Kate turns around she can see Sheila's long white body flashing in the sunlit stream.

A sleek head bursts from the water. "It's freezing," Sheila calls out.

Kate sits on the bank, dangling bare legs in the water. Why doesn't she go in? She would have as a kid, she knows. Well, maybe not skinny-dipping. She was always shy about her body. Kate looks around. No one is in sight. She stands up and slips out of her skirt and T-shirt, unhooks her bra, and in one quick movement steps out of her underpants.

She leans over the bank, trying to gauge the depth of the water. Sheila has swum off, her dark head barely visible in the distance. Like a child, Kate holds her nose and jumps in feet first. The water is icy, and Kate gasps and dives beneath the clear, still surface, swimming with powerful strokes. She is conscious of water entering her everywhere—her nose, ears, eyes, even between her legs as she spreads them in frog-like strokes. She surfaces after a minute, gasping for breath, and rolls over on her back. Closing her eyes against the sun's rays, she lets the water cradle her, kicking lightly occasionally to stay afloat. She's never swum naked in the full light of day. She dives down again; this time her nipples become erect as desire washes through her. If only Tom were here. She sees him swimming toward her, his body covered with dark hair. Now he is beside her. He wraps his legs around her waist and draws her to him. She opens her legs to let him enter her. They sink together, an odd sea creature with four arms and legs entangled. A cry of pleasure rises in her throat.

She surfaces and swims with fast, hard strokes, on and on, until she fights to breathe. Then she rolls over and gazes at the trees along the banks. The sun filters through the branches, warming her face. Her body is weightless, one with the water and sun. She lets herself drift back to the bank where Sheila now sits, drying her long hair. Kate waves.

"You look like a dolphin out there," Sheila calls.

"It feels wonderful. I never want to get out." Kate drifts next to the bank, dog paddling gently.

"I wonder if the princess swam here," says Sheila. As Kate emerges from the canal, Sheila turns away tactfully, reaching behind her for the cigarettes in her shirt pocket. Kate grabs her skirt and wraps it around her like a sarong. Sitting next to Sheila, she glances swiftly at the slender body stretched out on the grass. She tries not to stare at the scar low on Sheila's belly where her dark pubic hair begins.

Sheila smokes for a while as Kate lies next to her, her arms cushioning her head. When Sheila gets up to pull on her underpants, Kate can't help glancing at the scar.

"Oh yeah, I forgot about that," says Sheila. "A little souvenir from a botched abortion."

Kate can feel Sheila watching for her reaction. She tries to keep her face expressionless.

After several moments of silence, Sheila asks, "Are you shocked?"

"A little," Kate admits.

Sheila gives a short laugh. "Well, things have changed a lot lately, as Dylan says."

"Dylan?"

"Bob Dylan, a folk singer. Jesus Christ, Kate. Have you been on the moon all these years?"

"I guess so." Kate waits for Sheila to go on.

"I'm twenty-three, Kate, and I've had three lovers. One was serious, and the other two were . . . more like diversions."

"You don't have to explain anything to me."

"Oh, but I want to. Somebody has to get you into the twentieth century. Anyway, I got pregnant by one of the diversions. Went to a doctor in Chelsea who did abortions for a hefty fee. My parents knew nothing about this, so I went to my boyfriend's father and asked him for the money."

Kate notices the bitter set of Sheila's mouth.

Sheila continues, "Anyway, the guy wrote out the check there and then and I never saw his son again. The doctor made a mistake—had to go back in and clean it up. Thus the scar."

"I'm sorry." It is all Kate can think to say.

"So am I, believe me." By this time Sheila is dressed and raking her fingers through her long tangled hair. Her face brightens. "Say, does this count for confession?"

"I'm no priest, Sheila, but I'm glad you told me the story." She wishes she could tell Sheila her story. It lies inside her like a stone.

They walk back along the canal and catch Diane sleeping, stretched out on her back on a bench next to a picnic table. Flies buzz around the empty wineglasses on the table. Diane sits up. "Where were you guys? I thought I'd have to finish all this wine by myself."

"We went to Achirana. We went to see that which flows cleanly to that which is beautiful," says Kate, relieved that the somber mood has lifted.

"Well, what flows cleanly is this wine—so help yourselves, girls, and let's eat." While Diane begins unpacking the picnic bag, Kate grabs some cheese and bites into it, suddenly ravenous.

The afternoon stretches on, hot and shimmering. Kate lies back on the grass, feels the wine melting her arms and legs, and is soon asleep.

# Chapter Sixteen

~

*L*ater that same night, lying sleepless on a cot in the corner of the hotel room, Kate stares at a patch of moonlight across the foot of her bed. She hears the deep breathing of the two women. She kicks the sheet away from her body, plumps her pillow and stares, wide-eyed, into the darkness. She has lingered long enough in this playground. Her money is running out, and she has just enough to get a bus to Lima. Then what? She has been gone from Santa Catalina for—is it four or five days now? She's losing track of time. And worse, she is no closer to figuring out her problem than before. Would it have helped if she could have poured out her story to Sheila? There is a quiet intelligence in the young woman that Kate trusts. But she would probably think the whole struggle was silly.

She has found it impossible to love Tom and not desire him. In the moonlit room, she feels again the waters of Achirana swirling around her body, Tom caressing her. What had Christ said? If one part of the body offends God, cut it off. What could she cut off? Her body loves him.

Loving someone like this was new to her. She had been shy, tentative with Tom. She thinks back to those weeks after the exchange of their letters. She'd waited for Tom to return to

Juliaca from Lima, not knowing whether it was dread or longing that gnawed at her stomach.

After the trip to Copacabana in February, the rains came. Still she waited for Tom's answer to her letter. Kate knew this was really summer in South America, but it felt more like late autumn at home. She couldn't get used to the idea that the seasons were exactly opposite in the southern hemisphere. In the Altiplano, distinct seasons didn't exist. The cold was relentless year round. The only difference was between the sunny days with their brilliant light and the gloomy days when the storms rushed down from the mountains and swirled into the town with drenching wind and rain. Every morning she pulled on her long cotton underwear, grateful for its warmth next to her skin. Her room was not heated, and by the time she went down to stand in front of the gas heater in the living room, her hands were blue. Josepha and Jeanne Marie laughed at her as she stood huddled by the heater, for they had become accustomed to cold, or as Josepha put it, their hardy peasant stock made them more able to bear it.

Kate thought of her father who always claimed they were descendants of the kings and queens of Ireland. Could their castles have been as cold as this? As she put on her woolen cloak, wrapped a heavy black shawl around her head, and pulled on the rubber galoshes to protect her shoes, she thought she must look more like an Irish peasant woman than a queen. Then she followed the two sisters to church for morning prayer, meditation, and Mass.

Kate's prayers were fervent, even fevered, these days. She prayed for strength to live her vocation, asking God to guide her through the new land she was in, a land with no maps and no stars. Another hemisphere, for sure. She prayed for Tom whose face floated before her, always slightly out of focus. It was better, she knew, that he was away. It was easier to love him from afar.

With the rains, she had fewer students each day in school. But she enjoyed the smaller groups, in which the children formed a circle on the floor around her while she sat in one of the little chairs. She read to them, and they told her stories of the old ways of their people. They loved music, and she had them sing songs in Aymara, trying to pronounce the strange words with them, making them laugh. They taught her to say, "*Chaskiñawa*," pointing at her and laughing. It meant the one with stars in her eyes.

When she spoke to them about Jesus they were very quiet, their eyes shining. She discovered that Jesus' parables made sense to these children of farmers and shepherds.

One day she read to them in slow, clear Spanish with Elva translating softly into Aymara:

> If one of you has a hundred sheep and one of them has gone astray, does he not leave the ninety-nine in the open pasture and go after the missing one until he has found it? How delighted he is then! He lifts it on his shoulders and home he goes to call his friends and neighbors together. "Rejoice with me!" he cries. "I have found my lost sheep." In the same way, I tell you, there is greater joy in heaven over one sinner who repents than over ninety-nine righteous people who do not need to repent.

She'd waited for a long moment, looking at the faces gathered around her, solemn and unblinking.

"What do you think Jesus meant when he told his friends this story?" she asked. There was a stillness in the room.

Finally one tall boy who always sat in the back of the room spoke up. "If the man had a hundred sheep, he must be a very rich man."

Kate nodded her head.

"So, why doesn't he send his helper after the sheep instead of going himself?"

Kate was stumped. She had never taken the passage literally. But these children had been herding sheep with their parents since they could walk.

Kate was saved by Pilar in the front row who raised her hand, "I think Jesus means that we are all like sheep. And sometimes we go away from him and then he has to come and rescue us." The child stopped, overwhelmed by what she said, then added softly, "The shepherd loves the little stray one more because he caused him all that worry."

She looked up at Kate, unable to speak for a moment at the child's grasp of the parable. Now hands went up all over as each child thought of a story he knew about tending the sheep. Suddenly Kate remembered the boy by the roadside who had lost some of his father's sheep, his tear-stained face, his despair. She told the children that story, and they all murmured sympathetically at the boy's trouble.

Kate ended class that day by reciting Blake's poem "The Lamb" to them in English just wanting them to hear the sounds of the rhyme. Elva then wrote a translation of the poem on the board in Spanish. As the children bent over their notebooks, copying the poem in Spanish, Kate walked around the room, murmuring the words in English like a prayer.

> Little Lamb, who made thee?
> Dost thou know who made thee?
> Gave thee life & bid thee feed,
> By the stream & o'er the mead;
> Gave thee clothing of delight,
> Softest clothing, woolly bright;
> Gave thee such a tender voice,
> Making all the vales rejoice!
> Little lamb, who made thee?
> Dost thou know who made thee?

On her way to the convent for lunch that day, Kate dodged the puddles. The rain had stopped, and the clouds scuttled across the sky, leaving big patches of blue. Maybe she would write to Sister Antonia, her first great literature teacher, and tell her she'd discussed a poem by William Blake with the children of Juliaca, Peru.

She entered the house by the back door and threw a little ball she kept in her pocket to Tito. Marta turned from the stove and greeted her, and, almost as an afterthought said, "Padre Tomás is back. He's waiting in the front parlor to see you for a few minutes before lunch, he said. I told him lunch was at twelve *en punto*."

Kate was careful to keep her voice as even as she could, sensing a faint air of disapproval in the set of Marta's shoulders. "*Gracias*, Marta. I won't be late."

Her heart thudded as she walked to the parlor. She stopped at the interior door and pinched her cheeks. Smoothing her habit, she noticed that her hands were trembling. Then she opened the door, and Tom Lynch filled the room as he rose from the chair and in two strides stood before her. After a long moment he held out his hands, and she gripped them as a drowning woman grabs a lifeline. Still they said nothing. He was tanned and fit, bursting with restless energy.

"You look rested," she stared up at him, trying to match this face to the one in her dreams.

"Oh, that I am. I suddenly feel wonderful."

His grin was mocking. She blushed and looked around helplessly. "Well, sit down. Tell me about Lima," she said, taking the nearest chair.

He pulled his chair up near hers, and sat facing her, their knees not quite touching. "Lima was gray and misty and depressing, as usual. But I ate wonderful food, went out drinking with the lads at the Maryknoll House and lay in the sun in Chosica. Now cut the small talk, Kate, and tell me how the hell you are."

"I've missed you."

"That's better."

"Other than that I've been fine." She looked away now from the naked longing she saw in his eyes. Embarrassed, she rattled on about the trip to Copacabana, her class that morning, anything to fill up the silence. He was looking at her with amusement and a certain impatience. Finally, she paused. "Tom, it feels so strange to be with you. I don't know how to act."

"I love hearing you say my name."

"I say it all the time to myself."

They stared at each other. Then he got up from his chair and paced the tiny room, and she could only watch him stride back and forth.

"Kate, things are changing in Lima. The slums around the airport have grown. I couldn't believe the numbers. The people at first were only trickling down from the sierra. Now there's a torrent flooding Lima. Do you remember seeing the *barriada* called San Martín de Porres when you drove by the airport?"

"Yes, the sisters pointed it out to me but I was so scared by the traffic that I didn't pay much attention."

"I went out there with one of the men who works there, Jack Casey. It's a disaster. We've got to stop this exodus to the city by making things better for the farmers up here. They have no work in Lima." Tom stood at the one window in the room and looked out at the courtyard of Santa Catalina where the children were playing, their shouts ringing out in the thin air. He lowered his voice and turned to her. "While I was in Lima I went to the Ministerio de Agricultura. I tried to find out all I could about the new land reform bill. No one seems to know exactly what it will mean or how it will be implemented."

She was confused now. Why was he telling her all this? She had a hard time concentrating on his words, as she watched him move around the room, bursting with impatience.

He continued to speak, almost as if he were talking to himself. "Tomorrow I'll be going out in the *campo* again, probably for a couple of weeks." He turned as she gave a little moan.

"I have to, Kate. I'm going to talk to the men and women in the villages about the coming reform. They need to organize. I've been talking with people in Lima. What the people of the Altiplano need is technical know-how, roads, and cheap credit. But no one in the government is going to hand out these things. It's up to us to help them speak out." He glanced at her apologetically. "Sorry. I get carried away, I know. Can you understand why this is so important?"

She stood and faced him. "Of course. Part of why I love you is because you do care so much."

He laughed and laid his hands firmly on her shoulders, and for an instant held her in a cautious embrace. "Someday I'd like to find out the other part of why you love me." He held her away from him then, and she found she could not lift her eyes to his. Kate stared at his mouth, and her breath came in short jerks.

Abruptly, he turned from her and zipped up his windbreaker. As he opened the door, the bells in the tower chimed out the noon hour. Kate watched as he took the steps two at a time. He stopped, faced her and said with a grin, "It's great to be back. Great, because you're here. *Hasta la vista.*"

"*Hasta la vista,*" she called, her words fading in the quiet air. She sighed and straightened the chairs. So this is how it would be. He would breeze in every once in a while, completely upsetting her hard-won balance, and then take off again with a regretful but impatient air. She lectured herself sternly. *What did you expect? You yourself set the rules. Just be grateful for what you have.*

But it wasn't enough. Seeing him like this made it harder—like food placed just out of reach in front of a starving person. She joined Josepha and Jeanne Marie in the dining room, and as they stood with bowed heads for grace, Kate gripped the back of her chair in a silent appeal for help.

Now time played tricks on Kate. Gone was the steady rhythm of the days. She found herself jerked back and forth between long unending hours of waiting to see him and speeded up moments of sheer joy in his company. She tried to hide her love and wondered at the fact that everyone around her seemed so oblivious to the truth she was living.

One evening before the sisters said Compline, Jeanne Marie looked at her and said, "I can't get over the change in Father Tom."

Kate held her breath. Sister Josepha nodded and agreed. "Yes, he seems so much more relaxed since he came back from Lima. I guess the break did him some good."

Jeanne Marie went on. "It's not just that. He comes over to see us in the evenings now. I thought we'd never get rid of him tonight."

She laughed and yawned, but Kate could feel Jeanne's shrewd eyes watching her. Kate said nothing. His casual visits to them in the evening when he was not out in the *campo* were both a torment and a great delight for her. She longed to be alone with him but feared it, too. She usually managed to walk him to the door when he left, and in the darkness of the cold entrance parlor they would link hands and gaze at one another until she felt she would drown in his eyes. He always tried to keep the mood light. She thought her intensity frightened him.

Once he had grabbed her hand and brought her palm up to his lips. "Isn't there a line in Shakespeare that says something like, 'Let lips do what hands do,' or something to that effect?"

She looked up, willing him to kiss her. But he only kissed her hand and turned away. Her hand burned where he had kissed it. "*Romeo and Juliet*," she said finally.

"Oh, and look what a bad end they came to." His tone was light, but as he left that night he had looked back at her, his eyes dark and unreadable.

Later, lying in bed, Kate felt ashamed. She was burning up with desire while walking around in the habit of a nun. What had happened to her? She was luring on a priest, a man who had vowed celibacy not because he hated women but because it was the price he had to pay to be a priest. Maybe Tom had been right to want to break it off early, and now he was the one being careful, holding back. She would break her vow of celibacy in a minute if he wanted her. The icy clarity of that realization washed over her and she sobbed in the dark, muffling the sounds in her pillow. She tried to pray, but what would she pray for?

Kate reached for the crucifix she kept always by her bed, the one her father had given to her the day she entered the convent. The figure of Christ was silver, and the cross itself of a dark wood like ebony, framed in silver. She ran her fingers down the nearly naked body of the young Christ. *Help me—help me to not hurt him, to not hurt You. I'm not sorry I love him, though. I won't ever be sorry for that.*

When she woke up much later that night, the crucifix was beneath her, digging into her left breast. All the next day her breast was sore, and the pain was hidden and sweet.

By May, the rainy season was over and winter was coming on. Travel became a possibility once more. Jeanne Marie surprised Kate one morning at breakfast when she asked her if she felt like taking a little trip. "You've been up in the altitude for six months now. You could probably use a little break." Kate was cutting up a banana, and she looked over at the other nun to see if she was serious. Jeanne continued, "Once a year I go down to the Poor Clare nuns in Coroico for a week's retreat. Then I usually stay another week and help the nurse who's there. Father Tom drives me down there and says Mass and hears the nuns' confessions. They love to be able to go to confession in English once a year, although I can't imagine what they ever have to confess."

"Where's Coroico?" Kate asked, trying to hide her excitement at the news that Tom would be going, too.

"It's in the Yungas, about three hours out of La Paz. It's gorgeous, Kate—hot and humid with tropical flowers all over. I lie in the sun in the nuns' back patio with my spiritual reading and pretend I'm in Hawaii."

"Aren't the Poor Clares a cloistered community?" Kate had never even seen a cloistered nun. She thought then of Thomas Merton and her delight in his description of the monastery at Gethsemane. "Will it be all right with Sister Josepha if I go along?"

"Actually, she's the one who suggested it. She thinks you've been looking a little peaked lately, as she would say," Jeanne was grinning at her and Kate smiled back, trying not to look too eager. As she got up to clear the table, Jeanne added, "Of course you and Father Tom would only stay a day or two. He'll have to get back for the Masses on Sunday. I'll take a bus up to La Paz later and then catch a ride with someone coming back here from La Paz. Does that sound okay?"

Kate nodded and helped Jeanne clear the table, afraid to look up and betray just how okay it all sounded to her. She and Tom would have a whole day alone together. And this was all at her superior's suggestion, so she was merely being obedient. She felt a twinge of guilt at the casuistry involved in her reasoning, but no fine scruples were going to mar this one chance, she resolved.

They left at noon on Sunday, the twenty-first of May. Jeanne Marie and Kate had packed the jeep the night before with medical supplies from the States for the nurse in Coroico. Jeanne explained that even though the nuns were cloistered, they had received special permission from their Motherhouse in Philadelphia to open a clinic in one room of the convent every afternoon because there were no doctors in the town on a regular basis.

"The odd thing is," Jeanne said as they loaded the heavy boxes, "the nun who's the nurse, Sister Rachel, is Jewish. She converted to Catholicism in her late twenties, and then entered the Poor Clares. Her family is supposed to be fabulously wealthy, but she's really down to earth. We stay up late and tell jokes when I come. Sometimes I even smuggle in a few cigarettes for her.

Those women are really something, living in a little hilltop village in Bolivia, lost to the big world." She shook her head. "They're funny and smart, too."

Kate watched her short, stubby figure as Sister Jeanne Marie hauled out the last box. "You're pretty smart and funny yourself," Kate said, realizing how much she had come to appreciate Jeanne.

"Yeah, but I couldn't stand being cooped up like that."

Kate looked around and began to laugh. "Oh sure, you're really out in the big world here." She stopped when she saw a puzzled look on Jeanne's face.

"But this is the big world, Kate. There are hundreds of people who need me here and I like feeling needed. No one else is going to do the job if I don't. There aren't any backups here."

Kate realized she had hurt Jeanne, and she put her hand on her friend's arm.

"I know that. And I was just trying to say how much I admire you."

Jeanne grinned and slapped her hand away. "I forgive you. You still have a lot to learn here—and I do mean a lot."

Kate followed her eyes and saw Tom crossing the courtyard, his duffel bag slung over his shoulder. She gathered her skirts together and jumped into the back seat, crowded with packages, so that Jeanne could sit in front with Tom. They drove off in high spirits, like children playing hooky from school. Kate watched Tom and Jeanne as they talked and gestured in the front seat. The roar of the engine was loud, and she couldn't hear anything they said, but she was happy just to watch them, knowing that if she stretched out her hand she could touch the back of Tom's neck.

Kate sat back, letting the jeep carry her along as if in a dream. The winter sky burned blue above them, arching down to the purple snow-covered peaks of the Andes. The fields were golden brown; she saw here and there small patches of white and gray that turned out to be sheep grazing in the distance. When they were an hour outside of Puno, following the curve of the sapphire lake, Kate felt the jeep skid as Tom braked suddenly. She looked out to see a herd of llamas sauntering down the road in front of them. Their graceful heads held high, the beasts were unperturbed by the gathering trucks and cars on either side whose drivers beeped and honked in protest at the delay. Then Kate glimpsed two women trotting along beside the llamas, small black whips in their hands. They whistled and chanted to the beasts, and after ten minutes, finally got them off the road and into the near-by fields. Kate watched the scene framed in the back window of the jeep until it disappeared in the dusty road.

By four o'clock they were heading west into the setting sun. Tom shouted back to her that they would make a rest stop and eat the picnic dinner Marta had packed for them. Kate could see nothing except stony fields and the lake shimmering in the distance off to their left. Suddenly Tom pulled the jeep off the road, and he disappeared behind some rocks.

Jeanne looked at Kate and laughed. "I don't know about you, but I'm going to die if I don't go to the bathroom soon." They got out of the jeep, and as Tom reappeared, announced that they would be back as soon as they found a suitable private place.

The wind had picked up, and the setting sun's rays had weakened. Kate pulled her cloak tightly around her and then used it for a curtain when they found a good spot to relieve themselves. Suddenly Jeanne Marie laughed. "What would the mistress of novices say to us now, do you think? I don't remember that this situation was covered in the Custom Book."

Kate laughed, too, and, as the two of them took turns guarding each other, they would burst into laughter at intervals, thinking of the stern face of the elderly drill sergeant.

Tom was waiting for them by the jeep and looked up in surprise as the two nuns broke into a run and raced each other to the jeep. Kate's heart hammered in her chest. She had forgotten about the altitude, but her sudden gasps for breath reminded her that she was still in a different world.

They ate their meal inside the cramped jeep away from the wind, devouring the chicken sandwiches and candy bars and apples. Then the three of them sat quietly for a while. Tom handed a soda to Kate, letting his hand linger for an instant against hers. The look he gave her filled her with a rush of joy.

"Did I ever tell you I was in a gang?" Tom was stretched out in the front seat, smoking. When they laughed, he looked injured. "Sure and I was," he protested, "You know, when I was born in '32, the Troubles hadn't been over that long. So when we were about ten or so, then the middle of the War, some of the lads and I formed the Michael Collins Gang, with secret meetings and rituals. We spent many a night sneaking out of our houses to gather on the quays of Galway, looking for the enemy." He laughed, "The trouble was we weren't too sure who the hell the enemy was—the Germans or the British." He flicked his cigarette out the window, and asked Kate to drive for a while.

Jeanne curled up in the back seat and soon dozed off. Kate was nervous with Tom's eyes on her. Now in the dark, Kate felt as if the two of them were hurtling through a vast lunar landscape where no one else existed. They did not speak much, but once in a while Tom would point out a strange rock formation near the road or the way the moonlight was falling on the lake. After a while he put his head back and slept. Kate could look her fill, and seeing his unguarded profile, his head thrown back, his mouth slack, filled her with a strangely maternal tenderness.

When they had gone through the immigration control in Desaguadero, Jeanne took her turn at the wheel, and Kate climbed into the back seat again over Tom's protests.

"I'll sit in back," he said. "You two can pray your office together or something."

"Your legs are too long," laughed Kate. "You'd die of lack of circulation before we got to La Paz." Kate wrapped herself in a blanket and dozed fitfully through the night. Every time she woke up, Tom's face was the first thing she would look for. She felt warm and safe, safer than she had ever been before.

They spent the night in La Paz, Jeanne and Kate staying again with the Precious Blood Sisters while Tom went to the Maryknoll house. He was at the front door by nine o'clock the next morning, smiling and cheerful in light khaki pants and a short-sleeved red shirt. Kate had never seen him in anything but dark colors. He was usually bundled up against the unforgiving cold of the plains. Now she noticed that his arms were covered with fine black hair, and she had to stop herself from stroking it.

Jeanne laughed when she saw him. "You look more like a tourist going to Hawaii than a priest on his way to say Mass for some cloistered nuns," she teased.

"Yes, and you two are going to suffocate in those medieval robes when we hit the Yungas."

Kate knew that Tom thought their habits were ridiculous. He was always telling them about the many communities of nuns in the States that were beginning to discard the old-fashioned habit. Soon nuns would dress like anyone else, he predicted. Sister Josepha argued with him, saying the habit was a witness to the world of the consecrated life. Tom said their lives ought to be the witness, not what they wore.

Kate didn't know what to think. She hated the fact that she could always see both sides of a question. Since she was a girl she had loved the elegance and grace of the habit. But sometimes, she knew, the habit was a disguise or a costume, for it could cover up women who were selfish and catty, hard to live with. Lately she had felt the weight of its falseness on her. To the world, her habit spoke of her virginal dedication, but inside was this rebellious, anarchic love for Tom. Nothing mattered except him, and she was never more conscious of this split between appearance and reality than every morning when she put on each piece of the habit and prayed for chastity.

The jeep climbed slowly up the curved highway that led out of the city, and soon La Paz lay like an inverted bowl beneath them. Tom leaned back and shouted over the engine, "This is one of the worst roads in the world. It curves through the Cordillera, and we'll drop about 9,000 feet in fifty kilometers." He turned back to watch the road, but his eyes sought hers in the rear view mirror. "If you feel sick, just shout, and I'll try to pull over when I can."

Soon Kate saw what he meant. The road was narrow, trailing off into dirt and rocks at the edge where there were no guard rails. Now they gazed down sheer cliffs studded with scrubby trees and boulders. Trucks packed with workers hurtled by them, not slowing as they raced around the hairpin turns. Often as they climbed they had to pull over to let the traffic coming downhill have the right of way. Several times traffic backed up where a bus had gotten stuck in a narrow curve. A few men would jump out and guide the driver with shouts and frantic motions as he tried to avoid the precipice that yawned below. Kate wondered at the carnival atmosphere. Everyone on the road seemed unfazed by the situation, while at each mile she felt terror gripping her stomach. She fought against the nausea.

Focused on the road, Tom drove steadily, not fast, and a few times she heard muttered curse words. No one spoke. Jeanne looked back at her several times, and Kate smiled reassuringly, not wanting to be the first one to get sick. After a while they were descending, and now Kate felt the air grow heavy and sweet. She rolled up her sleeves, and pinned her veil back to catch the warm breeze through the open window of the jeep. She smelled flowers and saw cascades of blue and orange and red bougainvillea spilling from the rocks. There hills were terraced, with coffee and sugar-cane fields. In only two hours they had entered a different universe. Yet still in the distance the snow-covered peaks of the Andes mocked this temperate new world.

They passed several waterfalls, with steam rising from rocks overhead. She heard a sweet, piercing bird call and realized how much she had missed the songs of birds during her months in the high plains. White crosses dotted the road, and Kate knew they were placed there in memory of people who'd died on this road.

After three hours Tom pointed to white and red roofs in the distance. There, nestled between steep jagged hills, lay the town of Coroico. The scent of orange blossoms and lemons filled the air. How could this tropical world exist so close to the barren, cold world they had just left? Her back was sweaty now from the heat.

It was noon when they arrived, and the town's streets were quiet. Pots of begonia and roses bloomed in doorways and from small second-story balconies. They drove through the main plaza and headed down a shady side street to the Convent of the Poor Clares. There twelve nuns lived in a low, sprawling stucco building. On one side was a small room open to the public where the lay sister sold the peanut butter, biscuits, and wine the nuns made to support themselves. Tom beeped the horn lightly as they drove up, and Sister Marguerite, the one nun who was allowed to mingle with the public, came out wiping her hands on her apron.

"Ah there you are," she cried. "And wasn't I praying the whole morning for your safe arrival?"

Tom jumped out and hugged the little old nun, whose glasses fell down in the tumult. Her eyes shone up at her fellow Irishman; Kate could see the bond between them. His charm worked all over the countryside, she thought, yet he'd seemed so cold and distant to her at first and could be that way suddenly, without warning. She had seen him freeze up at a meeting when the discussion went on too long. He was still a mystery to her. Just then Tom turned and led the gray-and-black-clad nun over to the jeep.

"You know Sister Jeanne Marie, of course, and this is Sister Mary Katherine, the newest one in Juliaca."

He helped Kate step down from the back seat, and Sister Marguerite gazed up at her.

"Welcome to Coroico, my dear. We've got your room in the guest house all ready. You must be exhausted after that terrible road."

Puzzled, Kate turned to Jeanne, who smiled up at her and winked. "Poor thing," said Jeanne. "You have to stay in the guest house. Because I'm on retreat I get to stay in cloister. Well, I guess this is where I say goodbye. I'll see you when I get back." Jeanne followed the little nun up the path to the main entrance.

Kate looked at Tom. "Where do you stay?" she asked, trying to keep a creeping note of exasperation out of her voice.

"I'll be over at the priests' house in the village. Men aren't allowed to stay in the Convent." He grinned at her, and Kate felt like smacking him. Had she come all this way to be dumped off like baggage and locked up alone in the guest house?

Sister Marguerite picked up Kate's bag and grasped her arm. "I'll show you to your room now. You must be finished entirely by the ride down here."

She led Kate up a path on the side of the main convent to a low stucco building with a screened porch. As they stepped inside, the cottage smelled musty, yet every surface shone with polish. They passed through a sitting room to a hall with two bedrooms on either side. Sister pointed out the bathroom, and then took Kate to the last room, which looked out over the convent patio and garden. She put Kate's bag down on a wooden chair next to the bed, and stood in the doorway for a minute. "You'll hear the bell ring for Vespers at six o'clock. The chapel has an outside door that will not be locked. After Vespers, I'll bring you dinner over here. Have a nice rest, my dear."

Before Kate could think of anything to say, Sister had closed the door firmly behind her, and in a minute Kate heard the front door close and the silence of the place settled down upon her.

Kate unpacked her bag and laid out her few things on the wooden chest near the bed. Then she went to the window, standing for a long time to watch three sparrows splash in the stone birdbath in the center of the garden. They bobbed and dunked and shook their feathers in the shade of a small mimosa tree. Then she lay on the bed and closed her eyes, seeing again the winding road of the mountains and feeling the pull of the curves until she drifted off to sleep.

The clanging of the bell woke her, and Kate opened her eyes to a dark room. For a moment she thought she was back in the novitiate. Then she jumped out of bed and went over to the mirror to straighten her veil for Vespers. Her face was pale and her eyes seemed enormous in the gloom.

She followed the path to the small chapel on the other side of the convent. As she swung open the heavy door, she heard a single voice intone the opening of Vespers: *"Deus in adjutorium meum intende."* "O God come to my assistance," Kate prayed. Then a chorus of young women's voices answered the cantor, and the ebb and flow of the nuns' chanting began, soaring into the corners of the chapel. The voices came from behind a wooden grille carved with birds and leafy vines, but the nuns were invisible. She stood alone in front of the altar trying to sing along, but her voice sounded thin and reedy. Now she was angry. Why was she out here alone instead of being with the others as Jeanne was? Even Tom got to see the cloistered nuns face to face and could laugh and joke with them. She felt like a leper.

When the singing stopped, she listened as the nuns rustled and coughed on their way out. Then Kate knelt, closing her eyes tightly, trying to be calm. *Dear God, please help me.* She bent over the pew, resting her face on her arms. Sister Marguerite had to pluck her sleeve several times before Kate looked up into the fat, flushed face of the little nun.

"I'll be bringing your tray over to you in a little, my dear."

"Oh, can't you have dinner with me and keep me company?" Kate tried to keep the plaintive note out of her voice.

"I'm sorry, dear. I have to eat in the refectory with the others. But I'll stay and visit a little with you when I bring over your tray."

With that Sister shuffled down the center aisle, and Kate followed her outside and then headed back to the guest house.

She turned on the two table lamps in the sitting room and opened the single window that looked out to the convent garden. The scent of jasmine rose in the heavy night air, and Kate heard the sleepy last murmurings of the birds as they bedded down for the night. A few tree frogs croaked, and Kate thought she could smell the rain coming. She looked up to the sky, but the moon was hidden behind low clouds.

Restless, she turned back to the room and noticed a glass-fronted bookcase like one her parents had at home. She pushed aside the biographies of St. Francis of Assisi and St. Clare, and flipped through the History of the Poor Clares. Then she picked up a small maroon volume of the collected stories of Chekhov. She settled herself in the faded easy chair by the lamp, and opened the book to a story she had never read, "Lady with Lapdog." Her eyes fell on a passage:

> Anna Sergeyevna, this lady with the lapdog, apparently regarded what had happened in a peculiar sort of way, very seriously, as though she had become a fallen woman—so it seemed to him. . . . [S]he sank into thought in a despondent pose, like a woman taken in adultery in an old painting.

Kate could picture the woman so clearly, and she felt the callousness of the lover. She was almost sorry when she heard the key in the lock and looked up to see the little nun enter balancing a tray on one hip as she maneuvered past the half-shut door of the sitting room.

"I'm so sorry I took so long, but Reverend Mother gave us recreation at supper in honor of your Sister Jeanne Marie's arrival. Tomorrow she'll be in the silence with the rest of us."

She perched on the edge of the other chair and watched

approvingly as Kate tasted the steaming soup. Kate found she was famished, and she ate steadily, glad that they had sent two of the hard crusty rolls and not one.

"Try your wine," urged the nun. "It's made here from our own vineyards."

Kate sipped the white wine. It was cool and dry and tasted faintly of earth. "Wonderful," she said, and Sister Marguerite beamed at her. Kate finished every bite of the chocolate cake, and poured a cup of tea from a blue and white pot. Then she asked the little nun questions about herself and the other American nuns here she would never see. Sister chattered on happily, and Kate wondered whatever had made Marguerite decide to join a cloistered order. She seemed made to gossip.

Finally, Kate sat back and thanked her for the delicious supper; the nun rose and picked up her tray. "Sleep well, my dear. The nuns are all going to confession now to the darlin' father. He'll be working late tonight," she said with a wheezy laugh. "You'll hear the bell for Lauds and meditation at 5:15. Mass will be at 6:00."

Kate walked her to the door and peered out into the night for a moment as she watched the nun cross the dark yard.

Maybe Tom would stop by to see her on his way back to the priests' house. She realized that she had been hoping for this all day. What would happen? They would be alone in the tropical night, not a soul around. She stopped herself there, unwilling to admit what she was thinking. Once again she picked up the Chekhov. He would help her to pass the slow-moving time.

Finally she heard the crunch of footsteps on the twigs and branches outside her window. Then a pounding on the door, followed by Tom's voice. "Good night, Kate. I'll see you in the morning."

When she flung open the door he was already heading down the path toward the gate. "Tom," she whispered.

He turned and said nothing, just stood there looking at her in the doorway.

Flushing, she asked in a low voice, "Won't you come in for a little while?"

He came into the light then, and she could see his face. It was somber as he spoke quietly, "I don't think that would be a good idea now, do you, Kate?"

She flinched a little but recovered enough to say, "I never thought of you as a timid man, Father Lynch." She knew she was being childish, but by now she felt as though she were watching a play in which someone else was playing her role.

He stared at her for a long moment. When he spoke at last his voice was patient as though he were speaking to a child. "Kate, I'm going over to the priests' house now to turn in. I'm dead. I'll see you in the morning after Mass and we'll have time to do a little sightseeing before we head back. Okay?"

She nodded, not trusting her voice to remain steady. Then she slammed the door. She listened until she heard his footsteps on the path and the creak of the gate as he swung it open to leave the convent grounds. From somewhere in the nuns' garden, she heard the full, deep throb of a mourning dove's call and the sound echoed in the hollow place inside her.

She was furious with him. At the same time she was ashamed of herself, her pleading. She undressed quickly, her cheeks burning. She slipped the long white nightgown over her head, and threw herself down on the bed.

In the darkness she trembled. If he were here now, he would lie down beside her in this narrow bed. His hands would move up under her gown, and she would feel his body, strange and unfamiliar, stretched out beside her. Yes, oh yes, she would give herself to him. She kissed the pillow, pretending it was Tom.

Where were all those high resolutions now? They had been fooling themselves, or she had at least. She hated him for his virtuous distance.

Kate was sleeping soundly the next morning when the deep gong signaling the beginning of morning prayer wakened her. It was too late now; she had missed Lauds. She dressed slowly and walked outside for a few moments into the garden, still drenched with dew. The sky was gray and rose, and a low mist hung over the mountains in the distance. Her long habit brushed against the grass and she could feel its dampness in her shoes. Someone had planted a small rose garden with six thriving bushes, and she bent to smell a golden rose tipped with scarlet, a few drops of water in its center. Everywhere insects were busy. Lines of ants wound around piles of dirt and beetles scurried in the grass. She smelled the dark rich earth, and the scent took her back to her mother years ago, tall and slim in her old jeans, digging up the dirt for a vegetable garden. She and her brother and sister had been shorter than the hoes they carried, and she remembered their shock at all the worms they kept digging up. Dan had run inside for a jar, claiming that they would be good bait for fishing, and for days Kate watched the jar on the porch until all the worms had died.

She walked over to the chapel for Mass. The church smelled like spring, for the sisters had placed tall branches of white flowering bushes in vases before the altar. Tom came out in a white and gold vestment and began the Mass of the day. It was the week between the feast of the Ascension and Pentecost, and as he read out the words of St. John's letter, Kate looked down at her hands. "Beloved, since God loved us so much we also ought to love one another. No one has ever seen God; if we love one another, God lives in us, and his love is perfected in us. . . . God is love, and he who abides in love abides in God and God in him."

Kate had heard the words so many times before. Now they were life and death to her. She loved God; she had given herself to Him. She also loved Tom with everything she possessed. Kate rubbed her forehead. By loving Tom did she love God less? But a dry, Jesuitical voice inside her kept insisting, "Define your terms. Just what do you mean by love? If you really loved Tom, you would stay away from him, let him live out the difficult life he had chosen. You are fooling yourself, Kate. You want him for yourself; you are jealous of the time and attention he spends on everyone else."

She gazed up at the crucifix over the altar. It was not the dead, half-naked Christ but rather a radiant risen Savior, dressed in white with a gold crown, Christ the bridegroom. The nuns' voices soared as they chanted, "My soul longs for the Lord like a deer longs for running water." Longing was something she understood now; she was learning for the first time the reality behind the erotic imagery all through the scriptures. She was learning everything backwards. She should have loved like this before she came to the convent. Then she would have known just what she was giving up. Her timing was all off.

After Mass, Tom nodded slightly to her as he left the altar. When she met him on the steps, he frowned at her and said, "If you're still speaking to me, meet me out in front in about half an hour. We'll have breakfast together before we drive back." She tried not to smile, but she felt an idiotic, carefree happiness rising in her.

Kate packed quickly, and on a sudden impulse stuffed the volume of Chekhov stories into her bag. She told herself she was only borrowing it and would send it back next year, or sometime when Jeanne Marie came back for retreat.

She was waiting out in front when Tom emerged from the cloister with Sister Marguerite. The nun beamed up at Kate and embraced her tightly. "Now have a safe trip to La Paz and don't let this one be showing off for you on those turns. Slow and easy, slow and easy take it. I'll be praying my rosary for the both of you till I know you are safe." She thrust a package of jars and bottles at Kate. "These are some of our goodies for you all up in that God-forsaken place where you work. I wouldn't last a day there, I can tell you that." She stood at the gate waving goodbye as Tom turned the jeep around the corner.

He looked over at Kate. "Well. I'm glad you're still talking to me." He didn't wait for her answer, but hurried on. "We're just going next door to a great little restaurant called La Casa. They make wonderful breakfasts there, but I couldn't tell Sister Marguerite that or she would have been insulted we weren't having breakfast at the convent."

He pulled up in front of the restaurant and parked the car. They went in together, and Kate smiled to herself. "A date, we're having a date," she'd whispered to him and felt happy when he threw back his head and laughed.

They devoured scrambled eggs and bacon, toast with strawberry jam, and strong coffee made from the local beans. The owners were a German woman and her Bolivian husband. Tom joked with them, and they, in turn, seemed delighted to see him. The couple sat at their table for a while, and the conversation grew serious as they talked about the land reform going on in Peru. Santiago, the husband, said that revolution was always looming for them in Bolivia.

"If things get too bad, we will go back to Germany," and he looked at his wife.

She shook her head. "Never. I love it here. No revolution is going to spoil what we have here." She gazed at her husband, and Kate felt a pang of envy.

By nine o'clock, Kate and Tom were on the road heading back to La Paz. The windows were open, and Kate felt dizzy with happiness sitting close beside Tom in the fragrant morning. Her night terrors had evaporated. They spoke very little at first, and Kate watched Tom handle the jeep around the sharp upward curves.

After a while he broke the silence. "I guess it would be an understatement to say that you were mad at me last night?"

Kate shrugged. "That would be putting it mildly." Then she turned to face him. "It's just that I felt so lonely all day, shuffled off like that to the guest house. Then I thought you would stay for a little while after you'd been with the nuns all evening—"

"Kate, I was hearing confessions," he interrupted.

"I know." She was silent, not knowing what else to say.

"I wanted to come in to you last night in the worst way, and that's just why I didn't. I didn't trust myself. Kate, you do understand what I'm saying, don't you?" He looked at her helplessly. When she said nothing he went on. "Beneath this disguise, I'm just a man, Kate. I want you. It would be so easy to let myself go, and I know that you feel the same. Hell, it was so obvious last night when you looked at me. But it would be shoddy and wrong. If it ever happens, it's not going to happen like that."

Kate felt pity for him then. He, too, was facing the lonely struggle with conscience. "I know, Tom. When I saw you this morning on the altar I felt ashamed." She looked out the window so he would not see the trembling of her mouth. "It's been pretty humiliating for me to find out how lightly I regard my vows."

"Don't be ashamed. Never be ashamed of love." He looked fierce, as though he were talking more to himself than to her.

She laughed, "It's not the love part I'm ashamed of."

He looked over at her as if trying to judge her ability to take in what he wanted to say. "Kate, I've made a mistake in all this before. It happened about six years ago, when I was still fairly new in the Altiplano. She was a Peace Corps worker who came to help set up the school in Juliaca. Her name was Linda."

Kate felt her stomach lurch. She didn't want to hear the rest.

Tom lit a cigarette and waited a minute before continuing. "She was a strange girl, cynical and tough. I think I was sort of a challenge for her." He laughed and the bitterness curled his mouth in an unpleasant way. "I slept with her twice, and I've regretted it every day of my life. I broke my vow, and I hurt her, too." He looked over at Kate who was sitting very still. "I guess we used each other. And I don't want to do that again, especially not to you."

Kate didn't know what to say. She could tell by the slump of his shoulders the pain was still there. As they came around a bad curve, she saw three men waving their hands at them from the middle of the road ahead. A battered red truck, the paint almost completely peeled off the rotting slats of the back, was pulled half way off the road.

"Damn," Tom muttered. "Stay in the jeep," he ordered.

Kate watched as the men gestured excitedly. Finally Tom walked over to the truck, and his head disappeared under the hood. The men stood around the tall Irishman, waiting for his diagnosis. Kate wondered if Tom knew much about cars. She didn't really know much at all about Tom, she decided, as he walked over to the jeep now, kicking small stones in front of him.

He leaned inside the window to speak to her. "One of the belts is broken. They want to hitch a ride with us to La Paz. I told them we don't have room." His eyes were troubled. "I want to wait here with them awhile to see if someone in a truck will come along and give them a ride."

Kate nodded. She didn't want to give them a ride either. It was their only time together. Was a few hours too much to ask? Yet she could tell Tom felt guilty about turning them down. They really didn't have room. How could they all squeeze in?

Finally, after about fifteen minutes, Kate saw the men shake Tom's hand. He said something that made them laugh and headed over to the jeep. They stared at her as Tom got in, and she held her head up and waved, hoping they were not scandalized. Tom said nothing for a few minutes as he drove off, and finally Kate broke the silence. "We really don't have room, you know."

"I know, but that wasn't the real reason I told them no. I wanted this time alone with you. How's that for a Good Samaritan priest?"

"I'm sure they'll get a ride soon." She wasn't sure, but fervently hoped it was so for the sake of their peace of mind.

They drove steadily on through the morning. Sheer cliffs yawned below them at every curve. Clumps of blood-red hibiscus bloomed from green rocks, and the smell of lemons was in the air. Cataracts sent mist shooting up into the trees. The sides of the road were dotted with white crosses.

After a while Tom broke the silence. "I'm looking for a certain spot. There's a little pool under a waterfall. I want you to see it." Suddenly, he pulled the jeep over at a wide fork in the road. They had seen few cars and trucks during the ride, and now, with the engine shut off, the only sound was the cicadas' drone in the heat of the approaching noon. They got out and walked a little way into a small grotto beneath the trees. A waterfall spilled from the overhanging hills. Ferns grew along the side of the pool; the noise of the water was deafening. Kate felt the mist on her face, cool and delicious. Tom took off his shoes and socks and waded into the water. His feet, white and long, shimmered like fish in the blue green water. She sat on a rock in the shade and trailed her hand in the pool. Then she splashed him, and when he turned to look at her she couldn't breathe.

"I'll always keep this picture of you, with the sun dappling your face, and the white habit spread all around you." His voice was low and sad. She said nothing. Then he dried his feet on the grass and walked toward her. When he stood in front of her he reached for her hand and pulled her up. "Come on, we'd better get going." She held fast to his hand, and all at once he pulled her to him, murmuring her name. He framed her face in his hands and began pushing back the headpiece around her face. Her veil slipped off and soon he was stroking her short curly hair, burying his face in it. Then she lifted her face to his kiss and felt his mouth close over hers hungrily. Somewhere, far away, she heard falling water.

He was the first to pull away, and he grinned shakily as he said, "We'd better go. All we need now is those guys in the truck to come along, and their evil suspicions will be confirmed."

Kate followed him blindly to the car, her body heavy and strange. She rearranged her veil.

Tom kept looking at her. His eyes were happier now, and he reached for her hand, playing with her fingers as he drove. "God, we must look like a scene from the corrupt Middle Ages."

He drove on through the twists and turns until the heat and the motion made her dizzy. She was dizzy all right, dizzy with love.

# Chapter Seventeen

fter the trip to Coroico with Tom, time slowed for
Kate. She missed Jeanne, who had written to request
permission to stay in Coroico until the end of June to help Sister
Rachel set up the new addition to the clinic. Several local doctors
had committed their services to the Poor Clare nuns for one
day each week, and people were starting to come in with more
serious complaints. Josepha sent a telegram immediately giving
her consent. Now it was just she and Josepha in the convent.
Sister was kind but remote as she went busily about her duties.
When they prayed together, Josepha got on Kate's nerves with
the peculiar way she hissed the ss's chanting the Office each day.
Kate was irritable, restless.

Now she wished she had confided in Jeanne Marie about
Tom, but she had been afraid that Jeanne would have little sym-
pathy for her predicament. Once Jeanne had lashed out at priests
as the two of them sat together playing cards after supper. Jeanne
had complained about the pastor's insistence that only the nuns
should be allowed to work in the sacristy of the church, cleaning
and polishing the chalices, ironing the altar linens, preparing the
candles for Mass each week.

"It's a waste of my time. I'm a nurse, darn it." She slammed down the cards on the table. "The priests are really benevolent dictators. We're supposed to be a team, but by now you must see who makes all the decisions around here."

Kate was surprised by her outburst. She watched as Jeanne pushed her chair back from the table and got up to pace the room.

"And while I'm on the subject, there's something else that bothers me about the priests down here. You may have noticed this in language school in Cochabamba. I sure did." She looked at Kate a minute then went on. "Back in the States we never had anything to do with priests. But suddenly it's fashionable to have friends of the opposite sex. Well, a lot of women are getting hurt. These friendships heat up, and the priest walks away when things get sticky. I've seen it a lot."

Kate watched her for a moment and then spoke. "You can hardly put all the blame on the priests though. Don't you think the nuns or volunteers—or whoever you're talking about—share some responsibility?

Jeanne looked directly at her. "I think women who fall in love with priests are naive. They're the ones who get hurt." Then she gathered up the cards and said good night. Kate looked away, her face burning.

So Jeanne had seen something between Tom and her. Now there was no one to talk to. Loneliness closed in like the fog on the mountains. Now that she was back in the daily work of the parish, Coroico seemed like a dream. She relived those moments by the waterfall over and over, playing the scene in slow motion. Many nights she slept badly, waking up gasping for breath, as if she had been running. She had a hard time getting to sleep, and would lie in bed after night prayer reading the Chekhov stories until she nodded off. Once Sister Josepha asked her if she had been sick during the night. She had seen Kate's light burning at three in the morning.

Kneeling in church before Mass, Kate would feel her stomach churn as she waited to see which priest would celebrate Mass. It was hardest when Tom came out. To see him at the altar stern and distant was always a shock. Then he would disappear into the *campo* for days at a time, and she would feel relief. She was glad for her classes. She forgot about everything when she was with her students.

In the middle of June she got sick. Her period the week before had been heavy and painful. She hardly ever got cramps, but this time she had to go to bed. Marta fussed over her all day, bringing cups of *mate de coca* which Kate would pour into the cactus plant on her windowsill, hoping it wouldn't kill the plant. But when her period ended she felt worse. She was nauseated and weak. Her bowels rumbled, and she had to run to the bathroom down the hall all day. She felt guilty; poor Josepha had all the work to do now. Finally she began to feel better, but when she went outside, the glare of the sun in the courtyard hurt her eyes. Some nights, alone in her room, she couldn't stop crying.

Kate began to be afraid. What was happening to her? Nothing felt real. The day before she ran away had not been different from any other day. Tom had said Mass as usual at six o'clock. When she went up to communion, she looked into his eyes as he placed the Host on her tongue. When his fingers brushed her mouth, she felt a knife thrust of desire. Gazing up at him through the flickering light of the candles, she knew she could not go on. She was living a great lie. He was a priest, and she was—what?

That night she took off her clothes and looked in the mirror. She didn't recognize the haggard face. The body was the same, a little thinner, but tall and straight. She slid her nightgown over her head and arranged her things neatly for the next day.

Finally, she saw what she would do. She would go away from here. If she didn't leave soon, something bad was going to happen. Tom mustn't know. He would try to stop her. He would feel guilty, and for one sharp instant that thought gave her pleasure. She wanted him to be hurt too. His cheerfulness was maddening. Couldn't he see what was happening to her?

She felt calm as she slipped between the covers. It would be easy to leave if she waited until noon when everyone was inside at lunch. Should she pack a bag? But that would draw attention. No, she would just slip out. It would be so much easier to think if she were away from him. She could figure it out. She was Kate O'Neill from St. Louis, Missouri, she thought, her eyes burning in the dark. She would know what to do if she could just think clearly. In the open spaces, she could breathe.

In her dream that night she and Tom were in a car that was headed up Art Hill in Forest Park. The trees were full and green. It was a summer night, and the car windows were open. Tom stopped the car and took her in his arms. But when she lifted her face to his, he turned away.

When she awoke her gown was soaking wet and she felt the dry cold of the winter morning like an electric shock. She would leave that day. She dressed quickly and tore the sheets from the bed, stuffing them in the hamper. Swiftly, she went to the linen closet down the hall. She pulled out the clean sheets they had laundered the day before and tiptoed back to her room. She made the bed carefully, inhaling the fragrance of eucalyptus leaves Marta placed in the cupboards, tucking in the hospital corners as the novice mistress had taught her to do in the novitiate. When she looked around the room to see that everything was in order, her glance fell on the figure of the pregnant woman she had found there the first day she came. She thought about putting it in her pocket, but it was too bulky. She left the crucifix her parents had given her the day she entered the convent in its usual place on her pillow. Then she shut the door.

# Chapter Eighteen

## Tuesday, June 30, 1964

*N*ow waking from a fitful sleep in the hotel room in Ica, Kate knows it is time to move on. It will be easier to get away before the other two girls get up. She slides out of bed and picks up the habit she has not worn in two days. She closes the bathroom door and turns the water on very low. It feels strange to put on the habit again. The headband is tight around her forehead, and the veil is heavy. When she comes out of the bathroom, Sheila is sitting up in bed, and her eyes widen when she sees Kate.

"Well, I see it's Sister Mary Katherine again," she whispers.

They both glance at Diane, sprawled on her stomach next to Sheila, her mouth open as she sleeps on.

"Sheila, I need to leave. You've been wonderful to me. I don't know how to thank you." Kate walks over to the side of the bed and stands looking down at her.

"God, you scare the hell out of me in that outfit. I feel as if I'm back in third grade." Sheila swings her legs out of bed and motions Kate to the far side of the room near the windows overlooking the street. "Do you have any money?" Her eyes fix on Kate's intently.

"I have enough to get me to Lima. It's time to give myself up, I guess." She is trying for a light tone. "Tell Diane I'm sorry I didn't say goodbye." She stops, afraid she will cry if she says any more. She wants to seem to be in control of herself.

Sheila presses a card into her hand. When she glances at it, Kate sees that it is the address of the Peace Corps office in La Paz. Sheila looks embarrassed as she says, "I never really knew a nun before, Kate. You seem very human, maybe too human to be a nun. I wish you luck, whatever you decide."

Kate hugs her then, and Sheila puts her arms around her gingerly, as if afraid she will break. Kate grabs the jacket she took from Peter's car and slips out of the room without a sound.

Downstairs the lobby is still dark. But as she reaches the wide front doors, a figure emerges from the gloom. It is Pepe, and his eyes gleam as he sees her dressed again in the habit. She whispers to him, "Pepe, I'm going to need to catch a bus to town. Do you know when the next bus today will be passing?"

Pepe nods his head sadly. "*Que pena, madrecita*, there will be no buses for another hour or so. It is not yet six o'clock." Then he stops and turns to her with a grin. "The *señora* isn't even up. I don't think she'd mind if I ran you into town. I'll bring the car around to the front. You wait outside on the steps, *madrecita*." Before she can object he has disappeared down the hall. His sandals make no noise on the stone floor.

Kate unlocks the door, pulling back the great iron bolts, one by one. The morning is fresh and clear. The sun has not risen yet, but the sky is reddening in the east. Soon Kate hears the crunch of tires on the gravel, and a red Chevrolet pulls up to the porch. Pepe is dwarfed behind the wheel. Kate hopes he can see over the steering wheel to drive. She peers in at him. "Pepe, are you sure *la señora* won't be angry?" She is worried about the *señora*. She did not seem very friendly, and Kate suspects that Pepe is taking a big risk.

"Don't worry, *madre*." He motions for her to get in.

Pepe drives fast. Kate sees he loves handling the great powerful car. He speeds by the other cars and trucks on the road at a terrifying pace, and Kate worries that they will be stopped by any police out at this hour. How will it look? A runaway nun and a servant in the borrowed car of his employer. She seems to have a knack lately for getting into dangerous situations. In fifteen minutes, Pepe is pulling up in front of the bus station in the central square in Ica. The wheels screech, and people look curiously as he runs around and hands her out as if she is royalty.

Kate presses a few *soles* into Pepe's hand, and he looks down in surprise. He shakes his head and hands them back to her without a word. His head is held high, and the stern look on his face say it would be useless to insist.

"Thank you, Pepe." Kate shakes his hardened brown hand. "And thank you especially for telling us about the Achirana canal. It is a beautiful place."

He bows to her then, and Kate feels him watching her until she enters the bus station. She says a prayer that he'll get the car back in one piece and that the *señora* won't fire him.

There is already a line at the window with the faded gray sign: "Pisco. Lima. Chimbote." She waits her turn nervously, counting her money twice. A ticket to Lima is 135 *soles*. That leaves her only fifty *soles* from the money Peter had slipped in the jacket. She has to go somewhere tonight in Lima. It's the end of the road.

The ticket agent does not even look up when she asks for a ticket to Lima.

"*Ida y vuelta?*" he inquired automatically.

"*Ida, no más,*" she replies. She will not be needing a return ticket. What has she done? Up until now her flight has been an adventure, a dream. Luck has been with her, as the condor she'd seen that first night promised. In Ica especially, she had been lulled into a false sense of ease. Now she is more confused and afraid than she's been since the day she left the convent in Juliaca.

Lima is a big city; she can no longer count on the "kindness of strangers," as Blanche Dubois would say.

What is she doing in Peru anyway? She hadn't been prepared for this country; learning Spanish wasn't enough. She doesn't understand the politics. Her work in the Altiplano seems trivial in the face of great poverty. She remembers Lt. Vargas: "We alone will change Peru."

She buys a ticket for Lima. By seven o'clock that morning Kate is on the bus headed toward Pisco and the Pacific Ocean. They are leaving the green oasis of the valley. But as the highway heads north and west, the green gives way to great white sand dunes and she is in a desert. The landscape is moonlike, and the fine powdered rocks of desert sand blow against the windows of the bus, making sharp pinging sounds like hail. Through the dust a white chapel with two towers appears. The small crossing is marked "Pozo Santo," Holy Well.

By eight-thirty the bus pulls into the first stop, the station in Pisco. Kate looks out at a statue in the center of the plaza, shaded by dusty ficus trees. The station is crowded as people mill around between the buses and *colectivos* parked everywhere. Here the roads to Cuzco, Lima, and the South converge. Kate has never seen Cuzco and the ruins at Machu Picchu, and for a crazy moment wonders if she has enough money for a ticket there..

She gets off the bus and follows the other passengers into the wide-roofed station. Tourists, many of them American it seems, wait in line for tours by boat and bus of the Ballestas Islands. Josepha and Jeanne had stopped here once, and they had gone out to the islands covered with guano. They told her of the terns, cormorants, penguins, and the strange blue birds called boobies. The sea around the islands was black with seals and sea lions.

But she isn't a tourist. She is a poor runaway who is starving. She stares at a little boy who walks by chewing a roll. She can smell coffee and feels in her pocket for the few bills she has left. She walks back outside where the vendors are squatting on the ground in front of the bus station. She buys a roll and tries to buy a single banana. An old woman squints up at her, shading her eyes from the sun.

"Buy the whole bunch," she urges. Her smile reveals a gap where her front teeth should have been.

"*No, gracias, señora,*" said Kate. "Only one."

The woman's smile fades and she looks away. "I do not sell them like that. The whole bunch or nothing."

Kate knows this isn't true. Many people buy a single piece of fruit. The woman can see she is a foreigner. The fact that she is also a nun means nothing to the woman. Kate stands still a minute, trying to decide which is more important, her hunger or her desire to call the woman's bluff. She feels a flush of anger.

"*Señora,* I will buy the whole bunch. How much is it?"

"For you, *madrecita,* I will only charge five *soles.*" Her smile has returned, and she quickly wraps the fruit in a small piece of paper. Kate murmurs her thanks, and, slowly, knowing that the woman is watching her, tears off one banana and offers the rest to a woman nearby who is nursing her baby. The young mother accepts the gift stoically, with no motion of surprise or gratitude. Kate feels a twinge of shame at her gesture of charity, which was done to spite the vendor who angered her. Well, the mother probably needs the nourishment. Or maybe she will sell the fruit for something else.

She looks around for a place to sit and eat, when she notices the bus driver herding his passengers back in for the final push on to Lima. She runs across the street, stuffing her breakfast into the jacket. She had meant to buy some coffee, but now it's too late.

She boards the bus and takes a seat next to a window on the left side, so she can see the ocean. Then she sees a girl walking up and down beside the bus selling sodas, passing them up to the passengers seated on the bus. She stands up and leans her head out of the window to ask for a Coke. The girl's eyes are bright. Kate clasps her hand through the open window.

By now the bus is full, yet the driver lets more and more people on. They crowd the aisles, leaning over the seated passengers, reading their newspapers or stooping to look out the window. Kate is starving. She turns toward the window as far as she can and tears off a piece of bread under the jacket. It is delicious, and she tries to eat slowly. The bus winds through the narrow road out of Pisco, and soon they are back on the highway. Now Kate gives in to her hunger and devours the bread and fruit, not caring who is watching her. She drinks the warm Coke slowly, forcing herself to make it last. She is so thirsty. Bodies press in on her, smells of sweat and urine, even of manure. Someone in back has live chickens in a basket. Next to her sits an older man in a shiny navy blue suit. He is thin, and holds his newspaper close to his face, once in a while peering past her out the window.

Kate watches the gray swirling sea as it crashes into the coast. For miles she sees no one, just the restless movement of the waves. Later the sun disappears, and a gray mist covers the road and the surrounding dunes. The bus hurtles on through the fog, while the people sigh and sleep or speak in muffled tones, conversations that Kate cannot make out. She feels heavy, oppressed, and realizes that she misses the cold clarity of the high plains. There the air was clear, the mountains sharply defined making her feel buoyant, as if at any moment she could rise up off the ground and float away.

The traffic picks up as they reach the outskirts of Lima. Trucks pass them, loaded with bags of grain and corn, the workers piled on top. Sleek American cars, long and heavy, cruise by the bus, their dark windows faceless, menacing.

Through the bus's misted windows, she can make out huts in clumps along the road. Soon whole stretches of flimsy straw and mud hovels appear off to the right, clinging to the sandy hills like huge beehives. Smoke rises from the makeshift villages, and the stench of fire and rot fill the bus. Now they are passing men on bicycles, farmers driving their herds of sheep and a few scraggly, lean cows. She catches a glimpse of two women in the full skirts and brown derby hats of the sierra. She turns around in her seat, but she cannot see their faces as the bus leaves them behind.

She thinks now of Pilar, Rosario, Mercedes, the women in her afternoon group. Who had told them that the class would be canceled? How disappointed in her they must have been, after the long walk they'd had to get there. She can picture Josepha, trying to cover Kate's work, too, left all alone in the house until Jeanne Marie's return from Coroico. She cannot stand to think about the children, their eyes shining expectantly, waiting for her. She has been utterly selfish in her flight, wrapped in a cocoon of her troubles.

Now it is darker, and she looks up to see that the bus is winding through clogged streets, with tall buildings blocking out the light. Lima is gray and dirty in the late afternoon. Faded posters, half ripped from the walls, are everywhere. She sees APRA in red and black letters scrawled on buildings and buses. She isn't very clear on what APRA stands for; she knows that it is the party of the workers. Its opponents call it communist, but Tom told her it is simply the party of the disaffected, those with no power.

Now they are in the center of Lima, heading toward the Plaza de Armas. Well-dressed women stride by in high heels and short skirts, sometimes arm in arm. She sees students and businessmen in dark suits, and everywhere, quiet and small, there are the highland people, looking forlorn in the capital.

Before the bus comes to a stop, people stir, gather their packages and stand to stretch after the long ride. For the first time on her journey, she feels fear, heavy and real. A vague plan is forming in her mind, but she dreads the explanations she will have to give if she goes there. Somehow she has to get to the convent in Balconcillo. There is a Maryknoll parish there, and it is staffed by the Precious Blood Sisters from O'Fallon, Missouri, a small town not far from the Dominican Motherhouse in Chesterfield. Sister Josepha and Kate had stayed with the sisters from St. Louis for a few weeks when Kate arrived from the States. Has it only been six months ago? It seems a lifetime away now. Kate had liked the superior, Sister Domitia, a short, plump little nun. She was relaxed and kind, and her laughter rang out all over the house, most often at herself. If Kate showed up on her doorstep, Sister would not turn her away.

The trouble is that she has no idea how to get to the parish. She's pretty sure that they had taken two buses from the convent to go downtown to see about her visa, and Kate vaguely remembers that when they went back in the late afternoon, they had traveled east, away from the setting sun. Well, she would ask. Someone would help her.

Clutching the jacket to her, Kate gets off the bus, joining the throng of people jostling on the sidewalk. As she steps down, people shove past her, trying to get on. The driver is shouting, "*Despacio*, slow down; take it easy."

The noise of the city confuses her. Buses and taxis blares their horns routinely, and cars screech around corners. Many cars don't have mufflers, and Kate flinches as an old Plymouth belches smoke in her face. She walks blindly, hoping to see a street sign or someone she can ask for help. No one looks at her; she is invisible.

The sidewalk is lined with *ambulantes*, vendors selling everything from apples and shoelaces to cheap watches and polyester shirts. Many of the vendors are from the sierra. Amid all the noise, the laughing, animated Limeños, they are impassive and stoic. Women with babies in their laps gaze at the passing throngs. The gray mist of Lima casts a pall.

Kate crosses a bridge over red and gray stone cliffs. A trickle of water seeps through the dried up river bed. On the other side she stops to read the stone marker: Puente de Piedra.

She walks on, knowing that she is lost, not thinking anymore, just moving. The neighborhood is rough. Men stand around in clumps, smoking and drinking, calling out to women as they pass. A young man, swaying, steps out of a doorway and stands directly in front of her. He looks at her for a moment, then steps aside with an exaggerated bow. "God bless the breasts that nourished you," he mumbles, so close to her that Kate can smell the *chicha* on his breath. She crosses to the other side of the street where music blares from the doorways of restaurants and bars. Although it is only late afternoon, the street lamps have come on, the mist swirling in their yellow glow.

After a few blocks she comes to a ruined garden. Between crumbling marble statues, a double avenue of old trees stretches before her. As she enters the park, the noise from the street diminishes. She walks down the middle of the avenue, her steps crunching the gravel. There are couples in the garden, lying entwined under the shade of the trees on the edge of a deep woods. She tries to make out the statues, but they have decayed into unrecognizable shapes. Finally, she comes to the end of the walk where a large gate rises up in the gloom. "*Convento de los Descalzos*," the sign says. "*Diez soles. Cerrado los martes.*" She has come to an abandoned monastery, of Franciscans, she guesses, the shoeless ones. She doesn't have ten *soles* for the tour, and she starts to laugh. Now she's locked out of a convent, wanting to get in. The monastery is closed Tuesdays, but what day is this? She can't remember. She passes her hand over the stone gate and feels its roughness, solid and cold. The single step in front of the gate is worn smooth. The gate is closed to her now, the monastery empty, locked shut.

She turns away, retracing her steps through the park. Dusk is coming on quickly now, and she feels a damp chill rising from the grass. The leaves rustle in the wind, and she thinks she hears footsteps behind her. She walks faster, anxious now, toward light, people.

The blow comes from behind. Stunned, Kate drops to her knees as an arm circles her head and a rough hand clamps her mouth shut. She does not try to scream. Hot anger rises in her, and she scratches and claws at the hand that is gagging her.

"*Hija de la gran puta,*" a voice, low and musical, his breath hot on her face. Daughter of the great whore.

"No, Mother, Mother," she cries out. Then she feels a sharp, slicing sting on her arm, and looks down to see fresh blood blooming like so many roses on the white field of her habit. She kneels, motionless, her eyes closed as the man searches her clothes, running his hands over her body. He finds the envelope with the few *soles* she has left and yanks off a small silver cross she wears under the habit. Her grandmother had given it to her when she made her first communion at St. Roch's.

Suddenly an image appears of herself on that day, small and blond, brushing back her hair, squinting into the sun. Her mother stands beside her, tall, in a long skirt and a hat. Her grandmother is on the other side. She, too, wears a hat with a veil and her shoes are heavy and black. Kate is surrounded by their love, as warm and real as the spring sun that casts sharp shadows on the grass. Her father must have been taking the picture. She sees it all so clearly.

When she opens her eyes, the man is gone. Her arm stings, the blood seeping through her sleeve. She pulls back the sleeve to see the cut which is wide but not deep, and then looks around for the jacket to wrap it around her arm to stop the bleeding. It's gone, and for some reason this loss seems unbearable.

Kate staggers to her feet, trying to steady herself. Her knees are trembling. It's very dark in the garden now, but she can see the street in the distance. She walks stiffly, holding her arm with her hand, pressing down hard on the wound. As she emerges from the avenue of trees into the street, she feels dizzy. A voice, young and familiar, calls to her.

"Madre Catalina, what are you doing here?"

Kate turns to the voice. It is Magdalena, their Peruvian novice who had left the community. It does not seem strange to Kate that she has appeared like some dark-haired guardian angel.

Magdalena's eyes widen as she stares at Kate's habit. "What happened? There is blood all over you. Papi, help me. It is one of the nuns from the convent in Juliaca."

Now Kate sees a man at Magdalena's side. He is a big man, with a massive head of curly gray hair. She feels him catch her as she starts to fall. His arms are strong as he lifts her up, cradling her. He carries her for a long time when finally Magdalena whispers to her, "*Cálmate, Catalina. Ya estamos en mi casa.*" They enter a dark building, and Magdalena's father begins to carry her up the stairs. Kate is embarrassed and protests, but he shushes her and goes on, stopping at each landing to take a breath.

Then a door opens, there is light, and a woman's voice cries out. Kate hears Magdalena reassure the woman that everything is all right. Despite all the blood, the wound is not deep. The woman bends over her, and Kate sees another Magdalena in the mother, but her hair is graying and the face has the beginnings of delicate lines by the mouth and the dark eyes. The woman passes her hand over Kate's forehead in a gesture of infinite tenderness. Kate tries not to cry.

Later she is sitting at the kitchen table eating the stew Magdalena's mother has put before her. It is steaming hot, and the aroma of eggplant and tomato reaches her as she lifts her spoon for the first bite. Around the table the family watch her. Magdalena's two brothers have come home from school, slender young teenagers who stare at the sight of a strange nun in a blood-stained white habit sitting at their kitchen table. They watch her solemnly without saying anything.

Magdalena chatters on. Her father and she were just coming home after work. Magdalena explains that he is a teacher in San Miguel, a private school for boys in San Isidro, a wealthy suburb on the other side of the city. She has been working in the office of his school as a secretary until she can enter the Universidad Católica in the fall.

"We had just gotten off the bus in Rimac when I saw you, blood on your habit. I couldn't believe it was you, Sister!" Magdalena's voice rose.

"Rimac?" Kate looks puzzled.

Magdalena's mother cannot resist asking her now. "But *madre*, what were you doing in this neighborhood? It is not safe for any woman to be walking alone at night."

"*Chabelita*, leave her in peace. The girl is famished, can't you see? She can talk later." Magdalena's father is fingering a pipe, tamping down the tobacco carefully.

Kate looks at the him. Cristóbal Ruiz is a quiet man. He has been watching her steadily, and she notices now the furrows in his brow and the wide hands that are rough and callused.

"I must have taken a wrong turn when I got off the bus. I thought I was headed toward Balconcillo. I remember walking across a bridge," Kate finally manages to say as she looks around the room. The kitchen is large, and the big table in the middle is covered with a clean white cloth. Books and papers are scattered over a long sideboard that holds a silver tea set, polished and gleaming. Over the sink is a window, and a picture of the Señor de los Milagros, Lord of the Miracles, hanging over the arch that leads into the next room, a blessed palm tacked to the front of the picture.

Finally the father breaks his silence. "Where were you going?"

His eyes are piercing, and for an instant Kate thinks he must know her whole story, that somehow this wise and strong rescuer has been sent to deliver her from doubt and confusion, to show her the way. His name is Cristóbal, the Christ-carrier. But he just sits there, sipping his coffee, and waits for her answer.

"I was trying to remember how to get to the Precious Blood nuns' convent in Balconcillo. The parish is called Nuestra Señora de Guadalupe."

"That's near La Victoria," exclaims Martín, the youngest. "You were going the wrong way totally." He grins up at her, amused that a grown-up could have been so mistaken.

Kate looks around. "I really should be going now." She looks down at her arm. Magdalena's mother has washed and dressed the wound and wrapped it in a clean white cloth. But it still throbs dully.

Magdalena comes around to Kate's chair and sits close beside her. She motions to the rest of her family, and soon she and Kate are alone in the kitchen. Her eyes are gentle and she speaks softly, soothingly, as if to a child who has seen a ghost. "Catalina, why don't I call the sisters in Balconcillo and tell them you are with us, but that you would like to come over and see them tomorrow. Then you can get cleaned up here and get a good night's rest. They will be horrified if they see you with blood all over." She watches Kate to see how she takes this suggestion. "In the morning I will take you over there myself after they give me directions."

Kate begins to cry. She puts her head down on the table, and Magdalena pats her arm, stroking her hand and humming until Kate says, "Oh, I've made such a mess of this." She looks down at their two hands clasped together. Kate is sobbing now. "Everyone has been kind, but I've been so selfish, a coward.

"No, Catalina. I know something must have happened. You don't have to explain to me. Living in the Altiplano was not for me. She smiles now at Kate, and her face is radiant in the lamplight. "I'm glad I went to the convent. I don't regret a minute of it. But it wasn't my life." She got up from the table and began to gather the dishes. "*Bueno*, it's all settled then? You'll stay here tonight with us, we can share my room, and that will give Mami a chance to try to get those spots out of your habit. She has been dying to get at them all evening."

"Okay. But, Magdalena, don't call the nuns in Balconcillo. They'll just worry. When I get there tomorrow, they'll see that I'm all right."

In the bathroom that night, Kate peels off her stained habit and veil. She will have to wear the same things tomorrow. The hot water stings the cut on her arm, but she sinks gratefully into the tub. Her body is stiff now, and her neck is sore where the attacker had grabbed her. Why did he call her *puta*, whore?

The family explained to her that she was in the Alameda de los Descalzos, an old lovers' lane still used by couples in the neighborhood. "In the days of La Perricholi, all of fashionable Lima gathered here to walk in the late afternoon. It is a sad sight now, full of thieves and scoundrels." Cristóbal shook his head sadly. He remembered a different Lima, a city of close-knit neighborhoods where people shouted to each other by name across the street. Kate saw that he was ashamed of what happened to her. The city seems hostile to her, opaque. Maybe it is the mist, the *neblina*, that blurs everything, making it hard to see things clearly.

The Altiplano flashes before her, and she misses the fine sharpness of the air, the clean lines of the mountains and the dark that pulls down the brilliant stars like a great inky cloak. Would she ever see it again? Now it is hard to remember why she thought she had to leave. Tom, of course. She hasn't thought of him in many hours. She is conscious only of a dull ache, like a toothache, she thinks, that hurts all day but that flares up hotly only when you forget and bite down on something. What had Father Jack said on Lt. Vargas' radio? That Tom was out looking for her all night. She can picture his face, the lips drawn tight and angry. He was more angry than worried, she knows, furious with her for doing something so childish, so impulsive. Quick and decisive, he has little patience with weakness.

Why did she fall in love with him so swiftly, so totally? She didn't even like him at first, the cynical twist to his humor, the way his eyes narrowed and stared when she was saying something that all of a sudden in his presence seemed fatuous, naive. But that was it. He was a challenge, difficult, and she won him in spite of himself. Oh God, this is even worse than she thought.

Later she slips into bed beside Magdalena in the tiny immaculate room that the only daughter in the house has to herself. Magdalena is already asleep, and her perfume, sweet and pungent like gardenias, is on the pillow. For a long time Kate stares at the car lights flickering against the shade. She has been rescued, snatched up from trouble. She is safe and warm, but she doesn't deserve to be, she knows. She thinks of the smoke she saw this morning when they passed the slums of the *barriadas*, curling up black and ugly into the sky. It was a signal, an SOS sent to God. They all need help.

# Chapter Nineteen

### Wednesday, July 1, 1964

⟶⟶

*K*ate awakes to the sight of Magdalena examining her habit, the blood stains fainter now but still visible. The girl turns and sees Kate watching her. "*Buenos días*, sleepy-head. I thought you would never wake up."

Kate looks at the window. It is still dark. Magdalena is putting on her makeup, and Kate notices how lovely she's become since she'd left them in Juliaca.

"Mami tried to get all the spots out of your habit, but I'm afraid there are still some stains. But at least you won't look disreputable when the nuns see you." Magdalena is wearing a navy blue skirt and white blouse, and her high heels click against the wood floor as she passes back and forth across the room.

"Magdalena, have you been seeing anyone since you've been out of the convent?" Kate can't imagine that the men of Lima would not have noticed her.

"If you mean am I seeing a man, the answer is no," and she makes a face. "I am in no hurry to get mixed up with most of the men I meet. The good ones always seem to be married or unavailable for some reason." She looks at Kate, and there is a long pause. Kate says nothing. After a minute, Magdalena grabs her jacket and stands in the door. "I'll leave you in peace to get dressed now. Then we'll catch the bus to Balconcillo."

Kate crosses the room and takes her hand, "You have been so kind, all of you. I can never thank you for this. But I don't need you to go with me today. You have to go to work, and I'll be fine if someone will just put me on the right bus. Really. I mean it."

Magdalena looks at her for a minute and then nods.

When Kate comes into the kitchen dressed in her habit, Chabelo embraces her, holding her to her warm breast. Picking up the hem of Kate's habit, she looks critically at her cleaning efforts for a minute. "*Bueno*, it will have to do. At least it looks a lot cleaner than it did last night. How did you sleep, my dear?"

Kate embraces the woman again and feels her springy hair on her face. "I slept like a baby. Thank you for everything you've done."

"I am happy to have you. Maggie has told us how kind you were to her when she was still in the convent, up in that terrible place. I was so worried about her. She was *flaca* when she came back, but we are fattening her up now."

"She looks wonderful," Kate smiles at them.

"Now sit down and have your breakfast. There are fresh rolls, oranges, grapefruit, mangos, and some nice hot coffee. The boys have already eaten and gone, so we have a little peace and quiet."

Cristobal enters, and Chabelo lifts her face to her husband's kiss. He sits at the table, his newspaper folded neatly in front of him. Kate sees that his eyes are laughing as he looks her over, and she feels shy suddenly as she remembers how he carried her up the steps in his arms.

"And how did you wake up this morning, little sister?"

He motions toward her arm, and she pushes up the sleeve of her habit and pulls back the bandage. The cut is still raw. He nods toward his wife to take a look, and Chabelo holds Kate's arm up, examining the cut. Then she brings a bowl of some brownish red mixture and begins to apply it gently to the wound.

"What is that?" Kate feels the coolness on her arm.

"Oh, these are remedies I learned about from my mother and grandmother. This is a mixture of *malva* and aloe. It soothes the wound and takes away the sting. It helps the flesh to heal. But you may always have the scar." Her brown eyes stare into Kate's, and then she adds, "Such a shame to have a scar on your pretty arm. What will your mother say?"

Kate's stomach lurches as she thinks of her parents. During the attack she remembers crying out "Mother, Mother." Whom had she been calling? The attacker had called her "daughter of the great whore" with such pleasure, almost as if he had been whispering words of love or desire. She can feel his hands on her still, and she shudders. He could have done anything with her. There was no one around; he had the knife. What would it have been like if he had raped her there on the grass, in the Alameda de los Descalzos, her habit spread out beneath them like a fine sheet? She chokes on the bread and feels a wave of nausea recede. Someone has been watching over her.

Cristóbal and Magdalena walk with Kate to the bus stop and wait to see her safely seated in a front seat, right behind the driver. Cristóbal gets on and talks to the driver for a while, wanting to be sure he knows where Kate should get off the bus. The driver nods his head impatiently. As he pulls away from the curb, Kate waves to them and blows Magdalena a kiss. Then the bus enters a main avenue. Kate watches the morning traffic of Lima, a swirling sea of motion and sound.

The bus heads over the bridge and into the Plaza de Armas and circles the huge plaza, heading down the Paseo de la República. It stops every two blocks, until all the seats are filled and people still pour in, crowding into the aisles. She watches the schoolchildren, their faces shiny, the girls' hair slicked back in tight braids. Some wear the wool jumpers and white blouses or shirts of the private schools, where they are taught by the Religious of the Sacred Heart or the Jesuits. They chatter loudly and trade pieces of candy and gum as they balance themselves on the swaying bus, their book bags on the floor between their feet. Kate thinks of the children of Juliaca, so shy and quiet compared to these kids.

One little girl stands very close to Kate, her small hand gripping the back of the seat. When she looks at Kate, her green eyes are startling. This child could be her daughter. Her mouth feels dry as she watches the girl stare out at the street. The child wears tiny gold earrings that dangle from thin gold wires. Kate imagines the mother taking the child shopping for the earrings, or maybe they had been a gift from a grandmother. Kate feels a fierce pain at the thought of never having children, never having a child reach up for her in distress, moving into her arms for comfort. Suddenly the girl looks at her, a smile steals across her face revealing several missing front teeth, like any six-year old the world over.

"We're going to the zoo today," she whispers. "My whole class is going to see the llamas and alpacas and vicunas. They live in the mountains, you know. I have never seen them, only in pictures. Have you ever seen them?"

Kate can't speak and simply nods. Then the bus stops and the girl moves to the back with the other children, pushing and shoving.

"Good bye," Kate calls out to the girl. "Have a good time at the zoo." But it is too late. As the bus pulls away Kate watches the girl swing her book bag at her side, picking her way neatly through the vendors that crowded in front of the school. Then she disappears inside.

Kate is surprised at herself, the pang of longing the child makes her feel. She always loved children because secretly she feels as if she is still one of them. But when she entered the convent she didn't think much about giving up children. She was only eighteen herself. Now, though, the years stretch in front of her. She, like Josepha, would grow old loving other people's children. Maybe she would have nieces and nephews someday. Then she could be the doting aunt that the teenagers would talk to when they had stopped talking to their parents. She pictures herself older, much older, stooped and wizened. A shawl is thrown around her shoulders. She is looking out to the Motherhouse garden from her wheelchair, surrounded by the other old nuns. Her eyes are bad, she cannot read, and she never really liked doing the embroidery so many of the nuns do in their long hours of waiting. Is this how she wants to live out her life?

In the street, people scurry to beat the light. Long American cars are everywhere, old models from the 1950s. As the bus moves out from the center of Lima, the people seem poorer. Squat women lug bags back from the market. Everywhere, crowded together on the sidewalks so that people have difficulty walking by them, are the street vendors. Young men stop to examine the goods, and their shoulders are hunched against the cold in thin sweaters. The bus passes now through La Victoria, with shabby shops and throngs of street vendors. Most of the crowds waiting at the bus stops are going downtown, and the bus is now nearly empty. Finally Kate hears the bus driver shout, "Balconcillo." His eyes meet hers in the cracked rear-view mirror, and he nods at her.

She stumbles slightly as she goes down the steps. The door of the bus slams behind her, and she stands uncertainly on the sidewalk, gagging on the diesel fumes from the disappearing bus. The morning is still gray, but in the distance, just over the hills, a few pale specks of blue appear in the sky.

Now she begins to walk toward a starkly modern church she can see a block away—Our Lady of Guadalupe. Kate's mouth feels dry. The flight is over. Now she has to face the things she has been running from, or to.

She walks around to the left side of the church, hoping she won't run into anyone who might recognize her from the few weeks she had spent here a year ago. All the nuns will be in school. Maybe the cook will let her come in. She passes the front door of the convent and goes around to the back gate, which leads, she knows, into the patio where the nuns do their laundry. She rings the bell and then lifts the latch and slips in.

Someone has already done a load of wash that morning, and Kate threads her way among the nightgowns and towels that hang limply in the damp morning air. Kate knows it will take a day or two for these things to dry unless the sun surprises them with an unexpected appearance. She glances down at her own white habit, stained with dirt and blood. Her shoes are dusty, the heels worn. She tries to arrange her veil, hoping that she pinned it on straight that morning in Magdalena's bedroom.

Just as she raises her hand to knock on the kitchen door, it opens and she is staring into the eyes of Sister Domitia herself. The older nun gasps in surprise, then her eyes crinkle in a welcoming grin. She grabs Kate and hugs her, and Kate fights back the tears that always seem near. Then Sister pushes her back a few inches to study her. She stares at the stains on her white habit.

"Why, Sister Mary Katherine, what a surprise." She looks behind Kate. "Did you come down all by yourself?"

The question hangs in the air. Then Kate nods, and Sister Domitia looks worried.

"Come in. Why are we standing out here?" She pulls Kate into the kitchen. "Teresita has gone to the market, and I had a free period before my class, so I stayed home this morning to catch up on my correspondence. Is everything all right?" She falters now as she looks at Kate.

Suddenly Kate cannot find any words. She sits down abruptly in a dining room chair. Sister Domitia sits across from her, and folds her small plump hands neatly on the table in front of her. "Something has happened. You look terrible. What is it?"

Kate watches her face and struggles to begin. "Sister, I need to get a message to Juliaca. They don't know where I am. I need to tell them I'm all right."

She watches as Sister Domitia's reassuring nods stop. "What do you mean they don't know where you are? Isn't one of the sisters here in Lima with you?"

"No, I came alone. I left—it was about a week ago. I just walked out." Now she puts her head down on the table and begins to cry. The sobs are quiet, but they go on and on in the empty room. Finally she hears Sister Domitia get up and go to the phone at the other end of the nuns' living room.

"Henry? This is Domitia. Listen, I've got a problem here. I need to get a message up to the Dominican nuns in Juliaca." There is a brief silence. Then her voice lowers, "The youngest one, Sister Mary Katherine, just showed up at our door. She's distraught, and I haven't gotten the whole story, but—" The voice ceases. Then, "Yeah, that's right. She says they don't know where she is. We need to get a message up there immediately." Sister is quiet for a few minutes. "No, I don't think you need to come over just yet. Let her relax, sleep, maybe eat a little. She looks done for. I'll call you later. Okay, thanks, thanks a lot. Tell them she's fine. Bye."

Kate lifts her head now, watching the nun hurry back across the room. She feels heavy. She follows the nun up the stairs to an empty bedroom and sinks onto the bed. She hears the door click as Sister Domitia pulls it shut.

When she awakes she is confused. Where is she? She looks out the single window, but gray mist shrouds the courtyard below, making it hard to tell what time of day it is. She switches on the light. Someone has put a small stack of clean clothes on the chair by her bed. She gathers them up and the towel next to them and makes her way to the bathroom. From downstairs she can hear laughing and talking and the clinking of silverware on plates. It must be suppertime. She has slept all day.

When she comes downstairs in the gray skirt and blouse and the small token veil that the Precious Blood Sisters wear, the other nuns rise to greet her. She is immediately surrounded by their warmth, and someone passes a plate to her with a generous portion of chicken and rice. No one asks her questions, and the nuns carry on with their chatter of the day as if it is the most normal thing in the world to have a runaway in their midst. Kate is grateful for their tact.

After dinner she joins the nuns for Vespers in the living room. As they sing the psalms, Kate glances around at the group. Three of the sisters are over fifty, and the one young one among them must be about thirty. Their plain scrubbed faces are serene if a bit tired. They settle comfortably in their chairs, their feet stretched out in front of them, and Kate watches the easy way they handle their prayer books, caressing them unconsciously like familiar pets. Why can't she live like this? Why is she so restless, always wanting more? The words of the final hymn to Mary soar in the small room: "*Salve Regina, mater misericordia.*" Had it been to Mary she cried out in the night when the man attacked her, or was it a call to her own mother, tall and slim and so far from her these days? She feels a fierce ache to see her mother, to sit across from her and feel the love she had always taken for granted. After Vespers, Sister Domitia tells the nuns about the attack Kate has suffered. They were shocked at the sight of the ugly gash on her arm. She feels embarrassed by their pity, their unspoken questions.

After recreation the nuns go upstairs one by one until only Kate and Sister Domitia sit by the fire. Kate pulls her chair close, for the cold here, damp and penetrating, is different from that of the Altiplano. It feels strange too to be in a short skirt, without the long folds of her habit. The sisters had taken her habit to the laundry, and Sister Mary Agnes, the oldest of the group, had spent some time soaking the stains in a special mixture of bleach. She can hardly bear all their kindness.

Sister Domitia speaks gently to her, as if afraid at any moment Kate will take off. "Father Henry radioed Juliaca and talked to the pastor up there. He said they hadn't heard from you since Tuesday when the police radioed them from a station near Arequipa."

She looks at Kate now as if she is a stranger, and Kate cannot bear to lose the confidence of this kind woman who has taken her in with no questions. So Kate begins, haltingly, to tell her of the troubling of her soul, the long (or so it seems to her) struggle with her feelings for Tom; her desperate, unplanned flight, and of the luck in finding people who had helped her along the way. It wasn't until Lima that she'd run into serious trouble. "But I know I've been foolish. People have been worried about me. I've been selfish." She stops.

Sister is gazing into the fire, her sweater pulled around her shoulders. She looks at Kate now and her eyes are grave. "Yes, you've been very selfish. I can only imagine how Josepha must have felt all week worrying about you." She is quiet again, and Kate waits, not knowing what to say. Sister looks at her. "You are at a crisis in your vocation. Only you can decide the right way for you. Are you in final vows?"

"No. I'm supposed to make final vows this summer." Kate can see the logic of the question, and it shocks her. She has been floating in a dream of love, removed from all the practical questions. How can she go on being a nun? She stares into the fire.

Sister Domitia breaks the silence that has fallen between them. "Father Henry had a good suggestion. He said why don't you go out to the Maryknoll retreat house on the beach and spend a few days in the sun? You were due for an altitude break anyway after almost six months up there. The altitude does strange things to people who aren't used to it. Then you can decide what to do. What do you think?"

Kate gazes at the nun. They all think she is unbalanced. She is, in a way. That's exactly how she feels, thrown off balance. Somehow the center of gravity has shifted. Living at the high edge of the world was enough of a shock, but then she had to go and fall in love. Fall—the perfect word in her case.

Kate whispers, "That sounds wonderful if you're sure it won't be any trouble."

"Rubbish. What trouble could it be? The priests leave that great big house empty out there for weeks at a time. The thought of it scandalizes me sometimes, but I guess they need the rest. We'll drive out there tomorrow." She pats Kate's hand and gets to her feet with a little moan. "Oh, I'm half tempted myself to use the vacation house one of these days. These old bones give me trouble more and more. Good night, dear. God be with you."

Kate sits by the fire watching it die. She tries not to think of Tom. She has him tucked away inside somewhere, like a picture put in a locket and worn next to her skin.

With a sudden clarity she sees the truth. There is no good outcome to their love. Yes, she could leave the convent and hope that he would leave the priesthood and marry her. But does she want that? She would feel guilty forever of taking him away from what he dedicated his life to. He would come to resent her when things got hard. A spoiled priest—that's what the Irish called them. She thinks of what her mother and father's reaction to the news that she's fallen in love with a priest would be, much less the idea that she would leave the convent and marry him. Maybe after a few years they would recover and be cordial to him. But always underneath would be the thought of what he had been. They would secretly blame him for seducing her, she is sure. A spoiled priest and a spoiled nun.

She could go back to the community in the States and try to forget about him. She would never see him again, never write to him. That would be best for him. But for her? The thought leaves her frozen inside. She pictures herself in some parish in St. Louis, teaching her students, playing softball with them, turning into her old heroine, Sister Helene.

The one option that is out is going back to Juliaca to work with him. She can't stand it. They have tried to love each other and still be faithful to their vows. Suddenly it makes her furious to think that Tom seems content with the arrangement. She's the one who has crumbled. Doesn't he desire her? She'd thought men were supposed to be the passionate ones. He had succumbed to the other girl, the volunteer. It humiliates her to think that now—with her—he is so much in control of his feelings. Especially when she is not.

The fire dies. A wisp of dark smoke lingers in the hearth, but the embers are dark. Kate turns off the lamp, tired of her thoughts.

# Chapter Twenty

## Thursday, July 2, 1964

Sister Domitia's round face is the first thing Kate sees the next morning as the nun opens the door of her room. She has a sheaf of papers in her arms. She smiles at Kate, "I didn't wake you for Mass. I thought you needed the rest."

"Thanks, Sister. What time is it?"

"It's almost eight. I'll be back for lunch and then we'll drive out to Ancón."

"Is there anything I can do this morning? I need to pay for my room and board."

"Ask Teresita. There might be some vegetables to cut up. Oh, you could always do some ironing. These skirts and blouses are supposed to be wash and wear, but we don't like to wear them without ironing them. I'll see you later." A minute later Sister pokes her head in again. "I forgot to tell you that Pilar is bringing over a bag of clothes that some of the better-off ladies of the parish have donated to the clinic. Pick out a couple of things to wear at the beach. There might even be a bathing suit in there. I can't imagine swimming at this time of year, but you may be tempted to go in."

She disappears again, and Kate stretches and settles back down under the covers. This feels wonderful—she might stay in bed all morning. She dozes off and awakes to the scent of garlic and onions frying in olive oil. She dresses quickly and hurries down to the kitchen to greet Teresa, the Chinese woman who has been the sisters' cook since they came to Peru.

When Teresa sees Kate dressed in the simple skirt and blouse and small veil of the nuns, her eyebrows go up only a fraction. She says, "I didn't know when you would be coming down, so I just left everything out for you except the milk." Her voice is clipped and she keeps her back to Kate as she speaks.

"Corn flakes—I haven't had any corn flakes in a year." Kate knows her cheer is forced, but she chatters on to Teresa as if there is nothing strange about her unexpected appearance in the house. The cereal tastes wonderful, crunchy and fresh, and Kate thinks of home, the kitchen on Waterman Avenue with the plants hanging in the window and her father's motto over the sink: "Work is the curse of the drinking class." He still thinks it is funny and points it out to her every time she comes home.

When Pilar, the Peruvian social worker, comes over later in the morning, Kate is struck by her beauty. She is tall, with skin the color of cinnamon. Her features are Aymara, her straight dark hair coiled high on her head. Her dark, heavily rimmed eyes slant upwards. In a low, sweet voice she says, "I understand someone over here needs some clothes for the beach."

She is teasing her, and Kate finds that she doesn't mind it at all. They pick through the clothes together, laughing as Kate holds a tweed suit up to her body, and then a long, slinky red dress.

"I guess this would do if I went out in the evening," Kate says.

Pilar lights a cigarette and crosses her legs. "I think I had better go with you as a chaperone, Sister. You would be dangerous in that dress."

Kate laughs and tosses the dress back in the box. She chooses a pair of faded jeans and a navy blue sweater, along with a couple of men's shirts. "What I really need is a pair of sandals." She rummages through the clothes. "Aha, a nice pair of tennis shoes." She tries them on and admires her foot in the red canvas shoe. "They're Keds. I haven't had a pair of these since I went to the convent."

Squashing out her cigarette in a brass plate nearby, Pilar gets up and smooths her skirt down to mid-thigh. "Sister, I adore all the nuns. But I have never in my life understood what in the world would make a woman want to live like this."

"Like what?" Kate sees her looking around the living room.

"In a house with a bunch of women." Pilar pauses and grins up at Kate. "Without men," she whispers.

Kate hands the bag back to Pilar and watches as she makes her way down the steps of the convent, her hips swaying. Watching her, Kate feels awkward, boyish. No one would ever mistake Pilar for a boy. Now Kate realizes how in the convent, sexiness has been trained out of her. Day after day in the convent she had learned to move and to walk like a lady—"like Queen Elizabeth," the novice mistress would say. As new novices, they were trained to cross their ankles only, never their knees, and to walk with a glide. They were to practice custody of the eyes, keeping them lowered instead of staring about hungrily at the world. As Kate takes the clothes upstairs, she practices swinging her hips. Then she laughs to herself and feels lighter than she has since she'd come to Lima. Maybe the fog is lifting.

That afternoon as Sister Domitia drives to Ancón, a few miles north of Lima, the sun comes out and heat beats down on the van. They pass an area of one-story villas, partially hidden behind white stone walls. The waves boom steadily against tall rocks, a blue-green swirling mass. When Sister turns the van into a long driveway lined with olive trees, Kate is surprised. "How did the Maryknoll priests ever get a place like this?"

"Oh, I think it was a donation from an American couple who had lived here a long time. It's used quite a lot, I think. We've never stayed here, of course. It's supposed to be for people like you who are fatigued by the altitude in the Altiplano. Well, let's go in and get you settled. I want to get back before it gets dark. I don't like driving alone."

"Thanks for bringing me. I'm grateful to you, Sister." She's been a lot of trouble for everybody lately.

They are met at the front door by Carlos and Rene, the care-takers. Carlos takes the small canvas bag with the few clothes Kate has brought. Rene leads them into a long narrow living room, and Kate sees a wide expanse of white walls and windows that reveal the blue sea in the distance. The furniture is modern, spare and expensive looking. The bookshelves are crammed, and the coffee table is stacked neatly with old copies of *TIME*, *LIFE*, and a few *New Yorkers*.

"Is anyone else staying here now?" Kate has sensed the stillness of the house from the beginning.

"No, you have the place to yourself, at least until the week-end when a group from La Paz will be here." Carlos looks at her curiously. "How long will you be with us, Hermana?"

Kate glances at Sister Domitia, who gives a small shrug and says, "Not very long, Carlos. Perhaps just a day or two, if that would be all right."

"*Está en su casa.*" He bows to Kate and opens the slatted wooden door to the bedroom that would be hers. Its two windows look out over the garden to the ocean in the distance. She opens the window and the smell of the sea fills the room. The pounding waves roar on the beach. Now Kate can't wait to be alone.

"You're sure you'll be all right here by yourself? I know Carlos and Rene are in a wing right off the kitchen, but it seems a little lonely here to me." Sister Domitia joins her at the window. The sun is setting, the light playing at an angle on the water, glinting gold and red shards in the sea.

"I think it's just what the doctor ordered," says Kate.

"You look better already. Your eyes have lost that haunted look they had yesterday when you came." The older nun takes her hand. "I'll be praying for you. Remember, Sister, God made you the way you are. Everything He made is good. Don't be afraid. He loves you as you are." She sighs then, and turns to go down the stairs.

Kate stands in the doorway until the car swings around and disappears down the drive, scattering yellow leaves. When she goes back into the house she feels a surge of delight. This is a holiday. She can do whatever she wants. She has a place to stay, everyone knows where she is, and for the first time in a week, she doesn't feel guilty.

She takes the stairs two at a time and realizes that she isn't even out of breath as she would have been in Juliaca. She tosses the fussy little veil she has been wearing on the bed and peels off the borrowed skirt and blouse. The jeans she had salvaged from the charity box fit snugly, and she pulls the navy blue sweater on and laces up the Keds.

Kate hurries through the garden toward the iron gate that opens onto the beach. The air is velvet against her skin. In the lengthening shadows a white hibiscus glows. Now she is walking on the beach, and the wind lifts her hair. She shakes her head and breaks into a run, gulping in the salty air, the sand firm and wet beneath her feet.

The sea is new to her. Growing up in the Midwest, she had played in woods with deep ravines and gullies buried in piles of leaves. She had waded in cold streams in the Ozarks, watching the minnows dart between her skinny legs. But the sea is foreign, strange in its eternal pounding, its inexorable tides pulling everything out, far out from the shore into its glittering but dangerous depths. She runs for a while, darting in and out of the foam on the beach.

She slows to a walk. The sky is streaked with red in the west. A few high clouds, thin and fleeting, linger above the setting sun. She stands, hands on her hips, watching the sun grow to an orange ball as it nears the horizon. Then it flattens and spreads for a moment before the dark teeming sea swallows it whole.

The sky glows like pearls. Heading back, retracing her footsteps, she sees on a dune a flock of small terns. Gray and black, they stand in ranks staring out at the sea. Kate laughs out loud. They look like nuns, Dominican nuns, their hands tucked modestly in their sleeves, lined up for chapel. Far out, beyond the sand bar, sleek dark heads of some birds she doesn't recognize bob in the waves, riding their fury, impervious and serene. Overhead, a lone seagull drops suddenly earthward, skimming close over the waves. Then banking right, he lets the wind lift him into the darkening sky. She watches until he disappears.

Kate strides fast now, and her footprints are clear and deep in the sand. She takes great gulps of air. *I'm going to leave the order. I'll start my life over.* She says the words again, testing them aloud against the sounds of the sea. Leaving has nothing to do with Tom, and yet everything. What was it Sister Domitia said? "God made you as you are."

"You made me this way," she whispers into the wind. "You are the potter; I am the clay." Like the Prince in Sleeping Beauty, Tom has awakened her, but she knows for herself now what she is in her deepest core. She strides on. The air is cooling fast and the wind has picked up, but Kate is warm, her heart beating steadily with the waves.

When she comes to the gate of the house, she stands for a minute and watches the waning moon rising in the still glowing sky. Then she picks up her shoes and heads toward the house. Lights are on, spilling over the sand, signaling her way. She smells wood smoke.

When she opens the back door, Carlos steps into the light, startling her. In a low voice he says, "*Hermana*, there is someone waiting to see you in the *sala*."

Kate looks up as she brushes the sand from her feet and struggles to put on the tennis shoes. "Who is it?" She feels let down. She'd thought she had the place to herself.

"I don't know. He didn't give me his name. I think he is a priest."

Carlos follows Kate as she walks toward the living room. She stops in the doorway. Tom is kneeling by the fireplace, poking the logs viciously, sending sparks up the chimney.

She turns to Carlos then, surprised at the steadiness of her voice. "It's all right. It's Father Lynch. I work with him in Juliaca."

Carlos meets her eyes for a moment. Then he disappears down the hall as silently as he had come.

Kate closes the double doors and stands still. Without turning, Tom says, "I watched you walk up the beach for a long time before I recognized you." Then he rises and turns to her. "You little fool."

Her smile freezes; she cannot move. She notices a white line around his mouth, his cold eyes.

He stands there looking at her for a moment. "They told me a man stabbed you."

"It's nothing."

"Let me see it."

She walks toward him and pushes back the sleeve of her sweater. Then she pulls back the bandage gently. The wound gapes, red and livid, but a scar is beginning to form. "It doesn't hurt much anymore." She looks up into his face, searching for some flicker of feeling.

He takes her arm and bends to kiss it. She falls against him and lifts her face to his. Now he is kissing her on the mouth over and over, saying her name, "Kate, oh, Kate."

Everything in her rises to meet him. She feels his mouth on her throat, and then on her breast. She gasps and he kneels before her, thrusting his head into her body like a hurt child, wrapping her in his arms. She bends over him, stroking his hair, and the sight of his dark, shiny head against her sweater fills her with pity.

"Tom, stop it. Stop it. Let me go." Gently, she pulls herself free. His eyes are dark with tears.

A cold clarity has come over her as he caressed her. If she gave in now to her own desire, if they made love finally in this quiet, perfect place, he would hate her. Like some noble feudal knight, he would feel bound to her, obligated. He would renounce the priesthood and marry her. Then little by little resentment would begin to seep in, poisoning their love. She would never be able to make up for what he had lost.

She leaves him there on the floor like some wounded but still dangerous beast and curls up in a chair by the fireplace, watching him. For a while they say nothing. He hugs his crossed legs to his chest and rocks slightly as he stares into the fire. When he speaks his voice is low and unsteady.

"I looked for you all night the first night. I drove up and down the road from Juliaca to Puno. I called you every curse word I knew."

She smiles a little, relieved to see his crooked grin as he glances at her. "Tom, I had to get away. I was suffocating there, so close to you. I think—in the last few days—things are becoming clearer—"

"Wait, before you say anything, let me tell you something. I'm going home, back to Ireland."

Kate sits very still now. He continues, staring into the fire.

"My father is dying. He's been sick for a long time, but my mother's last letter sounded really grim. He has lung cancer. He's been smoking since he was twelve, and he's loved every damn cigarette he ever had."

"I'm so sorry, Tom." She wants to touch him but she is held fast to the chair.

"Anyway, I thought it would be a good time for me to go back. Two days ago I mailed a letter to Monsignor MacDonagh in Galway to tell him I'll be there to help out for a while." His words trail off at the end so faintly that Kate isn't sure she has heard them. Two days ago? So just like that—he was leaving. She tries to breathe.

"Your mother will be glad."

"Yes."

The fire crackles in the grate, and the flames dance. Kate can hear the muffled roar of the sea in the distance. She imagines the beach now in the dark, the moonlight trembling on the wild water.

"Tom, I've made a decision, too. I'm leaving the convent. I'm not renewing my vows."

He stifles a small moan, as if someone has kicked him in the stomach. She watches his face. "Oh God, Kate." He shakes his head as if to ward off her words. "Fuck it!"

She laughs then, she can't help it. He is scowling like a petulant fifteen-year-old. She goes to sit beside him cross-legged on the floor. Together they stare into the fire.

"Tom, listen to me. Don't feel guilty. I would have come to this decision someday even if I'd never met you. Knowing you, feeling loved and loving you, it's been the real thing. When I entered the convent, I was just a girl, not knowing myself. I didn't understand what I was renouncing. I see myself differently now. Oh, does this make sense?"

He turns to her and smooths her hair back from her face. "No, nothing makes sense right now except how much I love touching you, your hair, your neck." He kisses her then, and she tastes sadness like copper, bitter and metallic, in his mouth.

She leans her head on his shoulder. "I'm going back to Juliaca to finish out the year." She's surprised to hear herself say this. "The community spent so much money to bring me down here, send me to language school. Finishing the year in Juliaca is the least I can do. Then, when it's time to renew my vows, I'll go home."

"What will you do?" He watches her closely, and there is a tentative look in his eyes as if she is someone he's just met.

Kate shrugs. "I don't know. Probably teach somewhere."

After a long silence he takes her hand. "Kate, I can't say to you what I'm longing to—that I'll leave the priesthood and marry you."

She starts to protest and he covers her mouth with his hand.

"Wait, let me finish. There's nothing I want more than to wake up beside you every morning. But I just can't do it. Being a priest . . . it's who I am, damn it."

"Tom, I know. That last day in Juliaca, I watched you at Mass. You lifted the Host at the consecration, and I wanted to scream at God. He's got His hooks in you so deep that you'd tear yourself apart if you tried to get free."

He shakes his head wearily. "Shit, Kate. Sometimes I don't know if I even believe in God anymore."

This shocks her. She doesn't know what to say. Then he stands up and pulls her to her feet.

"I leave tomorrow."

She feels the blow right in her center. She looks away. He turns her face to his.

"Am I invited to stay the night?" The tone is light, joking, but she sees the trembling of his mouth.

"No, I don't think so."

He looks at her for a long time, holding her face in his hands. "You're a hard woman, Kate O'Neill. Harder than nails." His hands drop to his side then, and he turns away from her, searching for his keys. In the dark entrance hall he faces her again. His face is in shadows now and he stands very straight. His voice is a whisper. "I love you, Kate O'Neill. Wherever you go, know that I'm somewhere, loving you."

She nods, unable to stop trembling as if from a chill. Finally, "I love you, too, Tom. Always." She pulls his face down to hers and kisses him deeply, inhaling his scent, drinking him in. Then she releases him.

Still he lingers. His eyes are in shadow, but she can see the pain.

"Go," she whispers.

The door opens and he is gone. She hears the click of the lock and leans her face against the door. *Come back, please come back. I didn't mean it; you can stay.* For a minute she hears nothing. Then footsteps, a car starts, and lights flash against the stained glass window in the door. She listens for a long time until the only sound is the ticking of the clock in the empty hall.

# Chapter Twenty-One

### Friday, July 3, 1964

~~~

The *colectivo*, an old Chevy from the late 1950s, rattles and hisses as they speed south away from Lima along the Pan American Highway. Kate is crowded in the back seat with Señora Molina and her fifteen-year-old daughter. The plump *señora* is carefully dressed in a red and white polka-dot silk dress, nylons, and shiny patent-leather heels. Her hair is pulled back in a tight chignon, and beads of sweat trickle down her neck into the cleft between her breasts. She sighs often and wipes her face and neck with a lace handkerchief, offering a running commentary on the scenery, her daughter's willfulness, and the dangers the driver surely hasn't seen rushing to meet them. From Lima to Nazca she confides in Kate, seeing in the young nun an ally against the folly of youth. She and her husband, who sits stoically with his eyes closed next to the driver, are taking their daughter up to La Paz to study with the Madres de la Presentación in their boarding school.

"This girl is a little fool," she hisses, as if the girl isn't sitting next to her, staring at the Saharan-like landscape. "She thinks she has found the great love of her life, a fifteen-year-old delinquent who rides a motorcycle."

Kate glances at the girl. Her cheek rests on the window, her face hidden by a veil of long black hair. Kate has tried to change the subject several times, but the mother is undeterred. As she tells the story of María Luísa sneaking out of the house, the tricks she played to see the boy, the *señora* rolls her eyes in the direction of the silent husband in the front seat as if to say how useless he has been in the matter.

Kate pulls out the breviary Sister Domitia has loaned her and excuses herself to pray. Silence settles on the passengers, and she thinks she caught a grateful look from the driver as he nods to her in the rearview mirror. She pages through the book to find the psalms for Sext. It is afternoon, and the sisters in Juliaca will be finishing lunch now. She reads Psalm 8:

> O Lord, our sovereign,
> how glorious is thy name in all the earth!
> Thy majesty is praised high as the heavens. . . .
> When I look at thy heavens, the work of thy fingers,
> the moon and the stars set in place by thee,
> what is man that thou shouldst remember him,
> mortal man that thou shouldst care for him?
> Yet thou hast made him little less than a god,
> crowning him with glory and honor.

Kate looks out the window at fields of cotton. Marigolds are everywhere and their fragrance seeps into the worn car, mingling with the perfume and sweat of Señora Molina. The psalmist had it right. The immensity of the world stretches out before her. She is not the sun. She is only a tiny part of creation. The stars wheel on in spite of her pain. Her heart hurts, a real physical hurt. She tries to sit very still so that she can only feel a dull throb, not the sharp stab of loss. But on top of the pain she is floating free. Her senses sharp, she drinks in the vision of clouds scudding across a blue sky, the waves crashing on the beach, and the mysterious dunes, shifting and scattering in the wind off the sea.

Now they head inland, toward Arequipa. The whole journey to the Altiplano would last almost twenty-four hours, the driver has assured them, and they will stop only to eat or if someone has to go to the bathroom. Kate looks around. The Molinas are asleep. In the front seat the husband snores softly, his mouth open and his head thrown back on the seat. The daughter's head rests on her mother's broad shoulder. She is lovely, and Kate feels a rush of pity for her. Even the *señora* sleeps, her mouth closed firmly, one arm cradling her daughter.

It is dark by the time the *colectivo* pulls into the Plaza de Armas in Arequipa. Kate thinks of the night she spent on the hard bench of the church. How could she have run away like that? She feels strange to herself and humbled by her good luck. No, not luck; she has been protected, watched over. She pushes back the sleeve of her habit. The scar on her arm is still red. It will fade, she knows, but it will never disappear entirely, a reminder she'll carry forever.

The driver stops just off the plaza, saying they will take a two-hour break to eat. He'll get some rest, and by seven o'clock they'll be on the road to Puno. "It's better to travel at night," he says. "Fewer trucks to pass on the steep curves." He is a small man, slim and weathered, with a husky voice. He's smoked one cigarette after another, and he coughs now and spits on the sidewalk. He looks tired, and Kate hopes he really will take a nap.

"Madre, would you care to join us for dinner? There is a good restaurant in the Hotel Mercaderes. We would like you to be our guest." Señor Molina, much to Kate's surprise for she hasn't heard him say a word the whole trip, is charming.

"Thank you, I would be honored." She smiles at the three of them standing before her, and the *señora* beams and takes her arm. The father walks arm in arm with his daughter, and Kate can hear them talking softly.

It is early for dinner when they enter the restaurant; the waiters are just putting on their white coats and aprons. Their expressions are not friendly, but Señor Molina gestures grandly to one of them, and the young man scurries over to show them a table.

"*Oye, chico*, we're in a hurry. We are leaving for Puno in an hour or so. Do you think you can feed some hungry travelers from Lima?" Señor Molina is already tucking his napkin into his shirt collar. The waiter notices María Luísa, and suddenly his indifference disappears.

"Of course, *señor*. What will you have?"

Now both the husband and wife lecture Kate on the delicacies of Arequipa's cuisine. Their eyes shine as they describe the subtle flavor of *ocopa* or *rocoto relleno*. Kate asks Señor Molina to order for her, and soon they are drinking a red wine Kate recognizes from the winery in Ica. She mentions that she has visited the winery, and that starts the Molinas on a long and careful explanation of the superiority of Peruvian wines over Chilean wines. Kate watches María Luísa, for every time the waiter comes near, she raises her dark eyes to him with a peculiar gleam of conscious power. The waiter stumbles once and drops a basket of bread he was carrying. María Luísa looks at Kate and laughs, and Kate begins to think the parents are right in exiling this girl to a convent boarding school in Bolivia.

Are American girls like this? So sure of their sexual power? Kate knows she hadn't been. Her way with boys had come from being around her brother. She would tease and taunt them, but her banter was friendly and not charged with sex. Soon she will be going out into the world again—but as a twenty-six-year-old woman, not a girl. She doesn't know the rules of the game anymore. This fifteen-year-old is more worldly than she.

By the end of dinner they are all stunned with the food

and fatigue. Señor Molina, looking at his watch, suggests a short walk around the plaza. Soon they are out on the street, joining the jostling crowds coming from work, spilling into cafes and bars. Music floats from the open doors of bars, and in the distance the peak of El Misti pierces the darkening sky.

They walk to the corner where the driver told them to meet him, but he is not there. Señor Molina puffs on his cigar and watches with a slight smile the passing stream of office workers, school children, and young lovers walking hand in hand. Kate walks beside him in silence. Ahead of them, María Luísa is walking with her mother, her head high, her eyes never swerving to catch the admiring glances she draws from both men and women. "Your eyes are like the stars," one older man mutters, but neither the mother nor the daughter acknowledges the *piropo.*

The four of them wait on the corner for a few minutes before they hear the Chevy backfiring as it comes toward them.

"I'll bet he's drunk," says Señor Molina, trying to get a good look at their silent driver as he waits for them to get in without taking his eyes from the street in front of him.

"Ready?" he calls back to them. Then they are off, the tires squealing as they circle the plaza and head for the road to Puno. This time María Luísa sits in the middle, and Kate can smell her perfume, something delicate, violets.

As they leave the city, no one speaks. It is dark now, but on Kate's left the moon slips in and out of the clouds. Kate can see they are edging gradually across small hills and then they are crossing wide, flat fields. There is no sudden dramatic ascent into the mountains as she remembers on the road from Coroico to La Paz. Yet she knows they are climbing steadily, for her ears pop. Kate glimpses strange tufts of grass in the plains, like the feather dusters they had used to dust the convent parlor. Herds of llama move across the *pampa*, ghostly and silent in the moonlight. It is getting colder now, and Kate is grateful for the huddled warmth of the girl next to her.

When the car lurches to a stop, Kate wonders how long she has been sleeping. She cannot see her watch in the darkness. The driver gets out, and Kate peers through the dusty window at a small cluster of buildings. An electric bulb dangles over one hut. The Molinas sleep on. She hears voices outside and feels a scrape on the side of the car as the driver unscrews the gas cap.

The sharp smell of the gas fills the car stirring a memory of being back in St. Louis, with her mother and father on the way to a few summer days in the Ozarks. Then, too, she'd been crowded in the back seat, stuffed between Dan and Maggie. With the windows open, she'd lean out, and the wind would flatten her cheek. Once they stopped at a filling station out in the country. While Dan and Maggie had gone to the bathroom, she had stood by her father and watched the dark-haired teenage attendant fill the gas tank. "I love that smell," she'd said to her father. When she looked up she had seen a look pass between her mother and father, a strange look that she recognized now as desire.

What would her parents think about her love for Tom? She had described him in her letters in the half humorous tone she reserved for all the priests she worked with, but she had been careful not to mention his name too often. Her father was especially quick to pick up on her feelings. Now they would have to know. Or would they? She starts composing the letter: "Dear Mom and Dad, While I have been working in Peru, a wonderful/ terrible/unexpected thing has happened: I have fallen in love."

How can she explain running away? They would be horrified. They are already nervous enough about her being in Peru although they tried to sound cheerful in their letters, telling her the news of the house and the neighborhood, sharing her letters with anyone who asked about her. No, she will not write home about this.

She longs for home. It is July, winter here in the Altiplano. But somewhere back home on this night a screen door bangs, and that remembered sound is the essence of summer in St.

Louis. Instead here she sits waiting in a dark car, shivering in the dry cold air of the Altiplano. But it's the right thing to go back—back to the parish in Juliaca, back to the nuns and the children. She can stand it now. Tom is gone. The thought of his going has played around the edges of her mind all day. He is probably in Dublin already or heading across Ireland for Galway on the shore of the Atlantic, two oceans away from her. He would be hurting, she knows, and she remembers his eyes that last night, their puzzled angry pain, like those of a dog who can't understand why he's been whipped. He is going home to sorrow, the loss of a father, a mother alone. She imagines him in years to come, a priest still, caustic and impatient at the petty world around him. She loves him fiercely now, and the memory of his head in her lap makes her gasp. She closes her eyes, waiting for the image to fade.

Yes, she would finish out the year. Knowing she was leaving Peru in a few months made her want to see everything with that intensity that comes in knowing it's the last time. She will work hard, she vows; she will learn everything she could about the men and women of the sierra. The brilliant light that blinded her is gone; maybe now she will be able to see things more clearly. One thing has become very clear to her: she does not belong in Peru. She does not know enough of the culture nor of the history. She can't even speak Aymara! Sergeant Vargas's words echo: aren't there problems in your own country? She feels how presumptuous she's been in thinking that she could teach in the Altiplano, when actually, the Peruvian people have taught her. No, she will go back to the States and figure out her own path. Her Spanish is pretty good now, so maybe she can find a way to use this hard-won skill in her own country. She leans her head against the window, trying to picture her future.

They are driving again now, moving out of the village into fields of moonlight. She tries to pray, looking out at the dark. All her life God had been real to her. Faith was effortless.

She grew up in a world where His existence was assumed. Now came the test.

It would be easier to leave the convent if she didn't believe in God. For without God, that life made no sense. Nuns would just be a group of do-gooders living together in the uneasy way of women in groups. She stares out at the silent distant peaks of the Andes, and she senses a presence, feminine now, like the moon that has slipped behind the clouds. In the dark back seat, she whispers, "I'm sorry, Lord. But you made me this way. I know You are here with me even though I've been lost."

By dawn they are on the outskirts of Puno. Kate feels the familiar lightness, the breathlessness.

Señora Molina huddles in her overcoat, shivering and moaning, "Ay, my head hurts."

Her husband soothes her. "Now, now. In just a moment we'll go have a cup of *mate de coca* and you'll feel better." María Luísa is still asleep.

As they enter the Plaza de Armas, Kate sees the jeep from Santa Catalina. Sister Jeanne is standing beside it. Kate feels her stomach drop. She is embarrassed. How childish the whole episode must seem to these good nuns.

Jeanne grins when she sees her. They embrace, and Kate feels grateful as Jeanne begins to laugh. "Well, I go off for retreat, and you disappear into the mountains. Jeez, Kate, can't I leave you alone for a few days?" She has already grabbed Kate's arm and is heading for the jeep when Kate remembers the Molinas.

"Wait a minute. I want to say goodbye to the family I rode up here with." She turns back to see the three of them watching her. She holds out her hand to the *señora*, who takes it in both of hers.

"I am so happy we met, *madre*. I can't believe you really want to live up here. *No hay nada*." She looks around the Plaza, slick with the cold winter rain.

Señor Molina bows over her hand, almost kissing it. "Pray

for us all, *madre*," and his eyes shift to his daughter. Kate sees the worried frown.

María Luísa holds her face up to be kissed, and Kate looks into the girl's eyes as she embraces her. "Good luck in La Paz," Kate says. "Maybe I will come see you at the school the next time I get to La Paz."

The girl says nothing, staring at Kate and at Sister Jeanne who waits by the jeep. Finally the girl whispers, "Good luck to you. You will need it here."

Kate lifts her habit and climbs into the jeep. Jeanne starts the car and thrusts a postcard at her. "I can't believe it. You've been gone from us for only a week, and already you're receiving mail from a strange man."

Kate is grateful for the teasing tone. Obviously Jeanne has decided not to press her for the story of her journey, at least not yet. "This postcard is from an Englishman who lives near the Lake. I stayed in his house the first night I was gone. He gave me a ride to Arequipa." Jeanne nods, but keeps her eyes on the road. Kate reads the card aloud: "Greetings from Lima. I'm at the airport about to leave for London, but the thought of you wandering around (with my stolen jacket) makes me a bit uneasy. I hope by now you have arrived at wherever it was you were going. Perhaps I'll see you on my return. You're welcome, Peter."

"Stolen jacket?"

Kate sighs. "It's a long story."

"Save it for later. Sister Josepha and Father Jack are both pretty upset over the whole thing, so you're going to have to do some explaining." She glances at Kate. "I think I know why you left. It was Father Tom, wasn't it?"

"Yes." Kate finds she has trouble speaking.

"I tried to warn you." Jeanne's mouth is set in a tight line. She turns to Kate then. "I wish you had talked to me about what was bothering you."

"I do, too, Jeanne. But maybe I had to figure things out for myself."

"Are they all figured out?"

"Well, I have decided to leave the community."

Jeanne says nothing for a moment. When she speaks, she stares straight ahead at the road. "Is he leaving the priesthood, too?" Kate hears the note of contempt Jeanne gives to the pronoun.

"No."

There is a short silence while Jeanne swerves to avoid a flock of sheep at the side of the road. Kate tries to explain. "This is not about Tom, not directly, anyway. It's about what I've discovered about myself, about who I really am."

Jeanne says nothing. They drive on, and Kate can feel the sadness in her friend and her brave attempt to disguise it. She hasn't thought about that—how the sisters would react to her decision. How selfish she's been! Now she sees how her leaving for good will hurt them. It is the same pain she had felt as a novice years ago when someone left, a feeling of diminishment.

"Jeanne, I'm sorry. This has nothing to do with you or Sister Josepha. We've lived really well together, I think."

"I thought so, too." Jeanne's voice is wistful, a little tired. She rallies. "When are you leaving?"

"Not until next year when my vows are up. I want to finish the year working here, that is if you all agree." She stops. Maybe the nuns wouldn't want her here anymore after what had happened.

"Good." Jeanne's tone is brisk. "There's lots to do around here, and you were just starting to be useful." She looks over at Kate. "Besides, maybe you'll change your mind. Father Tom has gone home, you know. He doesn't know when he'll be back."

"I know." Kate stares out the window.

They are at the edge of Lake Titicaca now, and the rain has passed. Wispy clouds linger over the hills in the distance.

Then Kate sees them. Her hand clamps Jeanne's arm on the steering wheel.

"Jeanne, stop the car. Look at those people over there."

"What are you talking about?" Jeanne stares at her and then looks out the window.

"Over there. See that group of people. They're dancing. Can't you hear the music?" Kate is already opening the door. Jeanne slows to a stop and pulls the jeep off the road. Kate jumps out and strides across the field toward the group gathered on the shore of the lake.

Off to the right are the musicians, eight or nine men in the chill Andean morning, with their flutes and drums, their long reed pipes. The music wails, a plaintive melody that tells of suffering and loss. But over its insistent rhythm hovers a note of joy, a steady driving flight toward bliss. Against the deep blue water of the Lake, steam rising off it from the morning's rain and glistening in the emerging sun, the men and women dance. They are in a circle and the women twirl their full skirts, weaving among the men who call out to them, whistling and stamping their feet. Six women and four men dancing in the cold Andean morning, with no audience except the geese that fly low over the Lake and veer off at the sound of the flutes. She stands watching for a long time, the music rising and falling but never ending, the men and women tirelessly spinning at the lonely edge of the world.

# $\mathcal{A}$cknowledgments

$\mathcal{A}$ll quotations from scripture are from *The New English Bible with the Apocrypha,* used with permission from the publisher, Oxford Publishing Limited, reproduced with permission of the Licensor through PLSclear. For the hymns of the Divine Office quoted, permission was granted by the Sisters of the Most Precious Blood of O'Fallon, Missouri, from *The Music Supplement to The Liturgy of the Hours, 1979* (Benziger Brothers). The poem by Patrick MacDonogh, "Be Still As You Are Beautiful," is used by kind permission of Estate of Patrick MacDonogh c/o The Gallery Press, Loughcrew, Oldcastle, County Meath, Ireland, from *Poems 2001.* For the line from the song "Unchained Melody," permission was granted by Abby North of Unchained Melody Publishing LLC.

Writing a novel is a journey. Along the way, many people have lent a helping hand. For reading an early draft and for her incisive comments and suggestions, I thank novelist Christine Bell, author of *The Perez Family, Saint,* and her recent novel *Grievance.* Much gratitude is owed to Herta Feely and Emily Williamson of Chrysalis Editorial for their suggestions on the manuscript and their encouragement. Thanks to Tom Epley, an early agent for the novel. I am grateful to Brooke Warner, Shannon Green, and the team from She Writes Press for publishing the work. Special thanks to Sister Helene Rueffer, C.PP.S, with whom I worked in Lima, for her stories that she shared with me. Thanks to my dear son-in-law, Max Benitez, for developing a prototype of the map of Peru and Bolivia. Thanks to publicists Crystal Patriarche, Tabitha Bailey, and Hanna Pollock of BookSparks for their support.

Several close friends and colleagues have read early drafts and cheered me on. Thanks to Karen Sirmans, Mary Bozeman, Peg Wallace, Bill and Nina Burke, Ginny Vail and her mother from Peru, Graciela Rabines Kelly, and Sister Fran Raia, C.PP.S. I owe a huge debt of gratitude to the Sisters of the Most Precious Blood of O'Fallon, Missouri, for the eleven formative years I spent among them. Above all thanks to the wonderful people of Peru from whom I learned so much and whose literature, art, and culture I fell in love with.

My mother Margaret O'Shea and my father Tom O'Shea both read early drafts and were not too scandalized. My brothers Dan, Tim, and Matt; sisters Katie, Ellen, and Mary Grace; and sister-in-law Kay O'Shea urged me on. Finally, I thank my three wonderful children, Kristin, Tim, and John, who waited patiently for my attention over the years and who encourage me every day. Above all, I thank my husband, Michael, whose fine eye for detail in proofreading as well as his constant enthusiasm and patience saw me through the process. His love sustains me always.

# About the Author

Marian O'Shea Wernicke is the author of a memoir, *Tom O'Shea, A Twentieth Century Man: A Daughter's Search for Her Father's Story.* She is also co-editor with Herta Feely of a collection of short stories and memoirs called *Confessions: Fact or Fiction?* She studied under poets Derek Walcott, Maxine Kumin, and Mark Jarman at the Sewanee Writers Conference. A professor of English for 25 years at Pensacola State College, Wernicke also served as department head of English and Communications. As a nun for eleven years, Wernicke taught in St. Louis and in Lima, Peru. Married and the mother of three grown children, she and her husband now live in Austin, Texas.

*Author photo © Matthew O'Shea Photography*

# Selected Titles From She Writes Press

She Writes Press is an independent publishing company founded to serve women writers everywhere. Visit us at www.shewritespress.com.

*The Black Velvet Coat* by Jill G. Hall. $16.95, 978-1-63152-009-9. When the current owner of a black velvet coat—a San Francisco artist in search of inspiration—and the original owner, a 1960s heiress who fled her affluent life fifty years earlier, cross paths, their lives are forever changed . . . for the better.

*Shrug* by Lisa Braver Moss. $16.95, 978-1631526381. It's the 1960s, and teenager Martha Goldenthal just wants to do well at Berkeley High and have a normal life—but how can she when her mother is needy and destructive and her father is a raging batterer who disdains academia? When her mother abandons the family, Martha must stand up to her father to fulfill her vision of going to college.

*The Belief in Angels* by J. Dylan Yates. $16.95, 978-1-938314-64-3. From the Majdonek death camp to a volatile hippie household on the East Coast, this narrative of tragedy, survival, and hope spans more than fifty years, from the 1920s to the 1970s.

*Profound and Perfect Things* by Maribel Garcia. $16.95, 978-1631525414. When Isa, a closeted lesbian with conservative Mexican parents, has a one-night stand that results in an unwanted pregnancy, her sister, Cristina adopts the baby—but twelve years later, Isa, who regrets giving up her child, threatens to spill the secret of her daughter's true parentage.

*The Moon Always Rising* by Alice C. Early. $16.95, 978-1-63152-683-1. When Eleanor "Els" Gordon's life cracks apart, she exiles herself to a derelict plantation house on the Caribbean island of Nevis—and discovers, with the help of her resident ghost, that only through love and forgiveness can she untangle years-old family secrets and set herself free to love again.

*The Vintner's Daughter* by Kristen Harnisch. $16.95, 978-163152-929-0. Set against the sweeping canvas of French and California vineyard life in the late 1890s, this is the compelling tale of one woman's struggle to reclaim her family's Loire Valley vineyard—and her life.